I0563361

DARK TRESPASS
BOOK ONE
A NECROMANCER'S HEART

BY
MISTY D TACKETT

ISBN: 978-1-7373249-1-1

DEDICATION

Thanks to my dear supportive family & friends. I love you!

CONTENTS

Prolog 1

1 Who Needs A Heart 2
2 It's My Party 8
3 This Seasons A Bust 20
4 Two Old Ladies 32
5 Darkness & Despair 41
6 A Traveling Man 53
7 The Bitch Is Back 61
8 All Cooped Together 75
9 Dark Strangers & Leading Ladies 85
10 Desire To Devour 99
11 Grave Ambitions & Inhibitions 108
12 The Monster In Me 125
13 Bad Things 138
14 Confession of A High School Bully 155
15 Make No Mistake 168
16 Must Love Sunday's 181
17 Thick As Thieves W/Good Intentions 194
18 An Invitation 207
19 Dark Interpretations 218
20 Cold & Calculated 233
21 The Dead Move Swiftly 248
22 Deception & Revelation 265
23 A Puzzled Past 277
24 It's Hard To Say Goodbye 289
   Acknowledgment 300
   Author

Prolog
Roulette Table of Death

Endless tears dropped onto the hard wooden surface where my family sat around me, slaughtered. Their hearts, torn from their chests, lay in a circle like a roulette table of death. Their bodies slumped in their chairs while pale, glazed eyes stared at their hearts in disbelief. I sat with my wrists shackled to the table, defeated and in despair, as I awaited the monster from my nightmares to come and collect his prize. We had put up a good fight, and all was lost.

The commotion that started outside the bar an hour ago faded to silence. I couldn't believe they'd turned on us. As soon as word got out that the enemy was coming, the people we saved and called our friends attacked. After the fight and slaughter ensued, the remaining survivors fled. I knew it was out of fear of retaliation, but why would they cower to him now with the good news we had received? It just didn't make any sense. I wanted to bang my head on the table to wake up from this nightmare. The problem was I was wide awake.

The entrance door screamed on its hinges, and HE walked inside. His eyes went straight to mine, then my dead family seated around me, and he smiled.

"Hello, Tara! Having a rough night?"

Chapter 1
TARA

Who Needs A Heart

The mountains were beautiful this time of year. Fall colors draped across the majestic landscape—a kaleidoscope of yellow, orange, scarlet, and purple rolled through a never-ending divine canopy—a testament to mother nature and her abounding glory. To most, this scene would provide a feeling of serenity and wonderment. The dregs of summer give way to the excitement of fall and all the festivities to come.

For me?

I observed the last vestiges of flourishing life, the still clinging leaves losing the inevitable battle. Enter the season, which cast a dismal dread through my mind and wreaks havoc upon my countenance, too young at the age of twenty-two to have dark circles beneath my eyes and the deep crease between my brows due to the question I ask myself time and again.

WHY?

Why has my life ONCE AGAIN gone to complete shit?

Why is it that this time of year, since the tender age of twelve, has my life fallen to chaos, tragedy, fear, a mashup of mishaps, a shatter of broken hearts that have made me question the Almighty above time and again? Why me? But do I have time to feel pity for myself?

"No!" I shook my head.

From far too young, the responsibilities I took assured I kept myself second in life to everything and everyone. People have told me to move on, to let go of the past, but no one understands the gravity of letting go. The past is too deep within me. It's a part of my being; some may call it a crutch. But those people will never truly understand.

I dropped the visor and gazed in the mirror at my bloodshot brown eyes as my mind rehashed my latest travesty. I drug my trembling fingers down my face, cupped my hands, then screamed into the hollow darkness. Not much traffic came through this Smoky Mountain pass in the morning, so no one was around to hear me inside my truck on the rocky outcropping. A guardrail was the only thing that separated me from the sharp drop below.

"Get your shit together, Tara!"

I raked my fingers upward through my long dark blond hair, then worked through the knotted summer-kissed tresses and drew them back into a messy bun. I looked down at the ring on my finger and shook my head with the initial denial I had experienced many times. I should have known! Asher Ferris was a dream, a sweet one full of beautiful promises. Broken promises. Can my heart possibly take anymore before I've reached oblivion, to become dead inside?

I tugged the gold band with its meager diamond off my finger, pushed the button to let the window down, and contemplated chucking the piece of jewelry into the ravine. It no longer held the same meaning as once when Asher placed it on my finger with love in his eyes and words of faithfulness on bended knee.

I didn't even care about the size of the diamond. We weren't rich, but our love was strong, so all that mattered was us making our dreams come true for better or worse. And I could look beyond most things, but the temptation that proved to sway Asher so easily had him caught with his pants down, ass in the air, and laid atop my best friend.

NO!

Make that my ex-best friend, Gina! The bitch could have this trashy ring. I'm going to keep the truck! I tossed the ring into the ashtray as it now fits better anyway. Another dream went up in smoke and crumbled to ash.

I rolled the window back up and realized I had nowhere else to go. I restarted the roaring V8 engine of my black King Ranch F150 and pulled back on the road. The tires peeled and kicked up gravel in its wake.

I could only go back to The Hillbilly Roost, where I had just finished my late night shift a mere hour and a half ago. My uncle, Woody, The Rooster, Raybrook owned and ran the fine backwoods establishment and biker bar/church, where everyone drank and swore, but they had a friend in Jesus. Saturday nights were for partying, late Sunday afternoons for the three P's, preaching, prayers, and penance.

My adopted uncle, Danny, often had amends to make when the church bell tolled. He and my other adopted uncle, Cannon, aka Roadkill, got a bit crazy from time to time. And as crazed as my uncles may be, at least they're still a few people in my life that I could count on to have my back.

Without Uncle Woody, my life would be forfeit in this brutal world. He took me and my brother Rudy in after our mother was put in the state psychiatric facility after she murdered our step-monster, Dr. Lyle Durst. Her insistence that Lyle was indeed a monster of the demonic variety justified the actions against him in her mind. Unfortunately, the jury didn't see it that way. A ruling of insanity saved her from a life sentence in prison.

Dr. Durst had a good standing in the community. Documentation of self-harm and Lyle's many attempts to help me outweighed my mother's claims that he was hurting me when she walked into my bedroom that fateful night and shot him. She claimed she protected me from some terrible thing Lyle did that I can't remember.

I suffered from blackouts since I hit my head in a fall at twelve. That's when my life started falling to pieces, and there have been so many missing pieces of my life since then—the biggest is my father, Richard Raybrook.

Dad took me camping that fall, and he played his guitar and sang the comedy songs he wrote. We ate smores by the fire and laid out under the stars pretending to be cowboys of the wild west. On the second day, we went on a hike. We were climbing a slope when I heard a strange growl. Something rattled the nearby trees, startling me, and I lost my footing. The last thing I remembered was Dad shouting my name as he reached out to catch me. I saw the panic in his eyes as I tumbled backward. Then everything went black.

When I came to, my head throbbed terribly, and my vision blurred. I was alone in the night—the calls of the nocturnal creatures resonated in my ears. The shroud of frightening shadows made finding anything impossible. I went back to the campsite, but my father wasn't there. After tuning into the channel for the park ranger, I managed to call for help on the walkie-talkie.

For the longest time, I heard nothing but static. My chest tightened as I struggled to pull air into my lungs. By the time a response came, I had provided my location before falling back into the darkness.

I woke up in the hospital the following morning. My mother and Rudy were there. Mom explained that Uncle Woody had a search crew along with the police, and all they had found was Dad's pocket knife with blood on it.

Everything continued downhill from that point. Misinformation, false leads, and the town rumor mill spun out of control. After a year of searching, almost everyone gave up.

Not me. I still post pictures of my dad, knowing he was out there somewhere. I felt it in my bones. The events of my past ran through me as I drove the winding road, and dark clouds drifted my way.

"Fitting for a day such as this," I grumbled to the empty passenger seat. I might as well have an imaginary partner in crime as I thought of sweet vengeance. I could be the typical redneck girl and slash the tires of Asher's truck and smash in the headlights and windshield with Uncle Woody's Louisville Slugger, but then again, I was driving that truck right now. My mind began to wander back to an hour ago.

Asher ran out of the house behind me, holding up his pants with one hand as I threw my clothing and school book bags into the back seat and slammed the door shut.

"You can keep the ring, but I need my truck," Asher yelled.

"Really, Asher? You mean this truck under my name that I have made all the payments on since I signed for it?"

"Come on, Tara, you know I need the truck for my job. What the hell am I supposed to do, drive that rusted-out El Camino to the lumber mill? You got me that truck for my birthday present last year. As soon as we paid it off, we could afford to get you something nicer to drive."

"We? There is no WE anymore! It's you and Gina now. She can loan you her truck and drive your sorry cheating ass around. Besides, a big red bow and a birthday card don't prove ownership. So, let's just say you screwed yourself out of your nice ride."

Asher continued to yell after me as I jumped into the driver's seat and peeled out while flipping him off. Tough shit! I was so angry. The tears started, and I refused to let him see how much he crushed me.

Raindrops pelted the windshield, and suddenly a large shadow shot across the road. I screamed and slammed on the brakes. The truck swerved and fishtailed toward the bank before it jolted to a stop. I cursed, steadied my breaths, and rubbed my neck to alleviate the resulting whiplash.

"What the hell was that?"

It was the size of a large animal without a distinctive form. Grief and stress had me seeing things that were not there. Episodes like this have happened to me before, so I focused on breathing and talking myself through.

"This is all part of it. Get your bearings and drive slower. Get back to The Roost, and everything will be fine." I turned on the radio and tuned through the stations. Tina Turner belted out What's Love Got To Do With It.

"Yeah, exactly," I agreed.

Who needs a heart when it can be broken?

I sang along loudly as I pulled back onto the road and journeyed the remaining miles till I reached the turn-off down the long drive. The densely wooded acreage flanked both sides of the narrow gravel driveway to a clearing where The Hillbilly Roost sat atop a hill on my uncle's lake view property.

I parked, leaned back, closed my eyes, and listened to the rain continue. Break-up songs continued to assault my ears, so I turned off the radio and focused on the sounds of nature. A soft rumbling of distant thunder soothed my soul, and I reclined my seat to relish in this moment of peace.

Chapter 2
TARA

It's My Party

A knocking on my door's window startled me awake. I opened my eyes, noticing it had stopped raining, and heard Uncle Woody's muffled voice. His knuckles rapping on the window prompted me to push the button to open it.

"Huh?" I rasped.

Woody's eyes held mine with a look of concern. "I asked, what are you doing back here so early? Is everything all right?"

I rubbed my eyes and yawned loudly. "Uh, things are not so good."

"What is it? What's going on?" Woody folded his muscular tattooed arms across his broad chest. The thin line of his lips further conveyed his concern amongst his handsome, rugged features. He tugged at the beard hairs on his chin, then ran his hand through his thick dark blond wavy hair as he waited for further explanation. An explanation I didn't feel like giving at the moment. I was so tired. I needed to sleep if I was going to function behind the bar tonight.

"Uncle Woody, I'm kinda tired. Do you mind if I crash in the cabin for a while?"

"You know you're always welcome to it. But I need to know what's going on. Did that sonofabitch lay his hands on you?"

"No. I don't want to talk about it right now, okay?"

Hellfire sparked and flamed in Woody's eyes as he figured it out. "That little prick! I'm going to kill him."

"No, please! It's over between Asher and me, and that's all there is."

Woody's voice rose a few decibels. "No little piss ant is gonna break my baby niece's heart and get away with it!"

I flinched as the pain in my neck shot to my head. I wrapped my arms around the steering wheel, leaned forward, and groaned. I felt the tears in my eyes threatening to spill over.

Woody's voice softened. "Shit! I'm sorry. Come on out of there, will you?"

He opened the door, peeled me away from the steering wheel, then pulled me into his big strong arms, and I lost it. I'd gone to full-on ugly cry mode. As I sobbed into his black T-shirt, Woody continued to mutter curses and threats to Asher's life and manhood. He stroked my hair and held me tight, and I felt safe. My body shuddered until my eyes burned out the last tears I swore I'd cry over him, and finally, my muscles began to relax.

"Come on. Let's get you all set up in the cabin." Woody grabbed my keys out of the ignition, closed the driver's door, and guided me around the back of the truck.

I hesitated. "My stuff."

"I'll get it. You need to rest. You're off tonight," Woody insisted.

"I have to work. I need the money."

"Don't worry about that right now. I know you're a fighter and a grown-ass independent young woman, but sometimes you need to let others help you for a change." My uncle's voice was strong with a determination that brokered no argument.

But I lived around him and the biker gang influence long enough, and I wasn't going to stand for it if I was to stand on my own two feet. That's something he and my dad taught me.

He saw the look on my face that said as much and sighed. "Fine, but you're not starting till at least an hour later than usual."

I began to open my mouth, but he pinched my lips closed with his forefinger and thumb and gave me the I'm deadly serious look. My shoulders slumped beneath his arm, and I nodded as I gave in. He held my lips a moment longer and chuckled because I probably looked like a drowned raccoon with duck lips with my ruined mascara.

"Fair enough!" I mumbled.

Woody gave me a kind smile that crinkled the laugh lines around his dark eyes, then kissed my forehead. He pulled open the screen door to the open-room wood cabin with its small kitchen and bathroom and nudged me forward as if he expected further protest, but he would get none. I felt drained but would pull through this like I always do. Because when you're a redneck backwoods girl like me, you pulled up your big girl panties.

There was no crying at the party, even if it was my own. I didn't want questions and looks of pity, and I wasn't going to sit around and cry in my beer or anyone else's. No, I experienced enough waterworks for one day to last a good long while.

My eyes cracked open, surrounded by darkness under a cocoon of rat-tattled old granny quilts that smelled like home, and I heard the familiar rumbling of loud engines blazing up the roadway toward the clubhouse. From the sound of things, the house would be full tonight, and there was no way I'd leave my uncle hanging without the extra help. I looked to the bedside at the green neon numbers on the alarm clock and realized Woody hadn't set the alarm to wake me sooner.

"Dammit, Woody!" I threw the blankets off me and stumbled to the floor. I must have crashed hard because I wore soft fuzzy socks I didn't remember putting on, which caused me to slip on the hardwood and knock my knees on the unforgiving surface.

"Double shit." I pulled myself up, turned to sit on the squeaky mattress, and rubbed my knees. My neck still had a slight pinch, so I rotated my head. The relieving pop sounded in my ears, and tension in my neck released.

I used the bathroom, observing that I needed to hydrate. My mother would be chastising me about the importance of kidney and bladder health. I missed Mom, but I'd be visiting her next week at the far more pleasant accommodations of the Appalachia Hills Psychiatric Care Home. Uncle Woody helped get her in for aftercare at the end of her sentence from the state psychiatric prison. I insisted we use Dad's life insurance payout since the state declared him dead years ago. Mom was still locked in, but where she lived now was clean with a caring staff, decent food, and proper medical treatment.

My reflection in the mirror was frightening and made me feel like I should be checking myself into the psych ward. I had a quick shower and put myself together as best possible. I smoothed my damp hair back into a high and tight ponytail. A triple shot of Visine helped clear up my bloodshot eyes. I brushed away my rancid cottonmouth and then drank a bottle of water. I put on a heavy dose of concealer to hide the dark circles and fresh mascara and finished with a shimmery pink gloss.

My usual attire consisted of a black tank top over my most comfortable Walmart half-price pushup bra and stretchy black jeggings paired with my blood-red clobber-stompers. I wore my dangly bangles and flashy CZ earrings and decided I looked presentable to the public. I didn't have an appetite, so I grabbed a trail mix bar and another water and headed out. The smell of wet earth and trees eased my senses.

There's something special about the night and the crowd that comes with it. After a long day of wearing fake smiles to the public or busting their asses doing hard labor, everyone was more relaxed. I loved that part of my job included bringing out the best in people.

The music was hopping, and cigar smoke wafted through the air the closer I got to The Roost. I knew with it came the smiling faces that always greeted me with variations of bushy to well-groomed manly facial hair, tattoos, bandanas, tight Harley Davidson T's, and black leather.

My adopted uncles and Aunt Stella always greeted me with warm hugs and light-hearted quips about their day. The Hillbilly Roost was where things got real, and the patrons talked shit about their bosses, drank to their heart's content, and shouted curses at the football players on the big screen.

A loud chorus of "Tara Baby!" hit me when I walked through the door, and I could no longer contain my smile. That's right! 'Because sometimes you gotta go where everybody knows your name.' The Cheers reference was something Dad taught me since it was a television show before my time, but I appreciated it.

There was no mention of condolences over my broken relationship. Uncle Woody placed a firm hand on my shoulder, looked at me sternly, and asked, "You okay?"

"Yeah."

"Good. Get your ass to work!"

"Aye, Aye, Captain!" I saluted, and Woody smirked with that look that meant 'smartass.'

I appreciated my uncle even more for not calling me out. I needed this. It wasn't all about the money, but I needed to be productive to keep my mind from dwelling on the downside of life.

Uncle Cannon exited the men's restroom. The door had a sign made especially for his patronage.

If Roadkill exits, spray the Lysol in the sign of the Holy Cross before entering.

"Hey, Rudy's team is playing tonight. Switch to channel twelve," Cannon yelled. Woody grabbed the remote and changed the channel, and everyone booed as the Tennessee Volunteers were down by three in the last quarter.

"Come on! Quit dragging your dicks out there!" Danny shouted.

"Get your head out of your asses!" Cannon yelled.

I spotted my brother on the screen pacing, looking frustrated as the ref called a penalty. I couldn't focus on the game as much as I wanted to. I had to keep the beers, bourbon, and whiskey coming. In the background, the jukebox was playing Should've Known Better by Carly Pearce. Her words spoke of my internalized pain. I wiped down the bar of spilled alcohol. My phone buzzed in my back pocket, and I ignored it. I already knew who it was, and I didn't want to hear anything he had to say.

Just when I thought things couldn't get worse, my uncles started yelling in excitement, cheering Rudy on, and I turned to the television just in time to see my brother get knocked down in the end zone. The instantaneous snap of his leg, a gruesome sight, had me clenching my chest as my heart plummeted into my stomach.

"Oh, god, Rudy, no!" I whispered as this dismal sense crept through me, wondering if this whole day had brought a curse upon my family.

"Everyone shut up and cut the music," Danny shouted.

Uncle Woody turned up the television's volume, and all eyes turned to the screen as we listened to the announcer's commentary and watched the scene of Rudy in agony.

"Raybrook got the ball to the end zone for a touchdown. That didn't look good at the end of the play. He took a brutal hit by Warrens. That's a serious leg break. The trainers are taking a look. Raybrook, a junior from Tremont, is a solid wide receiver, and this is his first major injury in all the time he's played. Raybrooks' 4th touchdown of the season was looking promising for one of the Volunteers' top players. This injury is a major setback for Raybrook."

"Awe, fuck!" Woody grumbled next to me.

Rudy's prone form was loaded onto a bright orange stretcher and then transferred to the injury cart. His appearance was pale, and he appeared to be in shock. It was painful for me to watch my poor brother.

I squeezed Uncle Woody's hand, and understanding passed between us as he turned to face me with a pained look. Football was Rudy's life, and our family had supported him since Dad assisted in coaching the Pee Wee team when Rudy was six years old. The whole family put so much time and effort into backing Rudy.

Through hard work and dedication, Rudy was able to attend the University of Tennessee on a full football scholarship. And even though Dad and Mom missed his high school playing years, my uncles and I continued to stick by Rudy's side, cheering him on at all his games.

Rudy continued to push himself hard because he wanted to make Dad and Mom proud, honoring Dad's memory and showing Mom he still loved and believed in her.

"Tara!" Uncle Woody snapped me out of my reverie. "We're going. I'll drive. We'll take your truck. Stella, can you take over here?

"Of course, Woody," Stella replied as she hurried behind the bar.

"Cannon, Danny, take care of things while we are gone!"

"Go! We've got you covered." Cannon clapped Woody on the back.

"Let's go." Woody gave a light shake to my shoulder, and I came out of my grief-filled stupor. I blinked away the few stray tears, nodded my head, and followed after him.

The drive to Knoxville was an hour away, but Woody made it in forty minutes. He'd give any cops a chase because he wouldn't stop till we made it to U.T. Medical Center. We got the call on the way from the E.R. staff. I answered Woody's phone and let them know we were on the way.

My voice cracked. "He's in surgery. It's a compound fracture to his right tibia and fibula."

"Okay." Woody nodded. "He's going to be okay. You know how tough your brother is."

I nodded in response, but I knew it would be many weeks in the hospital for Rudy, not to mention months of rehab. And by that time, the season would be over. Rudy had a fighting spirit, but I couldn't help but wonder how so much time lost will affect him.

The surgical nurse came out to update us, and all we could do was wait. Woody handed me a coffee and a turkey sandwich and told me I'd better eat. He knew me too well. I didn't protest even though it was difficult to swallow the dry bread, and I needed the sustenance as my stomach had been growling on the drive. If it weren't for Woody's insistence, I would've just stuck with the coffee.

My phone buzzed again. I huffed in frustration and finally decided to look at my messages.

Asher: Tara, please!!! We need to talk.

Asher: Come on, Kitten. Pick up your phone.

Asher: You have every right to be angry with me. I'm so sorry, babe.

Asher: Shit! What I did was wrong. It didn't mean anything.

Asher: Tara, I fucked up, okay? I love you!!! Please call me!!!

"You're a narcissistic asshole, Asher." I was about to turn off my phone when it buzzed again.

Asher: I saw what happened to Rudy. Is he gonna be okay?

I bit my lips as my finger hovered over the call button. I looked at Woody sitting adjacent to me with his hand over his eyes and his body leaned back in the chair. The last thing I wanted Woody to know was my intention to call Asher.

"Uncle Woody." I nudged his knee.

"Yeah?"

"I'm going to the ladies and stepping out for some air."

"Okay."

I got up and walked toward the restroom but halted at the sound of Woody's voice. "Hey, Tara. Tell Asher he's not getting that truck back. I co-signed for it; as I see it, it's mine."

"I wasn't gonna call him." I insisted.

"Okay."

I started walking again when Woody cleared his throat. I froze because I knew what he would say next.

"Better hurry to the ladies; your pants are on fire, girl."

I didn't respond because I knew better. Woody always called me out on my bullshit. I splashed some cool water on my face, noting how tired I still looked. Did I want to talk to Asher? He and Rudy were friends in high school, and Rudy was happy for my and Asher's engagement. But I knew Rudy would want to kill him now, too, if he found out what Asher did to me.

I could call Asher to let him know he was on Woody's shit list. And though Rudy didn't know yet, he'd be on his too. He'd torn my heart in two; the least I could do was make sure Asher would be frightened for his life if he dared come near me with my uncles.

I walked far away from prying ears because I knew I'd raise my voice. I took a deep breath and hit the call button. Two rings later.

"Tara?" Asher exasperated in a desperate plea.

"Asher!" I responded in a flippant tone. I will not cry. Nope, not for him to hear. Cause if I did, that'd give him a way to wiggle back inside and play up the memories, to try to salvage the one good thing he lost.

"Hey," he responded, "I'm sorry…."

"For what? You know I don't want to hear any of your excuses."

"I realize I have no good reason for what I did. I mean, we both feel like shit."

"Oh, so you're covering for Gina too? She can call herself, but I have nothing to say to her either."

What nerve! She hasn't called or texted, not that I'd have responded. She broke my heart too. I was always there for her. I knew she'd recently gone through a bad breakup with Cam, but that wasn't any excuse for her part in this. She and Asher always had this light, flirty banter between them, and I was cool with it because I thought it was all fun. I'd never seen anything to indicate it meant more. We were like family. Not anymore.

"Look, Tara. I want to talk to you in person. I know you're at the hospital right now. Is Rudy alright?" Asher sounded genuinely concerned.

"He's still in surgery. Compound fracture of both bones in his leg. It's pretty bad." My voice choked, and I cleared it.

"Shit, I'm sorry," Asher responded mournfully. "Would it be okay if I come to see him?"

"Not tonight. I can't deal with seeing you with my brother's condition." I hesitated. I wasn't entirely sure how I felt. I could use some comfort, but it couldn't be from him.

"I understand. You're both important to me, Tara. I'll give you the space you need to deal, but I refuse to give up on us. I'll do whatever it takes. Counseling, therapy, you name it."

"The way I see it, you're in no position to be calling the shots, and if I were that important to you, you'd have told me we needed to talk before anything happened between you and Gina."

I started to shake with a fire coursing through my veins because he'd burned me in the worst way. He needed to realize this because I didn't feel all in to help fix what he broke. Maybe that's short-sided of me, but this wound was open and fresh, and it hurt, dammit!

"I've gotta go. The doctor is coming out to talk to us," I lied. Tears burned the backs of my eyes, and I had to cut this call.

"Woody's there? I mean, right there with you now?"

He's scared. Good!

"Where else did you think I'd go?"

"Tara, I."

"I have to go."

Chapter 3

TARA

This Season's A Bust

Another hour later, the doctor appeared and directed Woody and me to a recovery room where Rudy was asleep. The doctor explained what occurred during the surgery and told us to expect a long road ahead. Rudy would be in the hospital for at least two to three weeks. After his bones mended well, Rudy would have some grueling physical therapy. My brother wouldn't play the rest of the season, and I knew that would upset him the most.

Woody and I sat at Rudy's bedside and waited for him to wake. He was on a morphine drip to combat the pain. I observed the heavy cast on his right leg from knee to foot set in a sling suspended above his bed. The sight made my chest ache. The beeping sound from the pulse ox monitor and Rudy's calm, steady breaths kept me suspended in expectancy.

"Yeah, he's in recovery now," Woody spoke in a low voice on his phone to Cannon. "Hell, yeah, man. He's on the good stuff right now. He's still out, though."

Cannon said something in response to Danny, and they both chuckled. I couldn't make out everything, but I knew they were trying to keep everyone's spirits high at The Roost.

"It's gonna be a few weeks before he gets out of here," Woody said. "Yeah, I'll let him know once he comes round. Okay, see you tomorrow." Woody ended the call.

"Who all is coming?"

"Cannon and Stella will be here. We'll do a rotation, so everyone gets a chance. Rudy won't be alone for a moment unless he's sleeping. I'm sure he'll be pretty popular while he's here. Danny said he should snag himself up a sweet nurse if one gives him a chance." Woody chuckled.

I smiled. "Yeah, good luck with that! Mom got hit on by patients all to time. Especially the pervy old geezers."

My brother looked like Dad, handsome with dark brown eyes, thick dark wavy hair, and swoon-worthy masculine facial features. Football put a lot of muscle on Rudy, and his height at six' two" had all the pretty little cheerleader types shaking their pom-poms enthusiastically in his presence.

"I got a broken leg, and now I'm some old dude. That's harsh," Rudy responded groggily.

I jumped up and felt relief hearing my brother's voice. "What the hell, Rudy! You scared the shit out of me!"

"Hey, be nice. It wasn't Rudy's fault." Woody chuckled.

"Yeah. It's a chance all players take out on the field. I guess my luck ran out," Rudy's voice had a mild slur as he gave me a cheesy grin. "Hey, I got the touchdown. Did you see?"

"Yeah, I also saw your leg snap in two, jackass!"

"Yeah, that did suck balls," Rudy grimaced. "What did the doc say about my chances of getting back?"

"Well, Champ! You're finished for the season," Woody replied.

"To Hell with that! They don't know me! I'm not taking this bullshit lying down!" Rudy grumbled.

"Uh, did you see your leg?" I asked.

"Hell, yeah! I saw it and felt it. Hurt like a mofo. But I feel fine now."

"Ha! Just wait till they take you off the morphine drip. You'll want to eat the pain pills they give you like candy. And you gotta watch that because people become addicted to that shit," Woody said.

"I gotta high pain tolerance. Even my team knows not to haze me because it's pointless. I'm made of iron, like Superman!" Rudy popped his bicep and kissed it.

"Superman is the man of steel, Rudy." I rolled my eyes.

"Yeah, but I'm strong like him without the weakness of Kryptonite," he argued.

I laughed because I knew for sure he was going to be okay. His spirit wasn't broken, and he had as big a head as ever.

"You think Ma saw the game?" Rudy asked.

"I wouldn't know. It's not like Mom can call us, but I'm going out to see her on Tuesday," I replied.

Rudy looked at me imploringly. "Do me a favor, Sis. Unless Ma says she saw or heard about it somehow, don't bring it up, okay? If she knows, tell her I'm good. But you can say I made a touchdown for her."

"Sure thing." I placed my hand in his and squeezed. Rudy smiled at me, and I started to tear up.

"Hey, hey there! I'm going to be all right. You know that." Rudy squeezed my hand, then pulled it closer to his face. "Somethings missing. I can't put my finger on it now cause these drugs are doing some loopy shit to my head."

I kept my mouth shut as he studied my hand with my bare ring finger. I didn't want to tell him about Asher yet. He needed to rest. Hell, I needed to rest.

Later today, I thought.

The clock on the wall read nearly half-past five a.m. As I opened my mouth to tell Rudy to get some sleep, the doctor came in with a nurse.

"Ah, the young man has risen from the dead!"

"I wasn't exactly dead, doc," Rudy smirked and winked at the pretty blond nurse, who shook her head as she checked his vitals.

The doctor smiled mischievously. "No, and thank heavens, kid. You've been spared that fate; in the meantime, I'm afraid you're moving on nonetheless."

"I'm getting out of here already?" Rudy asked hopefully.

"Yes, Sir! You're movin' on up to the second floor. Have to make space for the next case. As for leaving the hospital, that's a no-go. You're in here for the long haul. Two to three weeks minimum, depending on how well you behave." The pleasant doctor winked, and the nurse chuckled.

On the other hand, I cringed because cheery, good-natured doctors gave me the creeps since having lived with Dr. Lyle Durst. My mind went into a flashback of the sweet-natured Dr. Durst. Lyle wooed his way into our family about two years after Dad went missing, and Mom gave up hope of finding him. Mom took on a position in Durst's office after finding the hospital hours too daunting, and she wanted to be there for Rudy and me.

Mom was sad and lonely, and she missed Dad desperately. Lyle's good nature and witty comments seemed the best medicine for her blues. Before we knew it, he took us on family outings, buying our affection with the latest electronics, clothing, and jewelry. And I hate to admit I bought it hook, line and sinker because I was only fourteen years old, and what teenager didn't appreciate the coolest new material items?

Lyle bought me my first cell phone. All the kids at school were drooling at the latest version iPhone in my hands, even my rival, Bren Taylor. Bren's flustered expression scored Lyle even more points in my book. Bren thought her shit smelled like Chanel No.5 and took every opportunity to rub it in my face. It felt good to pull all the attention from her pretentious actions. She always flaunted her body in her too-tight designer jeans and Vicky's Secret cami tops. Bren was a frigid bitch in heat as she snubbed any girl she deemed homely and teased the school jocks with her bountiful assets.

But back to Lyle. Once he established himself in Mom's good graces and talked her into an impromptu marriage, his behavior became questionable. Mom was too deep to see, but Lyle seemed excessively concerned about my health. Just me. Not Mom or Rudy. He became obsessed, and after I nearly passed out in gym class one day, he insisted on checking my glucose levels. He diagnosed me with juvenile diabetes, which shocked Mom as we didn't have any family history of the disease.

The next strange thing, Lyle insisted he was the one to check my blood sugar every day, even though I wasn't afraid of administering a finger prick to myself, and Mom could have just as easily done it for me even if I had been. Mom put her faith in Lyle as his patients sang his praises, so what was not to trust? I didn't question my mother's judgment as strange as it felt.

He never told me specific numbers; he said I was high, low, or normal. I researched it at school one day, and the weird thing was my body didn't show symptoms to match up.

Besides the gym class incident, I felt fine aside from being a little tired before I had my period, but I never mentioned that to Dr. Durst. I didn't need to give him an excuse to go there.

What made me feel more uncomfortable was when I snuck to check my blood, but he had somehow crept up without me noticing him enter the kitchen and firmly took over. After that, he locked up the meter, lancets, and test strips. He also administered my insulin shots, and when I began to feel uncomfortable with his hands always hovering around me, I tried to find ways to avoid him.

That backfired when he told me I needed meds for anxiety and forced me to take them before going to bed each night. He even prescribed Mom meds for depression, anxiety, and sleep disorder. He insisted she hallucinated when she mentioned having nightmares about our dad warning her about some dark evil encroaching upon our family.

"Hey! Earth to Tara!" Uncle Woody snapped his fingers before my face. I blinked out my pleasant trip down memory lane and looked around to see the nurse pushing Rudy's bed out of the room. The doctor left without my notice.

"Uncle Woody? Do you think Cannon wouldn't mind bringing my books, laptop, and a few changes of clothes with him tomorrow? I want to stay here with Rudy until I visit Mom Tuesday."

"I'll tell him. He won't mind," Woody replied.

"Do you think the hospital will allow me to stay overnight?"

"I'm sure they'll make an exception in this situation." Woody winked. I knew his power of persuasion with people, especially the female populace, whether heterosexual or otherwise. Woody put on a charm that oozed charisma that left even the sternest of Karens giggling and forgetting their reasons for arguing in the first place.

I woke in the reclining chair to the sound of rain. I groaned in discomfort from the awkward position in which I'd slept. I yawned and stretched, then put the chair upright. The dim light in the hospital room had a dismal feel due to the lack of sunshine as raindrops ran down the window. I heard the faint voices on the television and looked up to see the familiar crime show tied to unpleasant memories of my past.

Rudy's voice was rough. "You sounded like you were having a nightmare. Been having some of those myself lately." He pointed to the plastic pitcher. "Would you mind?"

"Normally I would, but seeing as you're a complete invalid right now, I suppose." I got up and poured a cup of water for Rudy and another for myself. My mouth was so dry. I must have been a drooling, mouth-breathing mess.

"Nice of you being a non-judgy, good Samaritan. So will you tell me what's happening or leave me hanging?" Rudy gestured to his hanging leg with a stack of pillows propped beneath.

I took a considerable moment to drink my water and held up my finger in a hold-on-a-moment gesture, leaving Rudy to give me the same 'smartass' look he'd adopted from Uncle Woody. After a long minute, I cleared my throat.

"You want the bad news first or the bad news?"

Rudy's eyes observed my hand holding the cup and nudged his chin in gesture. "Well, for starters, you can explain why you're not wearing your engagement ring?"

"I thought I might give Asher a chance to explain that to you so you can kick his ass. But you have to wait till your leg is better. He told me he wants to see you; I don't know when, but I'd rather not be here when he does. Then again, perhaps I should stay to prevent you from further hurting yourself when you're ready to lunge out of bed to murder him."

"In that case, he'd better not show up at all. What happened?"

"I caught him and Gina…Together," I blew out a breath of deeply held tension. I'd said it. What else was there to say? The details were unnecessary.

Rudy went dead quiet. His jaw moved back and forth as he ground his teeth, and his face morphed into that of a man on a mission set to destroy his enemy. He took a deep, cleansing breath and blew it out.

"The fuck-up better count his blessing that I'm laid up right now, or he'd be here instead. Shit, Tara, I'm in a lot of pain, but it's nothing I can't deal with. He hurt you, and retribution is a new goal to get me back in shape."

I sighed, sat down, and dropped my head in my hands. "You don't need to fight this battle for me. Asher and I are through. Gina is no longer my friend, and they can have each other as far as I'm concerned. Perhaps I was too blind to see any signs. I've been busting my ass working at The Roost, finishing school, and visiting Mom every few weeks. Asher promised to be there for me like I've been for him."

"Tara," Rudy said with concern.

"I'm through crying over him!" I lied to myself as tears rolled down my face. Dammit!

"Come here!" Rudy held his arms open to me. I carefully leaned into his embrace and let the silent tears flow onto his hospital gown. Without words, he had me scooch into bed by his side and held me while stroking my hair.

"Since when did my little brother become this man taking care of his big sister?" I mumbled into the crook of his shoulder.

"Tara, you've always placed yourself on the back burner, putting everyone else first. You make sure people in your life accomplish their dreams, and you'd start on yours once they make it. You're the most selfless person I know, and in some way, there's strength in that.

But most people in your life are grown-ass adults capable of choosing right from wrong. You are a guiding light, and Asher chose to crash into the rocks rather than making safe harbor, and that's his damn fault."

Rudy's words rang with truth. Losing Dad like we had made me feel responsible, and Mom killing Lyle made me feel this way, even more so, because she was protecting me. Uncle Woody made sure we had a roof over our heads, food to fill our bellies, and finished our high school careers, but I had turned into this mother hen tending her clutch with diligence and precisely doing what Rudy said. I placed myself second. I wasn't even sure who I was or what I wanted for my life.

I gave up on opportunities to do more or have better. The past still haunted me, and I was scared to step out lest something else came along to knock me over. It was safe to be the coach and not the player. But as it turns out, I can still get knocked over standing on the sidelines. There is no safety zone.

I heard a click, saw a camera flash on someone's phone, and looked at Cannon and Stella smiling down at Rudy and me in the hospital bed together. Stella had an endearing expression, and Cannon grinned as he lowered his phone.

"I'm posting this one on my page," Cannon said.

"Awe, look at the two of you," Stella cooed.

"Yeah, thanks, Cannon. That'll go over great with my teammates. I can't wait for them to start taunting me about our Appalachian backwoods relationship. They know what my sister looks like, and I haven't had a steady girlfriend in a few years. Those assholes like to make the worst assumptions," Rudy said.

"Don't get your panties in a bunch. I'll caption it, 'A sister's apology after running her asshole brother over with her truck.'" Cannon made the post, and Stella laughed.

"Here's the stuff you asked for, Tara." Stella set my bag in the recliner.

"Thanks, Stella," I murmured as I rubbed my runny nose on Rudy's gown.

"Ewe, gross!" Rudy complained.

"Sorry, I didn't have a tissue. You need a change and bath anyway. You kinda reek!" I sniffed and rubbed my nose with the back of my hand.

"I saw a cute little brunette out in the hall. Want me to wrangle her up to give you a nice scrub-a-dub, Bud?" Cannon asked with a wink.

"Yes, please," Rudy smiled.

I took the cue to exit. "I'll let you do your thing. I'm going to take my laptop and catch up on some work. I'll catch you guys later."

"Oh, Tara," Cannon called, "Stella and I rode our bikes here so Woody could head back. He gave me the key to your truck. Said you shouldn't worry about rushing home since he won't need you till Wednesday night." Cannon handed me the key fob. "You'll be stopping to see Lydia on the way? Tell her we're thinking about her."

"Yes, please send her our love," Stella said.

"I've never stopped," I replied. Cannon gave me a gentle hug. I grabbed my laptop and my book on business management. Before I headed out, Stella kissed my cheek.

"You need some girl company? Girls need to vent their ovaries from time to time; get away from all this testosterone, if you get my drift. I can give you some tips on hospitality in the leisure industry." Stella elbowed my side in jest.

"She just wants to talk some trash about me and initiate you into the old ladies club," Cannon smirked.

"I never say anything I don't already tell you to your face, and you know it," Stella replied.

Cannon and Stella have been together forever and a day, and I always found their banter entertaining. Once upon a time, before yesterday, to be exact, I hoped Asher and I would make the long haul and bicker at one another like my aunt and uncle. Anyone could see how in love they are, still after all these years.

They've always been faithful to one another. Their love story inspired me to believe true love exists. A woman has to be full of grit to handle a man like my uncle, and I've seen Stella put Cannon in his place when he started throwing a tantrum like a damn toddler. She has my absolute respect cause she had her shit together, unlike myself.

"Yeah, let's have a ladies' lunch," I said.

Stella stepped over to Rudy and leaned in to kiss his cheek. "You need anything, sweetheart?"

"Nah, I'm good." Rudy hugged her.

"Bring me a sandwich, chips, and a Coke." Cannon barked in command. Stella placed her hands on her hips and glared.

"Please, Sweetums?" The now sugary tone of Cannon's voice made Stella's lips turn up, and she tiptoed to kiss his lips.

"Better! Yes, Honeybuns. Your little bee will buzz away and cater to your whims." Stella sang.

Rudy and I laughed.

"Whipped!" Rudy covered his mouth with the fake cough.

"You got the bum leg keeping me in good graces right now, kid. You better check yourself, cause you won't be in a place of sympathy forever." Cannon pointed a threatening finger at Rudy.

"Bring it on, old man!" Rudy challenged with his fist shaking in the air.

"Go easy on him," I said.

"I won't hurt him. Yet!" Cannon replied.

"She was talking to Rudy," Stella said.

"Har-D-Har-Har, woman." Cannon folded his big arms across his chest, and Stella rolled her eyes, turned, and sashayed out the door with her hips swaying. Cannon whistled after her, watching her ass.

"I wanna ride on that swing set later," he called after Stella, and she laughed.

"Hot Damn, my lady is fine!

"Ewe! Awe!" Rudy and I exclaimed in unison.

Cannon laughed.

Chapter 4
TARA

Two Old Ladies

I sat at the cafeteria table and placed my food tray beside my laptop. Stella chewed and swallowed a bite of pasta and then slapped the table before me. When she lifted her hand, I saw my engagement ring and was surprised.

"Spill it, Tara! Woody didn't rat you out, said you were extra tired after your last shift, and let you sleep in a bit, but I wasn't buying it."

I sighed. "Everyone's going to find out anyway. I might as well tell you, and you can let everyone know because I don't want to talk about it anymore after I say it. Woody and Rudy already know."

"And that is?" Stella arched her brow and leaned toward me.

I looked at the people around us, overly engaged in their conversations to care. My mouth took that moment to dry again, so I took a sip of water as Stella's long electric blue fingernail began tapping on the table.

"Let's just say Asher and I are through. And Gina's not my bff anymore."

Stella sucked in a sharp breath and her eyes rounded in shock. "No!"

"Yep!" I shook my head. My body disagreed with the word coming from my mouth.

Stella slammed her fist on the table. "That little shit! I'll have his balls hanging off my bike plate. And that cunt, Gina, better watch out. I'll tear out her bitch balls and hang 'em like dice from my mirror."

I put my hand over my mouth to cover the water spray as I choked. The mess ran down to my shirt, and I quickly grabbed a bunch of napkins, wiped my chin, and started laughing my ass off. The visual of Asher's sack flapping in the wind as the heat of Stella's tailpipe burnt them to a shrivel sounded ideal to me. As far as Gina's ovaries, *ewe*. I couldn't see doing that to another woman, even if she was a lying, man-stealing cunt.

Some of the closer cafeteria patrons gave me a startled look, and Stella turned to glare at them. They then quickly averted their eyes. That's right! Biker chick in the house; even though she was gorgeous with her long blond braided hair, soft baby blues, and pouty lips, my aunt Stella was a force no one wanted to reckon with. She looked the part of femininity, but Uncle Cannon called her his 'brick house' in reference to an old song. He played it for me a few times, and I saw his meaning.

Stella turned back to me and smirked. It took me a moment to get the residual laughter bubbles to die. When Stella smiled at me sweetly and took my hand in hers, I sniffed as my tears of laughter took on a different emotion.

"Shit! I swore I was done with this already!"

"Tara Baby. Don't deny yourself the right to let go. Get it all out. It takes time, and this isn't something you get over in a day or two." Stella gave my hand a squeeze and a few tender pats.

"Thanks, Stella." I sniffed, wiping away my tears with the already demolished napkins. I blew my stuffy nose, balled up my mess, and dropped it before me, looking at the grotesque snot-riddled paper like it represented my whole life.

"I never told you this before, but the same thing happened to me long before meeting your uncle Cannon," Stella confessed.

"Really? How'd you deal with it? Get past it?"

"I didn't really. Least not till I met Cannon, and he rocked my world." She cracked an impish smile, and I laughed.

"Yeah, it turns out he'd been burned too. We both confessed it to one another, which resulted in us making a pact to treat each other respectfully. And if one of us felt the need to stray, we'd come clean before it came to blows.

But that fine man treated me so well, and I returned the favor many times; going astray never once crossed our minds. And you pretty much know the rest of the story."

"Yeah, no need to say more." I mimicked, putting my fingers in my ears, and Stella laughed. She reached across the table and pulled my hands away.

"You should know that you need to see this as an opportunity. One where you truly know who you want to be and what you want for your life—the kind of man you deserve. Slash that, a man who will put his nuts in a vice if it makes you happy. In the meantime, cry it out, get shit-faced. Hell, I'll join you!" Stella grinned.

"Nuts in a vice?" I laughed.

"Hey, it's just an analogy, but you get what I'm saying, right?" Stella winked.

"Yeah, I get it. You are my knight in shining armor."

"That's right! Your aunty Stella will always have your back. I love you!"

"I love you, too."

"Now eat and hit the books. I'm going to go buzz back up to my man and feed him. He'll need to keep up with me later at Hotel De La Bow-Chicca-Wow-Wow."

"La, la, la. Didn't hear that!" I laughed.

Stella beamed at me as she gathered her lunch, a brown bag, and a Coke bottle. She began walking, stopped, and turned to blow me a kiss, and I chuckled while shaking my head. I noticed quite a few men's heads turn along with a few women's as she left the room. I wished I had her confidence.

I ate, pushed my tray aside, and began cracking away at my schoolwork. After about an hour, my phone buzzed, and I checked it. A sigh of relief left me as I saw it was Woody checking in.

Woody: How's the lackey? Did you get what you needed?

Me: He's living it up in his new high-rise penthouse with a Loose Cannon and his ball and chain. And, yeah, I got everything I needed. Is everyone good there?

Woody: I'm hiring extra help. A live act is coming, and things will get extra busy.

Me: How come I'm just hearing this?

Woody: I just found out myself. I better not see you at work till Wednesday. Tuesday nights are slow, and it'll allow me to train up the new girl without you criticizing my methods.

Me: New girl?

Woody: Yeah, new girl! I'm an equal opportunity employer, and she arrived at the right time.

Me: Who is she?

Woody: Bren Taylor. She knows you from high school.

Me: Uncle Woody, NO!!!! She's a bitch! She was the bane of my existence! I can't work around her.

Woody: Suck it up, buttercup. I need the help, and she won't be with you behind the bar. If she causes too much trouble, I'll boot her.

"Fuck!" I said out loud. An elderly woman gasped as she pushed her walker by my table.

"*Sorry!*" I mouthed at her. She increased her pace, putting distance between her and me.

Me: Fine. She is trouble. Don't say I didn't warn you.

Woody: I eat trouble like a five-course meal. I think I can handle one girl.

Me: Don't let her tempt you to eat what she has to offer. That bitch spoiled a long time ago. She'll send you back here with a case of food poisoning.

Woody: Funny. See you Wednesday kiddo.

Me: Yeah, fine!

I felt betrayed! How could he? Woody knew I was already suffering, and he does this? Bren Taylor is a despicable, snub-nosed, elitist whore. I don't understand why she wants a waitressing job at a biker bar. She made my life miserable in high school. Every time I turned a corner, Bren was there spitting venom, making a mockery of me and any situation which put me in her spotlight of shame and humiliation.

And I could stand up for myself, but I'd never stoop to her level. After Mom got sent away for Lyle's murder, Bren took it upon herself to add salt to my open wounds. Bren shouted 'Snapped' every time she saw me. She got this from the television crime show depicting women who'd murdered their husbands, which became a popular topic after our town had a similar story.

Most of the students at school gave me pitying looks as they heard what happened with my family. Soon after, Bren started calling me Apple Snaps, insinuating the apple didn't fall far from the tree. I was so close to proving her right. But then, one day, I realized that Bren must be hiding something about herself. Because in many cases, bullies caused trouble for others to feel better about themselves when in reality, their lives were in turmoil. So perhaps Bren had some deep dark secret she needed to cover, and I was an easy target.

Gina, my one true friend at the time, sparked rumors about why Bren hung out at school long after hours. And one of Bren's extra-curricular activities entailed flaunting herself at the football players after practice. The more I thought about it, Bren seemed desperate. And desperate people do stupid shit, so I felt sorry for her somehow.

Suffice it to say, I'd suffered at the hands of evil much worse than anything Bren could do with her words, and on some level, I could relate to the emotional complexity that plagues a teenage girl's mind. Is it even possible for someone like Bren to change after four years? Why did she return? She had a scholarship and left to attend the University of Texas. I was so relieved when she went away.

I needed to stay behind to repay Woody for all he'd done and still does to help, and I wanted to be close enough to visit my mother. I chose to work for Uncle Woody when he offered the opportunity. He made sure my work schedule didn't conflict with furthering my education. I decided to get my business management degree to work in the Hotel and Leisure industry.

I dreamed of managing a luxury resort somewhere in a beautiful tropical paradise. I wanted Mom to live with me once she was well and free to rejoin society. Anywhere far away from here and a fresh start is something she deserves for all the hell she's endured.

I finished my class and completed my assignment while Rudy slept. A few of Rudy's teammates and coach came to visit, along with a few girls from the cheer squad. The girls went all out with a peppy cheer and dance, shaking their orange and white pom poms. Rudy's face got peppered with orange lip prints from the girls and the guys. He tried to fight off the boys, but they held down his arms. It was hilarious. I took many pictures and did a few close-up shots of his face to show Mom. If she didn't know about Rudy's condition, I would keep my promise not to tell.

The storyline: Rudy Raybrook got hazed. Soon Rudy's room was filled with balloons, flowers, banners, and get-well cards. A fun day filled with well-wishers tired Rudy and me out.

Uncle Danny showed up to keep us company in the evening. I knew it was Danny when I heard his approaching steps with the telltale sound of rattling chains and clinking spurs. I saw those infamous boots below the drawn curtain as Danny stopped and chirped. "Knock, knock. Anybody home?"

"You may enter, but beware!" I replied.

Danny pulled back the curtain. "Holy shit! Did someone buy out a party supply store? It looks like you had a wild one here, and I wasn't invited! What the hell?" Danny's brow dipped, and he postured his body in mock outrage.

"Sorry, I have no control over who shows up," Rudy held a giant balloon out to Danny as a peace offering. "You can have this if you want."

The balloon read, *'Your ass may be kicked, but your balls can't be licked'* along with a cartoon depiction of Rocky, the bluetick coon dog with a cone around his head.

Danny accepted with a gleeful smile. "Aw, thanks, man. I'm going to tie this to my handlebars."

"How's everything back at The Hillbilly Roost?" Rudy asked.

"Awe, let me tell you, this guy showed up at Sunday service. He looked nervous, so I asked his name, and he told me John Sceva. Man, I had to laugh," Danny chuckled.

"Why is that?" Rudy asked.

"Well, I told John Sceva, my name is Diablo Danny. The guy looked like he might shit his pants and asked me why a guy that goes by the Devil would be running church service, and I told him we all have our demons to exorcise. Just so happens in 1 John, some dudes named Sceva tried to call a demon out, and that demon was like, Do I know you pussies?" Danny laughed.

"Uncle Woody told me those Sceva guys called on the name of Jesus by way of Paul, but the demon called them out because they didn't know Jesus; they only knew of him," I added.

"What's the difference?" Rudy asked.

"Well, it's like gossip instead of the gospel. They weren't part of the grapevine, aka Jesus; they just heard Jesus' name. It's like telling a bully that a family member will come to kick their ass when they don't even know you exist."

Danny started laughing, and Rudy looked at him like he was off his rocker, which in Danny's case, is the gospel truth. "So, Sceva asked me to tell him the gospel and later asked to be baptized, so I took him down to the lake."

"The lake is nut-scrunching cold this time of year," Rudy said.

"Exactly. The guy had second thoughts, so I gave him a little extra incentive." Danny held up his lighter with a wicked grin.

I shook my head. "Oh, Uncle Danny, you didn't?"

"Yes, baby girl. I gave him a tiny taste of what Hell would feel like. I flipped my Zippo and lit his ass on fire. Sceva ran into the water, yelling, 'Save Me!' And while there, he officially took the plunge, and 'Cha-Ching' another soul shall make it through the Pearly Gates." Danny laughed like a loon, with Rudy and me chuckling along.

"I hope you repented after scaring the dude like that," Rudy said.

"I don't regret my methods. It got the job done. You know me. I'm a hot mess, and God knows it." Danny chuckled as he wiped away tears. "Besides I let Sceva dunk me and we prayed together afterward. We're all good!"

Uncle Danny was a prankster. Woody and Cannon performed water-board baptisms on him whenever he pulled fleece over their eyes. Eventually, Danny finally saw the error of his ways which meant 'don't prank Woody and Cannon,' so he pleaded for his brothers' forgiveness. That didn't stop him from moving on to unsuspecting fair game.

Before Danny left, he put my engagement ring in my palm and closed my fingers over it. "Stella told me to give this back to you and what happened with Asher. I'm sorry to hear. You know I'm here if you want to talk, but I get it if you don't. Stella said to tell ya, it still means something, but you should do with it what you wish."

I hadn't even realized she'd taken it with her after our lunch. My mind must have blocked that part out at the time. "Thanks, Uncle Danny." I hugged him.

"See ya back at the club." He saluted Rudy before turning to leave the room.

Chapter 5
TARA

Darkness & Despair

I was drifting in and out of consciousness. The room was dark, and I looked at my paisley and floral comforter covering me. The door to my bedroom creaked open, and the nightlight illuminated the hallway. A tall, dark shadow figure loomed at the foot of my bed. Fear took over, and my breathing escalated.

Total panic set in as I felt my body pinned and paralyzed. My bed dipped as the dark figure sat beside me. My comforter pulled away, and something sharp drew up and down my arm. My throat clamped tight as I struggled to breathe. I couldn't say a word. I couldn't scream.

Please, no! I begged in my mind. *Someone! Help! Me!* My lips trembled as tears ran down the sides of my face. A large hand reached up to push my hair back.

"Sshhh!" The figure attempted to soothe me. Creeping fingers traced my tears, and I shivered with fright. The cold, sharp tip traced a line down my lips, and a metallic smell permeated my nose as the blade grazed a straight path to my chin. Fingers roughly grasped my face, and I felt the claw biting into my bottom lip. I whimpered and struggled to move.

I tasted the blood on my mouth as the hand moved away, and I heard a wet sucking, followed by a popping sound as the hand drew away from the figure's face.

It had licked its thumb, obviously liking what it was tasting as a long, drawn-out 'Mmmmm' sounded like a groan of pleasure.

No! I started shaking violently. *P-please! Don't hurt me!* I begged in my head.

The shadow didn't speak, but I could hear excited, heavy breaths. I wanted to fight, scream, kick, and bite. Still, I remained frozen in place like a spell cast over my body. It felt like dark evil magic. I had to be cursed! What did it want from me?

The hand moved back down to my forearm, dragging the metallic claw slowly along my delicate flesh. I could not see a face in the darkness, void of any features; there was only a black smokey haze that blurred my vision and fixed my mind in a state of confusion. *Why is this happening to me?*

I felt increased pressure against my skin as the claw scratched, followed by a burning sting. I started sobbing inaudibly, then came the scream I could only hear in my mind as I felt the painful puncture of the claw's razor tip pierce my arm near my wrist. I was going to die; I just knew it. My arm was lifted and met with the press of cold, wet lips. A long tongue dragged from my wrist to the crook of my elbow. My stomach writhed with a nauseating urgency to vomit.

Then came a wicked chuckle. At this, I was groaning in agony, unable to release the screams clawing my throat, desperate to break free. The shadow leaned close to my face, and I screwed my eyes shut tightly, my breaths short and frantic. I felt a cold cheek press mine, lips next to my ear.

Cruel, taunting breaths hit me as a deep masculine voice whispered, "I'm coming back for you!"

I shot up from the recliner in Rudy's hospital room, breathing rapidly, and my heart nearly pounded out of my chest. I looked down at my arm finding nothing but the old scars that ran the same length from my nightmare.

My lip stung like a split fissure, and I tasted my blood. I brought my shaking hand up, pressed my finger to my lip, and pulled back, seeing the red smear on my fingertip. I moved my tongue back and forth and realized I must have bitten myself.

Rudy was sleeping. Early morning light peaked in between the slats of the closed window blinds. The curtain drew back suddenly, and I was startled.

"Sorry!" the nurse whispered. She did her job, checking my brother over and making notes on his chart.

I went to the bathroom and began getting ready for the day. My heart ached at leaving Rudy behind, but I knew he'd be okay with how people came in and out to see him. I'd be back next week to visit again.

I tended my lip, carefully brushed my teeth, and put ointment on the tender mark. I finished getting ready and came out to Rudy sitting up and his leg propped up on pillows. He tucked into his breakfast.

"When are you heading out to see Mom?" Rudy mumbled through a mouth full of eggs.

"I'll be leaving in an hour. Will you need anything before I go?"

"Nah, I'm good. I'll have more company this afternoon. Vera said she'd be back to give me a sponge bath." Rudy's smile grew.

"She was the one just in here? She's pretty."

"I noticed. Hey, if Mom gave Dad a chance, I figured I'd better try my luck while I'm here."

I smiled. "Well, I didn't see a ring on it, but I recall Mom saying she couldn't wear jewelry on shift. Best check and make sure. You don't want to get into a similar scenario I've been through."

"You gonna be okay?" Rudy asked with sympathy in his eyes. His ex-girlfriend, Cindy, had broken his heart a few years back, and Rudy took it hard. He took a hiatus from the dating scene for a time, and he was too much of a gentleman to seek out a rebound type of deal. I knew Rudy wanted something real with a good woman, and they were getting as hard to find as a good man nowadays. I thought I had the real thing with Asher. It turned out I was wrong.

"Well, I will be on a slow mend, just like you with your leg. But, also, like you, I'm tough, and I'll make it through. You and I have survived worse."

I began packing up my belongings. I had put the ring in the front zip pocket of my backpack. I wasn't sure what I'd do with it. Rudy and I talked for another half hour before I hugged him and kissed his cheek.

"Wooh-Wee! I'll be sure to tell Vera to get in here for that sponge bath, stat." I fanned my face as I backed away, and Rudy laughed.

I went to the cafeteria to grab a breakfast sandwich and a coffee for the road. I was glad to see the sun shining through the windows. I headed toward the hospital entrance and stopped when I saw the same elderly lady from two days ago. She wore a long pink dressing gown, and her silver hair strayed from beneath a sheer green headscarf. She sat on a bench outside the entrance and stared out. Her countenance appeared reminiscent.

I still had some time before I needed to be on the road, and I wanted to apologize to her for my outburst, which seemed to startle her when she walked by my table.

The automatic doors parted, and I stepped through. I didn't want to scare her, so I sat down a few feet away in case she was the type to lash out in fear or she was crazy. I set down my bag and cleared my throat, and she looked at me.

"Hello." I smiled.

"Hello, Dear." She smiled back. "It's a lovely day, isn't it?"

I looked at the blue sky with a few strati stretching across and back to her, meeting her blue eyes. "I'm Tara."

"I'm Abigail."

"Abigail. That's pretty."

"Thank you, dear."

"Abigail, I wanted to apologize for my potty mouth in the cafeteria the other day. It seems I startled you with my rude outburst. It's no excuse, but I've been having a tough week."

"Oh, Honey. When you've lived as long as I have, well, I am sure you've heard the saying before. I'm not easily offended. I had a strange feeling when I passed by; not your fault. I sense things, you see?" Abigail's blue eyes took me in, and I sensed something about her.

"Have we met before?" It seemed like I knew her from somewhere. My mind couldn't place her, though.

"No, I don't think so. I'd remember a pretty young lady like yourself. Though my memory isn't as good as it used to be. Getting old sucks, as you young people would say, and I'd have to agree."

I chuckled. "You know what? You're pretty awesome. And you're not old, at least not to me. You've got a young spirit."

"I suppose. It's the outside package that gets my goat." Abigail held out her wrinkled hands. She wore no jewelry, and suddenly I felt I should give her something—a gift. I leaned over, unzipped my backpack's front pocket, and sifted around till my fingers touched the ring. I pulled it out, held it up, and knew what I wanted to do.

"Does your family come to visit you often?"

"Well, no. Once upon a time, I had a wonderful husband and a son, but they're both gone."

"I'm so sorry." My heart went out to this lovely woman. "May I?" I moved closer to her and gestured to take her right hand. I gave it a warm, light squeeze when she offered it, then slipped the ring on her slender middle finger. Abigail's breath hitched. It wasn't a fancy ring, but as it turned out, Stella had been right; it did still mean something.

"I'd love for you to have this friendship ring. Will you still be here next week? I want to come to visit you."

"Yes. Room 409, like the bottle of household cleaner," Abigail jested, and I laughed.

"That will make it easy to remember." I got up and placed the strap of my bag on my shoulder. "I'll see you next week, Abigail."

"I look forward to it, Tara." She smiled sweetly at me. I began walking to the parking lot when Abigail called, "Tara!"

I turned back, curious as to why her voice sounded panicked. "Yes?"

Abigail looked at me nervously. "I remember now. What I sensed when I passed you in the cafeteria."

"What is it?" I asked in a gentle voice.

"You've been having terrible nightmares. Something dark wants you. Pray, dear child. I'll be praying for you."

My mouth dropped as I was dumbfounded by what she revealed. How could she have known this? My body shook as I tried to play it off. I nodded to Abigail with a faked smile and confidence I no longer felt. "Thank you. I'll take all the prayers I can get, but I ask you not to worry about me. We will talk more next week, and I want to know more about you. You are an intriguing lady."

Abigail looked once more into my eyes, and a feeling of dread filled me. Not because of her, but her words hit my heart like an all-too-real warning. She then nodded and looked away into the distance like I had first found her.

It was nice to see my mother wearing the flowy, yellow satin gown I'd brought her last Christmas, even though it was under the thick, plush robe with a rubber duckie print Rudy gifted. Mom always liked ducks.

She and Dad used to take us to a park with a pond full of the feathered foul when we were little kids, and we'd feed them corn and peas. Some of the greedier ducks would eat out of our hands, and I remembered the feeling of their bills.

The frantic movements pecked and pinched as they gobbled up the offering. Rudy and I laughed; the sensation didn't hurt, but we found it too funny to watch. Dad would imitate Daffy Duck saying, "It's mine! All mine! Give it to me! Num, num, num!"

I smiled at the memory and observed my mother. Her dark blond hair had soft curls, and she had a radiant glow to her serene features. She breathed in the crisp cool air and lifted her chin to let the sun caress her face. Her contentment made me feel happy.

"You look beautiful, Mom."

"It feels nice to be outside with my beautiful daughter. So, tell me what's been happening in the rest of existence."

"Rudy scored a touchdown Friday night, winning the game. He got showered in orange lipstick." I showed Mom the close-up and Rudy's face with the orange lip prints, and she laughed.

"Rudy is so much like your father, quite the ladies' man. Does he have anyone new in his life?"

"Not that I'm aware. Oh! Woody has a live act coming to The Roost so that things will pick up."

"Perhaps, Woody should give you a raise. You've been working hard and deserve it."

"Well, he hired on a new girl I know from high school, and let's just say we were never friends. So, unless this act brings in the dollars, I don't foresee getting a raise since he has to pay her. But, you're right, I bust my butt there, and I should receive some extra compensation from having to put up with the new girl's presence."

"Who's this girl?"

"Bren Taylor. My evil tormentor."

"I remember you telling me about her. What was Woody thinking?"

"That's what I would like to know! I told Woody she's trouble, but he dismissed it."

"Maybe she's changed, grown a conscience. That can happen after high school."

"That's what I'm hoping," I agreed. "Danny baptized a new church member. It's a funny story, and he literally lit a fire under this guy's ass."

"I can see Danny doing that." Mom chuckled. "He's a bit of a pyro, used to scare the crap out of me sometimes. But, where there's fire, there's ice, and I got him with a bucket full while he slept in a tent on one of our family camping trips."

I laughed. "I remember that. Didn't Dad unzip his sleeping bag, you doused him, and Dad zipped him back in nice and tight?"

"Yep, that'd be the time. You and Rudy were so young then; we all were. I miss those times." Mom sighed. "How's Asher doing?"

I swallowed nervously. I tried to keep our visits neutral to happy, and I didn't want to take our time together in the opposite direction. But she asked, and I didn't want to lie to my mother even though I knew this might break her heart.

"Tara? Where is your ring?"

"I didn't want to bring you bad news, but I ended things with Asher. He cheated on me."

"Oh, Tara! I'm so sorry. You were so good to him; Asher never deserved you. I didn't want to say this before, but I always had a feeling he wasn't the one. You kept the truck, though?" Mom smiled knowingly.

"Damn straight, I did!" I laughed.

"That's my girl!"

We sat in silence for a moment. I looked at my mother, Lydia Raybrook, the woman who gave me life, raised Rudy and me with all the love in her heart, and saved me from a monster. We were practically twins. She had a few fine lines on her soft, lovely face. I watched her and could sense the gears turning in her mind.

Her expression reflected internal thoughts looking for some solution. I wanted to put my mother's mind further at ease. She didn't need any added stress.

"Stella and Cannon send their love. Stella told me how she went through the same thing and how to deal with this time in my life. Her advice helped put things into a positive perspective." I squeezed Mom's hand reassuringly.

Mom smiled. "I'm so glad. Stella is a wise woman. Stella and Cannon are wonderful people. Tell them I love them too."

"I always do." I paused for a moment of reflection. Mom needed to hear that I had more good things than bad in my life.

"Another good thing happened today. I made a new friend. She's a sweet elderly lady."

"Where did you make friends with an older lady?"

Ooh, I hadn't thought of that. I didn't want to tell her at the hospital because she'd want to know why I was there. She didn't mention hearing about Rudy's accident, and I couldn't tell her the whole story. I made a promise to Rudy. So, I went with the following plausible explanation. "I met her at the park we visited to feed the ducks, you remember?"

"Yes, of course!" Mom smiled. "What's your new friend's name?"

"Abigail."

Mom went quiet. Too quiet.

"Mom? Is everything okay?"

"Y-yeah. I think I'm just getting tired." She nodded her head with an unsettling jerky movement.

"Oh, okay. You want me to help you back inside?" I offered. I felt Mom wanted to say something, but she was trying to protect me as I had been with her by choosing safe topics. Something triggered her, and I wanted to kick myself. Perhaps she was more concerned than she let on when I told her about my break-up with Asher.

I helped Mom stand and led her back inside and up to her room on the second floor. I wrapped my arms around her. "I love you, Mom."

"I love you, Tara."

"Do you need me to get you anything?"

"Some water, please."

I went to the hall, pulled a paper cup to fill at the water cooler, and brought it back to her room. Mom was lying on her side facing the wall. I heard her soft peaceful breaths and didn't want to disturb her, so I placed the cup on her bedside table. I unfolded the blanket at the foot of her bed, draped it over her body, then leaned in and gave her a soft kiss on her cheek.

I went to the nurses' station and asked for a piece of paper and a pen, and I wrote a note.

Mom,

I'm sorry our visit was short. I hope you feel better soon. Please know that I'm going to be okay. Perhaps next time, I can bring you a strawberry shortcake, the kind with the chocolate-dipped strawberries you like. Till then, I promise I'll do what is needed to take care of myself; please do the same for me.

Love, Tara

I folded the note in half and returned to her room to lay it atop her bible. Mom looked peaceful. But then, as I turned to leave, she began to moan and mumble, and I stepped closer and strained to hear what she was saying.

"I'm so sorry. I had to save her."

My chest tightened. *Who was Mom talking to?*

Chapter 6
DEAN PERRISH

A Traveling Man

I always enjoyed taking the back roads on my travels. There's less traffic, and my brother Zane and I enjoy the scenery. We also find the best biker bars and honkytonks along the way. It also helps to have fewer witnesses and sparse law enforcement officials around when Zane decides to party. When Zane steps out, all hell breaks loose, and people go missing. I have to put a leash on my brother the closer we get to the populace. If Zane gets thrown in the clink, I'm stuck with him. A sad reality I must face. I can't get away from him, which drives me up the wall.

I allowed Zane a little leisurely time in Miami, and now we're on the lamb rumbling North toward Atlanta on my midnight black Heritage Soft tail. Going several hours straight, we were in the clear, so I pulled up to a roadside dinner.

"Hey Dean, you think I could get a rare steak here?" Zane asked.

"Didn't you get your fill back in Miami? I think I've had enough of what you want, and I'm going to need a lot of alcohol to get the taste out of my mouth. Zane, your last bender is why we had to leave, and you know I don't appreciate your voracious appetite killing what could have been a good time. Reel it in, won't ya?"

"Look, I'm trying my best here. Can we at least make this one small compromise? You know when you hold me back for too long, the lust takes over. Next stop, and I promise I'll behave for as long as possible."

"Let's see. While in Miami, you had Cuban, Puerta Rican, Mexican, Panamanian, and a little Brazilian side dish. I'm just glad it wasn't spring break." I threw my hands up in frustration.

"Well, shit happens during spring break, and people get injured and go missing all the time, which creates more of an advantage for plausible alibies," Zane argued. "We should hit Mardi Gras next season. I wouldn't mind a little Creole dish."

"Only if you can behave till the time comes," I offered.

"Done, Brother."

"We will see about that."

I turned off the engine and put the kick-stand down just as another bike pulled in across the lot. Zane's head turned, and our eyes zeroed in on the deep purple Triglide Ultra.

"Would ya look at that! Mamacita has got her tight catsuit going on! Rar Ow!" Zane salivated, and I reached up to close his mouth. Before I could gain control of the situation, Zane was dragging me along toward his next prospect, and I groaned.

"I knew it was too good to last."

"Don't sweat it. I'm just going to make conversation."

"No, you're not. You're going to keep your damned mouth shut, or I'm going to knock you out of commission so hard and hide your teeth where you'll never find them again," I threatened.

"Fine, but.."

"Nope."

"But!"

"I said zip-it, Zane!"

"Fine!" Zane pouted. But then his smile returned as I continued our approach toward the rider on the trike. The matching purple helmet sparkled in the late afternoon sun and read, 'Like What You See?' Upon closer view, the tank had a design with shooting stars and the name *'Qweenie Martini'* in a scrolled script.

"Me likey what I see very much!" Zane said, and I abruptly shushed him. The rider dismounted, wearing rhinestone high-heeled boots, and turned our way.

"Oh my!" the rider exclaimed in a deep effeminate voice. "Well, don't you look like young Brad Pitt and MGK had a love child? Honey, you can join me for dinner, and I'll even let you buy. What's your name, cutie?"

"Dean Perrish," I replied.

The rider pulled fingerless gloves off her large brown hands with long glittery red claws. Her Adam's apple bobbed as she swallowed, taking us in from head to toe. She then removed her helmet to reveal a light brown clean-shaven face with a masculine bone structure, large false lashes, and a soft coppery shimmer shadow framed dark brown eye—shining red lip gloss painted a set of full luscious lips.

A silver sequin scarf tied back at the nape of her neck and covered short-cropped black hair peeking around her face. The black leather catsuit hugged a body with broad shoulders, a narrow waist, and hips.

Nice legs! I thought.

"Oh, I forget my southern manners! I do apologize." Her voice turned full-on manly. "Let me introduce myself; I'm Trey D. Ryder."

The soft feminine twang returned before Trey added, "But you can call me Martina Dollyounce' because I have only loved four women in my life. Mariah, Tina, Beyonce, and the queen of country herself, Miss Dolly."

I was not expecting Trey or Martina, whichever persona they decided to stick with for the rest of our conversation, to continue assessing Zane and me as if they knew something was different about us. But there was no telling my twin and me apart. We were pretty much one in the same person, much like Trey and Martina.

But one wouldn't know by looking at the one man standing before them. Because just as Trey and Martina shared one body, so did Zane and I. We were born this way. I absorbed Zane in the womb, and I was his gracious host. Zane is my parasitic twin. And though it isn't evident by our outward appearance, we share this body.

Inside?

Two hearts and two sets of circulatory systems pump two blood types through our body. One brain shares two minds. I have no idea how to explain that one. One thing is for sure; I know I do not suffer from schizophrenia or multiple personalities.

In public places, it's easier nowadays to have full-on audible conversations with my brother. People may look at me strangely, but I point to the Bluetooth device in my ear, and they look in the other direction. Before modern technology, people avoided me as I appeared to walk down the road ranting at myself like a crazy person.

"It's a pleasure to meet you, Martina?" I decided.

"A pleasure, for sure." Martina offered her hand.

I decided to be a gentleman, placing a light peck on her soft brown skin. Sorry to say, she was not my type in the sexual department, but I couldn't help but appreciate the authenticity and boldness of the character she currently portrayed.

"My treat then." I smiled at Martina as I gestured the way toward the restaurant entrance.

As we entered the front door, the loud clinking of silverware on plates and conversation ceased. All eyes were on us, or should I say, Martina, as she looked for an available table. She must be used to the attention because she didn't bat an eyelash at the offensive glares.

"Oh, there's a table open over there." She pointed with her long fingernail. We headed that way, and I noticed the Butcher Bounty Brotherhood on the backs of large hulking shoulders sat around a set of pulled-together tables. I pulled out a seat for Martina when suddenly I heard one of the gang members speak up.

"You can't sit there. Table's reserved!"

I turned to the fat bastard in question. "I don't see a sign."

Oh, hell yes! Let me take him, brother! Zane spoke in our mind.

The shit-stain tub of lard stood up and barked, "This is your sign!"

He came to stand face to face before me. His rotted teeth and breath reeked of putrid decay. He had a few inches of height advantage, but I could tell he was slow by his movements. I was gearing myself up for a fight when Martina cleared her throat.

"Look, gentlemen. We are cut from the same cloth. I'm sure this is a minor oversight. Tubby, be a doll and sit your fat ass back down, and we can all enjoy our meals in peace."

"What did you call me, you freak faggot?" Lard shit-stain for brains asked.

"You want me to smack the last three teeth out of this guy's face, Martina?" I asked.

At that, seven more Butchers stood up at once; the loud drag of scraping chair legs had everyone in the restaurant turn their attention our way.

"That won't be necessary, honey. There are women, children, and senior citizens in here." Martina nudged me aside. She stood up to the fat asshole and pointed a red claw at the Butcher.

"You best back your wide load, homo-transphobic ass back into your chair if you know what's best for you, Chacheeto. My man, Trey D, can be here in one second, and he's dying to put on a show." Martina sneered.

The fat Butcher's eyes widened with fear. "You don't mean Trey D. as in Trey Danger?"

The gang standing in comradery began looking at one another nervously, and I had to say the sight brought a newfound appreciation for sweet Martina.

So Caliente! Zane said, and I smirked.

"That's right, bitch! Don't make him break loose and then have to drag your two-ton waste of space to the Rooster." Martina poked her claw into a lumpy man-boob.

"You don't mean Woody 'The Rooster' Raybrook?" Dumpy's voice quivered, and the rest of the gang immediately sat back down in their seats.

"Tried and true, I certainly do!" Martina placed her hands on her slender hips to emphasize her point.

"Look, Miss?" Dumpy Butcher questioned.

"Martina Dollyounce," Martina provided.

"Miss Dollyounce. You're right! It was an honest oversight on my part." Dumpy ass hurried over to pull out the chair from our table, and Martina sat as he slid the chair forward like a gentleman.

"I apologize for the misunderstanding and my insult to your person."

Zane and I were barely containing our laughter. Even a few of the Butchers were snickering.

"That's alright, baby. We all make mistakes. Finish your meal, and I'll give you the number of an excellent orthodontist, and she will fix you right up. In the meantime, mouthwash, honey, okay?" Martina nodded.

"Yes, Ma'am," Dumpy said. He returned to his table, and his crew started laughing their asses off.

"Shut the fuck up!" he yelled.

They quieted down to low snickering before resuming their meal, and I heard the mention of this Rooster guy's name pass amongst them.

"Mmm-hmm!" Martina began to hum as she picked up her menu as if the confrontation hadn't happened. Everyone in the diner relaxed and continued to mind their business after the scene they had witnessed.

"Baby, I'm straight as an arrow, but I think I'm in love." I laughed.

I concur, Zane said. However, she didn't hear him, as he behaved himself for once.

"Where are you heading after this, sugar?" Martina asked.

"North, I guess. Where ever I can find some adventure."

"Well, Dean, baby. Call me Dolly and follow me in those 'painted on jeans' cause I got your ticket to a new adventure." Martina held her hand out. "Your phone, sweetie."

I reached into my leather jacket, pulled out my phone, and handed it to her. She started to put in her info. "I'm doing a show tonight at The Kiss Club. It's not far from here. From there, you're free to follow me if you wish. I will be premiering at The Hillbilly Roost for some time after. I've got my family there, and I'm long overdue for a visit."

"I like the sound of that." I overheard the Rooster's name from the Butchers enough times, and so intrigued was I that I couldn't pass up the opportunity to see this guy myself. So, I was more than willing to follow Martina/Trey to their next destination. My gut had a strong feeling there was more to this guy than I had already heard, and I had a feeling it had something to do with my abilities. Abilities that no mere mortal could ever begin to understand.

As my brother and I shared one body, so did our demons, one that took life, and the other awakened it. And neither was a good thing.

Chapter 7
TARA

The Bitch Is Back

I noticed the red Camaro in the drive as I pulled up to The Hillbilly Roost. I had never seen a car like it here before. As I got my belongings out of my truck, I eyed the license plate, noting it was out of state. I passed the sporty car on my way over to my modest accommodations.

"It's only temporary, Tara," I told myself. I noted the Texas plates. There was also a bumper sticker with the shape of a longhorn head and the word PROUD in bold orange.

"Great! I'm back in Hell," I grumbled.

This car could only belong to one person, the person I detest with my entire being. Bren Taylor is here at The Roost, and I was to swallow my contempt like a spoon full of acid. What was it my uncle Woody told me? 'Suck it up, buttercup.' I contemplated scenarios where I could turn the phrase on my dear uncle.

I quickly walked toward the cabin, as I didn't want anyone to see I had returned, other than noting my truck was there. If I didn't make my presence known, one may guess I could be anywhere on my uncle's one-hundred-acre property. I did enjoy a run around the lake when the weather was decent.

I made it to safety and closed the door. I knew I was acting like a chicken tucked away in a coop, but I wasn't ready to face Bren. I had to get my head in the game, as Rudy would tell me whenever faced with a situation beyond my control. I needed to prepare mentally so I didn't lose my cool.

I didn't have to work till tomorrow anyway, so I could use this time to give myself a pep talk and bolster up my defense. I hoped Woody didn't call me out to face the enemy sooner. I had a feeling he'd want me to give Bren a few pointers on how I handle rude or handsy patrons.

When I started working at The Hillbilly Roost, I bussed tables, washed dishes, swept, and mopped, as I was not old enough to serve alcohol. It wasn't a hard job per se, but the patrons liked to get a bit grabby. At first, I'd get upset and flustered, and my uncles would throw offenders to the curb, threatening to remove any body parts that came in contact with mine. It wasn't long before I could hold my own as Stella taught me how to handle these situations.

Mostly, I only had to threaten my offenders that I'd be telling their old ladies their men were acting like pigs. For those single pinpricks with dicks for brains, I could insult the integrity of their manhood. And if that didn't work, I'd 'accidentally' spill their drinks in their laps and show them I could light their world on fire with the Zippo Uncle Danny gifted me.

Soon enough, those who had been my worst offenders gave me a wide berth while minding their manners. Derogatory terms like 'sweet thang' and 'sugar tits' quickly changed to 'miss' till they learned my name, and everyone called me Miss Tara. Only my family could call me Tara Baby.

The visit with my mom played over in my mind, and I couldn't help but wonder if mentioning Abigail had triggered the apology in my mother's dream. Mom had said, 'I had to save her.' Was she talking about a friend, a patient, family, or me?

But then I recalled the strange feeling of déjà vu I experienced when I approached Abigail, that feeling we'd met before. I'd blocked out so much from my past. It's a possibility; I'd seen her, even if briefly. I had trouble recalling any scenario we'd had an exchange before the hospital, and I couldn't shake the feeling she connected to something.

I would soon revisit the matter, as it nagged my brain, but I needed to switch gears and concentrate on my schoolwork. I could jump ahead on some reading and finish my weekly assignments. Perhaps have some downtime, me time, something I rarely experience nowadays.

Hours passed without interruptions, and no one came knocking on my door to check on me. I didn't even get a phone call or text till now when Bad To The Bone alerted me to Woody's text message.

Woody: You didn't let me know you made it back. You, all right?

Me: Yeah. Just catching up on school, and I'm pretty tired. Going to get some rest.

Woody: Ok, kiddo. Making a quick run to the store. Need anything?

Me: My usual healthy snacks, please.

Woody: Okay. The new girl is working out well, and Stella is helping behind the bar. You can breathe easy tonight.

Me: Thanks.

I looked out the window and saw Bren's car, and I stewed in belligerence. Tuesday nights weren't the busiest. Still, I usually worked. Aside from the late afternoon church services, The Hillbilly Roost remained closed on Sundays, and Mondays were Woody's day of rest. No alcohol was served or consumed on those days except for wine during a communion service.

I wondered if Bren would be attending church. She hadn't seemed the type in high school. If she had a clue about 'an eye for an eye, tooth for a tooth,' she'd probably want to run away.

I wouldn't be surprised if there weren't a line of people waiting to pull a tooth from her mouth with pliers in hand. And if she dared to stab me in the back, I might consider taking an eye.

Lord, help me. I'm still so sour because Bren was so salty. I guess forgiveness didn't come so easily for me. Did it make me a bad person for not letting go of the past? It certainly made me a less trusting person. I've been through the wringer because so many people have hurt me. And perhaps Bren may have changed, but her past actions put a heavy weight on my shoulders.

I heard a knock at the door, and I paused the movie, which mainly served as background noise as I was near falling asleep. I figured it was Woody with his hands full of groceries, but no one was there when I opened the door. Either I was hearing things, or someone was trying to prank me. Assuming the second, I looked around and listened for Uncle Danny's boots, but all I heard was the faded music from the club.

"You better not be trying me, Danny," I yelled.

The wind picked up, and I felt a chill run deep. It was an eerie sensation, like the creepy feel of entering an old abandoned haunted house. I shut the door and secured the deadbolt and chain. I looked out the window to see Woody hadn't returned yet. Danny's bike was missing, so it couldn't have been him trying something. I recognized the few vehicles and bikes in the lot; Bren's the only new addition.

I sent a text to ask Woody if he was on his way back with no response. He wouldn't respond if he were riding. I didn't want to call him just because I was feeling paranoid. I went to the bathroom, and when I came out, the television was off. I didn't recall turning it off. Perhaps there was a power flicker I hadn't noticed, but then the alarm clock would be flashing, needing to be reset.

Perhaps I did turn it off. I was about to fall asleep; my mind had been a blur. I grabbed the remote and turned the television back on to distract myself, but I continued to feel on edge. I decided to call Stella. Business was slow tonight, and I could use some reassurance. I listened to the phone ring and ring.

"Hey, Tara! What's up?" Stella asked.

"Hi, Stella. Has anyone wandered out of the bar? I see all the regulars are here." I could match each person to their mode of transportation to know who was in attendance tonight.

"No. All the usual faces are here. Why do ya ask?"

"It's nothing really. I just heard a knock at my door, and no one was there. I thought Danny might be pulling a prank, but his bike isn't here."

"Sit tight. I'll send Cannon to check on things. Okay?"

"Okay, thanks."

"Stay on the phone with me till he gets there."

"I'm here. How's everyone doing? Is the new girl causing any problems for you?"

"No. Everything and everyone is fine. Why do you ask?"

"I'll explain later." I spotted Cannon's hulking frame as I peeked out the window. His body language was a warning sign to anyone looking to cause trouble; he wasn't someone you'd want to try.

"I see him now. Thanks, Stella."

"No problem. Don't ever hesitate to call for any reason, understand?" Stella's voice was stern.

"Understood."

Knocking sounded at the door. "It's me, Tara. Open up," Cannon called.

"He's here. I'm gonna let ya go," I told Stella.

"Alright," Stella replied, then ended the call.

I opened the door, and Cannon stepped inside. He didn't say anything as he began doing a sweep around the room, checking the bathroom, then looking out the back window.

"I'm going to check around outside. It may have been an animal. Damned raccoons are getting into the trash again and knocking things around. I found this a few feet away from the door." He held up an empty can.

"I'm coming with you."

"Here, take this, and stay to my left." Cannon handed me Uncle Woody's baseball bat, and he pulled his gun from the holster on his belt.

We went out the door, and I locked up before heading around the side of the cabin. Cannon shined a flashlight into the trees as a gust whipped through the air stirring the leaves around us. A few broke free from the branches, falling to the ground as a growing bed of debris crunched beneath our steps.

The darkness beyond the light stirred up a feeling of mystery deep in my veins, beckoning something inside me to awaken. It felt like something I could almost recognize. There was a kindred calling, like a whispering spirit carried by the wind. And it made me feel as though my destiny was knocking. Perhaps that was the knock I heard at the door.

Something was coming my way. Something dark. But somehow, my heart told me it was something I should not fear. Perhaps it was something that would save me, somehow.

"Did you feel that?" I asked.

"Feel what?" Cannon asked.

"I don't know. The wind."

"Of course, I felt the wind."

"No, I mean there's something else like, I don't know how to explain it, but an attachment. It feels like something spiritual." I heard a cracking in the distance like a footstep on a fallen tree branch, and Cannon immediately swung his light and gun in that direction. Suddenly a large shadow darted away from the light. It looked human, well over six feet tall. I watched as the figure darted behind another tree.

"Who's out there? Show yourself!" Cannon yelled.

I quickly covered my ears as Cannon fired a warning shot into the trees. I could see it again in the darkness as if my eyes became more acute. The figure morphed into a large four-legged animal with no distinct characteristics to define it as anything recognizable. It zipped away with unnatural speed, and I stood frozen in astonishment.

"What the fuck was that thing?" Cannon asked.

"I don't know, but I've seen it before!" I flinched as Cannon fired another round.

"You better keep running, you sonofabitch!" Cannon yelled.

"What the hell is going on out there?" Uncle Woody yelled. Footsteps approached with the telltale sounds of chains and spurs from Danny's boots.

"Hold your fire. It's just Danny and me," Woody called. Cannon and I turned and lowered our weapons.

Woody shielded his eyes from the blaring flashlight. "Lower the damn light! What are you doing out here firing a gun into the woods at night?"

"There was someone, something out there," Cannon replied.

"I heard a knock on my door before we came out here to investigate," I told Woody.

"Let me see your phone," Woody demanded.

"Why do you need to see my phone? What does that have to do with what happened?"

"Just hand it over, Tara." Woody held out his hand. Cannon and Danny looked as confused as I felt. I gave Woody my phone, and he pulled up my recent calls. He hit dial, and I heard Asher's voice.

"Tara?" I heard a mix of question and hope in his voice.

"Not Tara. Where are you right now?" Woody asked.

"I'm home. What's this about?"

"Proof it!" Woody demanded.

"How?"

"Facetime Tara's phone."

"Fine!" Asher's face was on the screen, and he looked tired like he hadn't been getting any sleep. "What's this all about?" he demanded.

"You don't get to ask any questions. Show me your surroundings," Woody boomed.

Asher walked with his phone, and I could see the familiar home interior where we'd shared a life for the past three years. "I'm home. You satisfied?" Asher snarled.

"Watch your tone, kid," Woody warned. "Now tell me this? Have you been stalking my niece?"

"NO! I would never do that. Tell me, what's going on?"

"Let me ask this again. Are you or anyone you know following Tara around?"

"Shit no, Woody, I swear. Honest to God, I didn't, wouldn't do that!" Asher's voice rose in anger.

"If I find out you or anyone affiliated with you is coming around trying to scare or harm Tara. You'll need to pack a bag real fast and run for your life," Woody yelled.

"Fuck, Woody. Calm down! I swear. If anyone is doing that to Tara, I'll hunt the fucker down myself! Now, please, tell me what happened. Is Tara okay?"

"She's fine, and that's all you need to know." Woody hung up. Asher tried to call back, but Woody turned off my phone and handed it back to me.

"I get it, Uncle Woody, but I know it wasn't Asher," I said.

"What made you come to that conclusion? He's lied before. What's to say he doesn't have someone checking you out and making plans to kidnap you or something? You can't be too careful about something like this."

I huffed in frustration. "I know Asher is a first-rate douche, but he wouldn't do something like this. He's too scared of you, Danny, and Cannon, and he doesn't have a death wish."

"She's right," Cannon agreed. "Besides, what we saw out there wasn't human."

"What the hell? You mean you saw an animal?" Woody's brow arched in question, and he folded his arms across his chest.

"Sort of," I replied. "It stood upright and looked human but then shifted to something animal-like. I saw it once before."

"When? Where?" Danny jumped into the conversation. All three of my uncles stood looking at me with arms folded and demanding stares.

"Look, I didn't think anything of it before because I thought I was hallucinating. It was just after I left Asher and on my way back here. I saw a big dark shadow of an animal dart out in front of my truck. It happened so fast; I couldn't make out any details."

"Just after you left Asher? And that doesn't sound suspicious to you?" Woody asked. "It seems like whatever that thing is, has followed you here."

"You're not getting it. What does something without distinction, be it human or animal, have to do with Asher? And why I saw it before and why it's here now could be a coincidence. There's a lot of wildland out there," I argued.

"So, you're not concerned that that thing was what possibly knocked on your door, and you find it lurking in the woods behind the cabin?" Danny asked. Woody and Cannon stood in agreement with that assessment.

"I never said I wasn't concerned. It just seems highly unlikely Asher is involved. I'm going inside!" I started back toward the cabin.

My uncles followed me, discussing the situation amongst themselves. They did another check around and inside, and Danny ended up staying while Woody and Cannon headed back to the bar. I didn't complain and felt safe with Danny here, but I couldn't sleep the rest of the night. The image kept playing in my mind, and the more I thought about it, the more it seemed whatever it was, was more afraid of us than the other way around.

The movement of the shadow seemed inquisitive. I didn't feel threatened and recalled the kindred connection I felt looking into the darkness before the shadow creature appeared. But, if it had knocked on my door, why was I its person of interest?

This change of season in my life brought more questions than answers. Everything was happening at once, but I feel less crazy knowing Cannon witnessed the same thing. Eventually, I fell asleep as the sun crept up over the mountains.

I woke later in the afternoon with a need to find out more. Cannon and Danny went with me to explore the woods to look for the creature or any clues it may have left. We were out for a few hours and found nothing extraordinary. Perhaps it moved on, scared off by the gunfire and Cannon's threats.

We returned to the cabin, and I saw Bren's car and two new bikes. One a dark purple trike and the other a black Heritage.

"Who's here?" I questioned.

Before Cannon or Danny could answer, a grey Chevy truck pulled up. "Gina? What the hell is she doing here?" I walked toward Gina as she exited. I was almost happy to see her when the visual of her naked beneath Asher flashed through my mind. I stopped and folded my arms; my mood snapped into instant bitch mode.

"Why are you here, Gina?" I scowled at my former best friend, and her face sunk in shame. Still, she approached and stopped several feet before me. She looked down in remorse and trepidation as she shifted her boots through the gravel.

"I didn't come here to cause trouble. I came to apologize and let you know I'm leaving town. But there's something you need to know," Gina's voice quivered. Perhaps she was afraid I'd lay her out in the parking lot. The thought crossed my mind, but I did want to hear what she had to say.

"Okay. I'm listening." I replied calmly.

"First off, I feel sick to my stomach for how I betrayed you. We are; well, we were best friends, and perhaps in time, things could go back to the way they once were if you could find it in your heart to forgive me. But I understand if it never happens. I'm ashamed of myself and that I let this happen the first time...."

I held up my hand to halt Gina's speech. "Wait! First time? Are you telling me you slept with Asher before the time I walked in on you both?" The heat in my veins rose. "You dare to come here to let me know you and Asher have been sleeping together behind my back for how long?" I rooted myself in place. If I moved, I might attack Gina and tear out her bitch balls; after all, forget female comradery.

Another car tore down the drive and stopped abruptly behind Gina's truck. I couldn't see who it was at first. I heard a door slam, and whoever arrived began running. I heard Asher's voice yell my name with an urgent plea of desperation.

"Too late, Asher, she knows," Gina yelled.

"Damn it, Gina! I told you to stay out of this," Asher yelled. He stopped between Gina and me. "Tara, I was gonna tell you, okay?"

"What does it matter anymore? I already said we are through, and this," I motioned, pointing back and forth between Gina and me, "Just put the final nail in the coffin. Do you think this information coming from you would have made any difference? How do you think Gina could stay out of this when she was already involved? The both of you deserve each other. I could care less anymore what either of you has to say. You screwed each other and screwed me over."

My teeth clenched, and my hands balled into fists. I was ready to throw if either of them took another step closer. Gina took a hint and backed a few steps. Tears streaked her face, but those tears weren't for how she did me wrong. She felt guilty only because she got caught. It sounded like they had been cheating for some time.

On the other hand, Asher, the douche wad took a step, and before I knew what I was doing, I swung with all my might. My fist connected the Asher's nose, and he yelled out in pain as the distinct crunch of bone sounded at impact.

"Ah, fuck!" Asher's hand went to his nose, and blood seeped down his chin. Asher's pain somehow brought me a feeling of satisfaction.

"That's the least you deserve, Asher!" I yelled. I heard the crunching of multiple footsteps behind me, and I knew Woody, Cannon, and Danny were at my back.

"Tara, I'm so sorry. There's no excuse," Gina cried.

I looked at Gina, and I could tell from her reaction she could see the fire in my eyes. She'd tuck that bitch tail, turn and run if she knew what was best. "You're right about that part. You broke my heart, and I have cried all the tears I'm going to over losing my best friend. You killed our friendship, dug the grave, and now count yourself departed from my life. I've got nothing else to say to you."

Gina hung her head. "I'm gonna go." She turned away and got into her truck, then drove off. Asher was still clutching his nose. No one offered to help him as he stood waiting in expectancy for sympathy; he wouldn't find it here.

"You're bleeding all over my driveway. You'd better go before you find yourself bleeding some more. Consider this a mercy that a busted nose is all you received," Uncle Woody said.

Asher ignored Woody. "Tara, please! Gina is gone. I hadn't seen her at all after you left. Not till now. I miss you, kitten. I can't sleep. I'm dying without you. I miss you. We can still fix this."

I folded my arms and pinned Asher with an unyielding glare. "The only thing that has a chance of being fixed is your nose. Did you not hear what Woody told you? Leave! Now!"

Asher looked angry. He took a menacing step toward me.

Wrong answer!

Woody and Cannon stepped around me, grabbed Asher by his arms, and lifted him bouncer style. They escorted Asher to the rusted green El Camino, and Danny followed. Asher was struggling and cursing. "Fuck! Tara, I wasn't going to hurt you! I just want to talk. I swear."

Danny opened the car door, and Woody and Cannon tossed Asher inside. "Goodbye, Asher," Woody said.

"Buckle up now!" Danny taunted.

"You fucking assholes!" Asher screamed.

Cannon pointed his large finger at Asher's face. "I would punch you, but you need to be conscious to drive. If you're not gone in the next thirty seconds, my boys and I are going to dump this piece of shit along with its occupant into the lake."

Asher started the engine; the tires spun and flung rocks as Asher turned the car around and drove fast down the long drive.

Chapter 8
DEAN

All Cooped Together

Zane and I followed Trey through the winding mountain roads of southern Tennessee. It is beautiful here this time of year with the trees changing. A sea of yellow, orange, red, and scarlet gives me a sense of serenity and wonderment, and I feel like life is going in the right direction for the first time in a long while.

A pull of energy called to my soul, and I know Zane also sensed it. For once, he was quiet and calm. As I kept my eyes on the road, I pictured Zane's closed as we breathed in the fresh mountain air. My pinkie finger tingled where I wore my ring with a deep red garnet etched with the symbol representing my power. I was one with the darkness that presided over death, and the same power kept Zane's monster in check. We rolled through Tremont, making a few turns until we reached a long gravel drive flanked by acres of woodlands.

"This looks like a good place to lay low for a while," Zane commented.

"Yeah…Perhaps you could hunt for some wild game. A palette change would be ideal while we are among our brethren."

"You feel that too?"

I nodded. "There is a deep spiritual connection here, more benevolent than our nature. If you grow careless and reveal your inner demon, we may be at odds with the people here. Best behavior, brother."

"You know I don't care for wild game. It tastes, well, gamey. Blah!" Zane stuck our tongue out in disgust.

"Well, you'll have to make due for the time being. This Rooster guy might not be able to kill us, but I'm sure he can do some lasting damage."

A sweet wood log tavern sat in a large open clearing ahead. The sign read, **Welcome To The Hillbilly Roost. Leave your spurs at the door.** Trey pulled Martina's trike up by a row of nice bikes, and I pulled beside them. A pretty blond woman came running outside, squealing with excitement.

"Trey D! Oh, praise the Lord! The voice of the angels has arrived!"

Trey dismounted, and the woman threw herself into his arms. "Hey there, Stella Bo Bella!" Trey laughed. "Where's the rest of the calvary?"

"Woody is in the office. Cannon, Danny, and Tara are in the woods searching for something strange they saw last night."

The woman called Stella looked at Zane and me. "Who's your cute friend? New love interest?"

Zane and I laughed. "Names' Dean Perrish, Ma'am."

"Ewe, don't call me ma'am. Normally, I'd slap a fellow for that, but I'll let it slide since you're new. Stella is my name." She held out a hand, and we shook. Her grip was firm, assertive. Stella was a woman no one would dare try. I'd be keeping on her good side. Zane took note, and I was glad we agreed for once.

"Stella is Cannon's old lady. Don't call me ma'am," Trey mocked. "But she's fine with 'old lady.' A contradiction if I ever heard one."

"You know there's a difference," Stella argued, "I may be Cannon's old lady, and I am a lady if you're a gentleman, but I'm no ma'am."

"Ain't that special," Trey replied with snarky sass, to which Stella barked a laugh and gave a genteel slap to his arm. Trey flamboyantly gestured with Martina's stylishly manicured hands from head to toe. "Well! This lady needs to go inside and make some preparations for tonight. Martina doesn't show up on stage without her full face, her hair and wardrobe in pristine condition, and her vocals well-tuned."

"Come along, girlfriend. Your parcel arrived a few days ago, and I took it upon myself to prepare your dressing room. I must say I'm a jealous bitch, cause your wardrobe is hot." Stella led the way, her hips swaying in tight leather pants and kick-ass high-heeled boots.

"Nice ass," Zane commented in a low voice.

"And that ass is private property. You don't want to mess with that, let alone the old man who claimed it; I can assure you," I told Zane in our private conversation.

Martina and Stella were too busy chatting to notice my whispered discussion with Zane, whom neither had met. I was always the first to initiate communications as Zane often put his foot in our mouth. I'd eventually introduce him once I established a mutual rapport with these people. I looked as though I was commenting on my surroundings to the casual observer.

Once inside the tavern, I took a moment to check the place. A well-stocked polished bar with all of Zane's and my favorites lined the glass shelves in front of a mirror with The Hillbilly Roost's emblem.

Wall-mounted televisions played a variety of sports and music video channels. Numerous round tables provided views of the televisions and a stage with instruments and a karaoke player.

A sizeable dancefloor sat below the stage. A side room with pool tables and dartboards finished my brief scope of the establishment. I looked to the wide doorway where Martina and Stella had disappeared and saw a swinging kitchen door. I looked up and down a hallway. To my right were restrooms, and to my left was an office. On the men's room door was a sign that read, **If Roadkill exits, spray Lysol in the sign of the Holy Cross before entering**.

Zane laughed. "I wonder who this Roadkill guy is? He sounds like a big scary dude with a delicate constitution."

"Sounds like an appropriate assumption," I replied.

The kitchen door was pushed open, and a young woman with a large tray of drink glasses stepped through. She didn't see me standing there as she bumped into me and let out a startled yell. I caught the tray and righted it before all was lost. I caught two glasses with my free hand as another three crashed on the floor.

"Ah, shit!" she cursed. "Are you okay? It's my second day on the job, and I'm already screwing up."

"Here, let me help you," I offered. I held the tray balanced high on one hand and continued to the bar before placing it down. I set the two extra glasses on the tray and turned to look at the pretty brunette with green eyes.

"Dibs!" Zane exclaimed.

"Dibs?" the girl questioned, and I quickly covered for Zane's loose tongue.

"Dibs on the first toast of the night." I lifted a glass off the tray and held it in the air. "A toast to close calls and nice saves." I gestured to the tray.

"Oh!" She laughed. "I'm Bren. It's nice to meet you?"

"Dean," I supplied.

"Thank you for saving me back there. I've been prone to catastrophic failures of epic proportions lately." Bren flashed a dazzling smile.

"Glad to be of service." I bowed, and she giggled.

"You're adorable, Dean." Bren's cheeks colored bashfully.

"What happened here?" a deep, authoritative voice boomed. A man of impressive stature was looking our way with his big arms crossed across his broad chest. Suffice it to say; he looked like he lifted the logs to build this place. He looked at me with a questioning gaze.

"Sorry, Woody. I was leaving the kitchen with a full tray and wasn't watching for anyone in the hall. I bumped into Dean, and he managed to save the day," Bren explained.

"Well, don't worry about it, Bren. Accidents like this happen all the time around here. Just pay more attention around the kitchen door. And don't worry, I won't dock your pay over a few broken glasses." Woody smiled and winked.

Bren deflated a breath of relief. "Thanks, Woody. I'll be better about watching for people."

"Lesson learned. Sweep this up and hop back to it, kiddo," Woody said.

"I can help you with that!" Zane eagerly jumped the leash I usually kept.

"No. It's okay. Thanks again." Bren shyly tucked her hair behind her ear as she walked away.

So, this is the infamous Woody 'The Rooster' Raybrook. However, the words didn't leave my mouth.

"So, this is the infamous Dean Perrish," Woody said as if he were reading my mind.

"Nice to meet you, Woody." I held out my hand, hoping for his offered acceptance of brotherly solidarity.

Having friends of such magnitude is nice in low places, and I have had many. Sadly, many have grown old and moved on to the hereafter. It's the other reason I never stay in one place too long. People are bound to notice when you've been around as long as Zane and I have and still look in your late twenties.

Woody clapped his large hand into mine, and I felt an immense burst of energy flow through me. It seemed he felt the same as me as he held my hand in a tight grip, and his very intense eyes held mine. I felt a strong kinship that stretched back through the ages. It was like we'd met before, in another life. I knew there were others out there like me. The only exception was no one was exactly like Zane and me.

A moment of silence gave Woody the advantage of studying me. He knew something but couldn't precisely place his finger on what. I held his eyes with mine. Locked in a stare-off of testosterone-fueled display of prowess, we sized up our likeness and searched for any weakness. It seemed Woody didn't find me wanting as he gave my hand a pump and let go.

"It's nice to meet you as well, Dean. Trey tells me you stepped up in Martina's honor, making you an honorable man in my book."

"Yeah, well. Nobody messes with my lady." I grinned.

Woody burst out laughing. He had one of those contagious laughs that made everyone want to join the party. Zane and I laughed along. Stella cracked up, and Martina folded her arms over her chest.

"Woody's just jealous he hasn't found his knight in shining armor," Martina huffed.

Suddenly there was a commotion outside. A car's brakes slammed to a halt, and a young woman yelled. Then a man yelled. Woody, Stella, and Martina ran outside, and I followed. Woody held his hand in front of Stella, who looked ready to charge into action.

"Hold her back, Martina," Woody said. He then walked out to join two other imposing men, and they came to a halt behind the girl whose voice I heard. Bren approached and stopped by my side. Her eyes widened with concern as she watched the show.

"What does it matter anymore? I already said we are through, and this just put the final nail in the coffin. Do you think this information coming from you would have made any difference? How do you think Gina could stay out of this when she was already involved? The both of you deserve each other. I could care less anymore what either of you has to say. You screwed each other and screwed me over."

Wow, she's a spitfire if I ever saw one, Zane spoke in our mind. I nodded in agreement because this girl had a fire in her veins. Her heat radiated out through her aura. I hadn't seen her face yet, but it took one to know one, and this girl was more my equal than she had yet to comprehend. She exuded a power that she probably didn't realize flowed through those veins—a life force of blood, darkness, and light.

It's what I felt from Woody, only stronger. And as she gave the man and woman standing before her words filled with deeply held vitriol. I realized it was her. Hers was the energy that pulled me here like a magnet. She was my destiny.

The man she called Asher was a first-rate dipshit. He called her Tara as he desperately tried to hold his ground, quickly sinking himself in quicksand as he advanced on her, and she reared back and slammed an impressive jab to the guy's nose.

He covered his nose with his hands and whined like a pussy as the woman she called Gina conceded and got in her truck to leave. The asswipe looked around imploringly for someone to come to his aid, and no one budged a muscle. Woody and the two men stepped up behind Tara.

"You're bleeding all over my driveway. You'd better go before you find yourself bleeding some more. Consider this a mercy that a busted nose is all you received," Woody said.

Asher ignored him. "Tara, please! Gina is gone. I hadn't seen her at all after you left. Not till now. I miss you, kitten. I can't sleep. I'm dying without you. I miss you. We can still fix this."

Tara folded her arms and pinned the asshole with an unyielding glare. "The only thing that has a chance of being fixed is your nose. Did you not hear what Woody told you? Leave! Now!"

Asher must have thought he had balls of steel as he advanced on her once more, and my whole body jerked as I felt the need to charge him and take him out for good. I smartly held my ground and noticed Martina holding a seething Stella back.

"Let me go, Martina. That shithead's balls have a date with my switchblade."

Remind me not to piss that woman off, Zane said. I nodded in agreement.

Woody and one of the other men grabbed Asher by his biceps, gave him a courteous lift to his shitty old El Camino, and threw him inside. The third guy opened the door then slammed it closed in Asher's face.

"Goodbye, Asher," Woody said.

"Buckle up now!" the guy who slammed the door taunted with a chipper tone.

"You fucking assholes!" Asher screamed.

The biggest mother effer of the three men pointed his finger at Asher's face. "I would punch you, but you need to be conscious to drive. If you're not gone in the next thirty seconds, my boys and I are gonna dump this piece of shit along with its occupant into the lake."

Asher had the right idea to look scared as he started the engine, turned the car a complete 180, and drove away like the devil was chasing his tail. My lips curled into a wicked smile at the satisfaction I felt. It was like a cup of coffee that settled a person with ADHD.

I could feel Tara's energy rolling off her in a tidal wave. When Tara finally turned around, I was granted a vision of beauty as tendrils of her dark blond hair with natural highlights caressed her sun-kissed complexion. Her eyes were a gorgeous brown that reminded me of the deepest shade of a Charlie Brown Orchid. Her full lips, a lovely shade of pink, completed a palate of perfection.

Tara walked toward Stella's outstretched arms and leaned into the offered embrace. "Good job, Tara Baby," Stella praised.

Tara sniffed, and she let tears fall onto the woman's shoulder. I could feel Tara's heartache, and it royally pissed me off. How could some asshole treat her like a piece of trash and be allowed to continue to breathe?

I was ready to go after this Asher guy, tear his heart out and let Zane feast on it. Tara pulled away from Stella and nodded when asked if she would be okay.

"Yeah, Stella. I just need some rest before tonight."

I noticed Bren nervously wringing her hands as she was still by my side. When Tara looked our way, Bren quickly dropped her head and turned to go back inside. I wondered what that was about, but then it no longer took precedence as those beautiful brown eyes locked with mine, and Tara looked surprised. A moment passed between us, and I knew she felt the energy sizzling between us like a million blazing white sparklers on the fourth of July.

She looked embarrassed as she averted her eyes and quickly wiped at her mascara-streaked face. I wanted to go up to her, tenderly hold her face in my hands, wipe away her tears and kiss her lips.

She walked toward a small wooden cabin and closed herself away from the world. I was left standing with my heart bleeding in my hands as I pined for Tara. I looked around and saw that Zane and I was the only body left standing outside.

"Shit, you've got it bad. I can hear your heart hammering like a freaking woodpecker; it's giving me a damn headache," Zane said. I felt the tension in my temples and messaged the sides of my head in a circular motion. I took a deep breath and willed my heart to slow down.

"Thanks," Zane said appreciatively. "So, how in the hell is this going to work? I'm jonesing for the brunette, and you are already in love with the blond."

"Well, you certainly aren't in love with Bren. I know she's just another conquest for you."

"That's harsh. How do you know what my heart is feeling? There could be something between Bren and me," Zane contested.

"Your history proves you incapable of true love. You only love the chase, the bloodlust. You present the idea of love to draw a woman's heart just to get her in your temporary hold till you're sated. Then you leave them like broken dolls."

"Well, maybe things will be different this time around. I don't want you to lose Tara before you even have a chance with her, so oblige me the same courtesy, would you?"

I shook our head. "This is a catastrophe waiting to happen."

Chapter 9
TARA

Dark Strangers and Leading Ladies

Who was that guy? The tall, dark, excruciatingly handsome man with striking blue eyes hit mine with an intensity that made my heart beat madly. His facial structure was unmistakably model-worthy, with a straight nose and those perfectly kissable full lips. A mess of wild blond finger-length locks and a shadow of facial hair didn't exactly make his features dark, but he had a dark essence, like the epitome of the perfect bad boy.

I only saw him for a moment, but it was enough to see his tall frame with taut, lean muscles beneath his white t-shirt and black leather jacket. He had been standing next to Bren, and I was shocked by her reaction. She looked lost and sad as she averted her eyes, then turned and walked away, leaving me holding the man's gaze. Intense energy rolled through me like a tidal wave. Surprise ruled my features, and I could tell he felt the assault of white-hot flames that burned and sizzled between us.

I realized he had witnessed what happened between Asher and me, and embarrassment hit. I looked away from this stunning dark creature and wiped at the angry tears that streaked the ruined mascara down my cheeks. I was a mess which certainly didn't give a great first impression. I walked to the cabin and felt his eyes follow me. I had a strong feeling he'd be around when I worked tonight.

I only managed a couple of hours of sleep. The image of Asher's anger morphing into an actual green-eyed monster kept me tossing and turning till I managed to succumb to my fatigue. I got ready for tonight, putting extra effort into my appearance, hoping my second impression with the dark stranger went better than the first.

I didn't see the man anywhere when I went inside the bar. Stella was preparing the bar for a busy night, and Bren was stocking the bins with assorted cut fruits for the extended beverage menu only served on occasions such as tonight. I approached quietly. My mind was still in limbo as to whether or not I wanted to say a single word to Bren. Stella looked over and saw me standing in hesitation.

"Hey, Tara. How are you feeling?"

"I'm fine. We expecting a large crowd tonight?"

"Supposedly so. It seems Martina has quite the following."

My eyes widened in surprise. "Auntie Martina is here?" Why hadn't I noticed before? Of course, that's who drove the purple trike parked out front.

"Where is she?" I asked excitedly.

Stella smiled. "Backstage in the dressing room. She's been dying to see you. Of course, you were understandably sidetracked earlier."

"Shit! I feel like an idiot for not noticing." I hurried to the dressing room, relieved that no peep came from Bren. I saw her glimpse my way before quickly returning to her work. I was beginning to feel she probably had changed. Either that or she was on her best behavior with my family around. After the show with Asher and Gina earlier, Bren might be too scared to try me.

I knocked on the dressing room door adorning a glittery purple star with 'Martina Dollyounce' scrolled in fancy script.

"You may enter!" Martina announced like royalty.

Auntie Martina was also my Uncle Trey; their personas were mighty and fierce. Martina looked up from her mirror at the dressing table, and her big brown sparkling eyes with fluttery dark lashes greeted me with love.

She stood up with her feet tucked in fluffy purple boa slippers and stretched out her toned muscular arms on show from her sleeveless black dress. Martina's lush red-painted lips curled into a tender smile. "There you are, my beautiful brown-eyed girl! Come, give Auntie Martina a hug."

I wrapped my arms around her waist, and the figure-hugging black sequined dress rubbed uncomfortably against my arms, but I didn't care. Martina gave the best hugs and advice. I felt the motherly warmth of her strong embrace as she pulled me in.

"Auntie Martina. I'm so sorry I didn't notice you earlier. No one told me you were coming. Woody said a live act was coming; I'm so happy it's you." I smiled up at her. Martina took my hands in hers.

"It's alright, baby girl. You were lost in the moment and needed to breathe. I understand. But, look at you, all grown up into a fine young woman." Martina turned to move a stack of garment bags off a chair, letting them fall to the floor. She pulled the chair closer to the dressing table and patted the cushion.

Martina went back to applying her make-up. "Come and sit a spell and talk to me, Sweetie."

"Well, you saw what happened earlier? And as you already know, Asher cheated on me with Gina."

"Duly noted. You handled yourself with grace and dignity. Have no doubt the beauty of a tigress, for her ferocity is her beauty and her beauty is also her strength. And you, my girl, are a tigress. Look out, world, my baby niece, is now a woman; hear her roar." Martina swiped her red claws at me playfully, and I laughed.

"You think I'm a tigress?"

"Baby, make no mistake. You've got your daddy's strength and your mama's tenacity. Woody helped pull you out of your timid shell and made you bold. There's a fire in you, girlfriend. Now tell me something good."

"Well, I made a new friend at the hospital. Abigail."

"Yes, the hospital. I saw what happened to my poor baby Rudy. Woody told me he would be okay. I'm going to visit in a few days we could go together. You can ride on my trike; it'll be fun." Martina brushed blush on her cheekbones, making them look even higher. "So, tell me what Abigail is like?"

"Mysterious."

"Ooh, well, I do like a woman of mystery. I wouldn't mind meeting her too. Have you seen your mother lately?"

"I did; I saw her after leaving the hospital. She looks beautiful and serene. She wore the lovely yellow gown I got her last Christmas with the duck print robe Rudy gave her. She even curled her hair. You'd be proud of her."

"Well, I don't know about the duck robe, but it's nice to hear she's feeling well and making some effort."

Should I mention how Mom's demeanor changed after I said Abigail's name, and Mom's cried pleas for forgiveness?

"I can see a question in your eyes. Spill it!"

"Martina, when I told Mom I'd met Abigail, she froze up. At first, I thought it was a delayed reaction to my break-up with Asher. But when I took her to her room and heard her talking in her sleep, asking forgiveness from someone, I felt it was an odd coincidence because I recalled feeling something when I met Abigail like I'd seen her somewhere before."

"Honey, I'm afraid I don't know anything about that. But listen to your instincts, Baby Tigress. A woman's intuition is spot on most times. Believe me, I know. Mine have never led me astray. Now, how did Auntie Martina do?" She turned to me, fluttered her lashes, and flashed a dazzling smile.

"You always give great advice," I told her.

"Tara Baby, I know that! Do my make-up and hair go well for singing Tina tonight? How's my dress look? Does it make my ass look big?" Martina stood and turned around to show her backside.

I laughed. "You look fabulous as always, Martina."

The club was filling up with many new faces—men, women, men as women, and the other way around. The Roost has never seen such a colorful crowd like tonight, and they were all there to see Martina perform.

The drinks I was making were as colorful as the crowd, with the addition of little umbrellas. Woody, Stella, and I were behind the bar when Bren came up. She looked flustered as she dropped used glasses into the soapy water.

"Table four wants two Hanky Pankies, a Cosmo, and an Amaretto Sour. Table seven wants two Jacks and a Heineken," Bren called. "Man, I'm getting slammed out there!"

"Tara, I need your help on the floor for a bit. We're short a server tonight," Woody said.

"We're getting slammed back here too," I huffed.

"I need to go to the lady's room. I've been holding it for the past hour, and I'm about to burst," Bren said.

"Go use the one in my office." Woody handed Bren a key.

"Thank you!" Bren took off, and I saw the line to the restrooms spill out the hallway.

Stella set the order on the tray. "Out you go, Tara. These drinks go to table four."

I carried the tray of concoctions and weaved through the crowd. "Hi, ladies," I greeted the group of glamorous gals with their big hair, dramatic make-up, and designer outfits.

"Oh, hey, Doll! You're not the pretty brunette who took our order."

"Afraid not. If you wouldn't mind telling me whose drink is whose, I'd be greatly appreciative." I put on my best genuine smile despite feeling compared to Bren.

"Sure thing, Sweetie. Just hand them to me, and I'll sort it out."

I passed the drinks one at a time, and everyone was satisfied. "Thank you, darling," the women said in unison.

"You're welcome. Enjoy the show." I smiled.

"Oh, we will! Martina is singing Tina tonight, our favorite." The quartette clinked a toast and cheered. "To the Queen of Queens. Long live Qweenie Martini!" Their praise of Martina warmed my heart, and I let go of the pretty brunette comment.

The happy atmosphere was just what I needed after my day. I went to retrieve the next round. Bren was on the other side of the room, busting her ass; she looked panicked as she tried to keep up. I don't know why I was feeling sorry for her. She'd taken no pity on me in the past, and I went through an actual crisis. Still, as I watched her struggle, I decided to put aside the past and head in her direction.

Someone bumped into me from behind, and I lost balance. My tray tipped, and a strong set of hands grabbed my waist as the drinks spilled.

"Awe, hell!" a man groaned. Two more began laughing, and I recognized Cannon and Danny.

"Looks like the drinks are on you tonight, Dean," Danny joked.

When I finally saw what had happened and who it happened to, I gasped. The hands that had me by the waist belonged to the dark stranger, and the drinks I spilled soaked his white t-shirt, revealing a defined chest and abs. Ice cubes fell between his legs, and his dark denim jeans looked like he had wet himself.

"Oh, shit. I'm so sorry!" I pulled the towel from my apron and hurried to soak up the mess on his shirt, and then I worked my way between his legs without thinking. When his hands covered mine, I realized what I was doing and where my hands were now situated. I quickly pulled away; my cheeks flushed with embarrassment.

"I think it was worth it." His voice was deep and smooth, like Tennessee Whiskey. Danny and Cannon were still laughing their asses off, and I shot them a menacing glare.

"Tara. Get Dean a t-shirt from behind the bar," Cannon said. I nodded and turned to walk away. When I got to the bar, I asked Stella to remake the drink order for table seven. I squatted down to shift through the stack of t-shirts to find a size large. I stood up, turned around, and screamed.

Dean stood inches before me. "Sorry. I didn't mean to startle you."

"You didn't have to follow me! Do you make of habit out of invading someone's personal space?" Good grief! My heart was slamming into my ribs. It wasn't only because Dean scared the shit out of me; it was his dangerous proximity.

He removed his ruined white shirt, and save my soul, I wanted to lay him out flat and rub myself all over his body like a cat in heat and high on catnip. I didn't realize I was gawking until I felt his hand tug at the new shirt. I blinked and shook my head to clear the lust-filled haze.

"Oh. Sorry. Here." I offered the shirt. As Dean pulled it over his head, my eyes went to the tattoo on his left pec. It was a silhouette of two figures sitting back to back, heads bowed and knees drawn to their chests. They were black and white like yin and yang with words above and below.

The Light In The Darkness. The Darkness In The Light.

"That's cryptic." *Crap! Did I say that out loud?*

"What's cryptic?" Dean asked.

"Shit!" *I didn't mean to say that aloud either.*

Dean smiled. "Shit is cryptic? Well, I suppose there is some pretty cryptic shit out there."

I laughed. "No, I meant your tattoo."

"Oh, yeah, I suppose it is," Dean casually replied.

"It's your tattoo, wouldn't you know for sure?"

"I do, and I'll explain it to you if you'd like to join me for a drink. Drinks were on me anyway." He grinned mischievously.

"Tara. Get your ass back to work. You'll have time to chat later." Stella smiled knowingly.

"Sorry, Stella." Dean and I apologized in unison.

"I better get back to it." I motioned with my thumb over my shoulder at the bar. Dean smiled and nodded and turned to walk away. He stopped and looked back at me.

"Later then?"

"Yeah, later," I agreed with a smile.

I watched Dean walk away and couldn't help but admire his backside. The t-shirt I gave him stretched tightly across his broad shoulders and hugged his lean torso. And I had to admit he filled out his tight jeans mighty nicely.

Stella whispered in my ear. "You're drooling, girlfriend."

I shut my mouth and turned to look at Stella. She laughed and handed me a tray with drinks. "Table seven," Stella chimed. "Let's see if you get it right this time."

"I was bumped," I protested.

"Yeah, well, by the looks of it, you wouldn't mind getting bumped again." Stella smacked my ass. "Go get 'em, Tigress!"

"You been talking to Martina? Did she give you the tiger talk?"

"Honey, I taught Martina that."

I laughed, returned to my lucky table seven, and managed a successful drink delivery. Cannon and Danny lifted their drinks and smiled.

"Thanks, Tara." Dean's fingers touched mine as he took the bottle. Dean's touch and voice sparked my libido. How was I supposed to make it through the night if I kept having encounters like this?

The stage lights dimmed and talking lowered to soft murmurs. I looked around the floor, and everyone's attention was front and center as a spotlight lit the middle curtain. Music started playing an introduction.

"Waas up, Bitches?" Matina yelled into the microphone, and the crowd went berserk. The curtain burst open, and the music for Proud Mary blasted from the speakers. Martina shot forward, flanked by two backup dancers.

The three queens started to shimmy shake; the black sequins on their dresses bounced and flashed, reflecting the light in a sparkling display. Queens and kings jumped to their feet, screaming as Martina sang.

I stood with my mouth agape at Martina's production. I had seen her practice routines when I was much younger, but she was now on top of her game. The whole floor was on their feet, dancing and singing along. I had never experienced something so exciting before. The atmosphere was electric.

I felt a breath on the shell of my ear, and I shivered as I heard Dean's voice. "She's fabulous, isn't she?"

I turned my head to agree, but my mouth grazed a stubbled chin just below a pair of succulent lips. I felt a zap of static charge, and I put my fingers to my lips, feeling somewhat embarrassed but mostly energized. Sparks zinged through my core. This feeling was something else I'd never experienced before.

"Sorry." I apologized. I didn't intend to bump into Dean again, especially not like that, but he had this habit of being so close every time I turned around. There was an intense magnetism I couldn't deny.

"I'm not." Dean smiled. He made me feel timid, and this intimate exchange made me feel shy and bold at the same time. Dean lowered his face to mine and captured my lips in a searing kiss. The empty tray slipped from my hand and clattered as it hit the floor. Caught up in the moment, I turned my body to Dean's. My hands traveled up and around the back of his neck.

What am I doing? I just met this man and haven't exchanged more than ten words, or, hell, I don't know how many. This was, was. *Don't overthink this! Just go with it, Tara!* So, I did. I allowed Dean to consume me like the most decadent chocolate, which felt sinful and right. I felt his warm hands move around my waist and then to my back, and he pulled my body closer to his heat.

Lord, help me. Don't let me drop my panties too.

The music ended, and with it, so did our kiss. Dean pulled away, and I was left standing dumbfounded. I snapped out of it when Martina's voice boomed over the speakers. After her opening performance, everyone took a seat, and Martina addressed her adoring fans.

"Wooh, this crowd is hot tonight! Let me tell you something, ladies and gents. The Hillbilly Roost is where I started ten years ago, and tonight just so happens to be the anniversary of my first show. I want you all to give it up for my brothers, Woody The Rooster Raybrook, Roadkill Cannon, and Diablo Danny, who not only opened this fine establishment but took me under their wings. And I couldn't be more thankful to these men who accepted me as their brother and queen. Stand up, brothers, and let us all give them a round of applause."

The spotlight swung around and landed on Cannon and Danny as they stood and waved, then on Woody behind the bar. Everyone clapped, whistled, and cheered. After picking up my tray, I clapped along. My mind was still abuzz from the effects of Dean's kiss.

Martina continued. "But really, folks. Tonight is special. And I want to bring someone dear to my heart on stage to sing a song for you. Tara, where are you?"

Oh no. I wanted to hide. *Martina, why are you doing this to me?*

I sang karaoke alone in an empty bar, not on stage in front of an audience. Everyone started clapping and chanting my name as the spotlight swung around the room, searching for me. The only place I could immediately hide was behind Dean, who sat at the table to my left.

As I made my way to duck for cover, the spotlight landed on me mid-squat with the tray I held up to shield my face. I realized how ridiculous I looked as I saw Dean looking at me with a big grin.

He pointed at me and shouted. "She's right here!"

The murderous look I gave Dean only made him burst into laughter. Danny and Cannon joined in, and I could hear Woody chuckling behind the bar. I spotted Bren, trying to hide a smile with her hand.

Ah, there was the bitch I knew and loathed.

I decided at that moment to give her a show that would wipe that smile off her face as I stood and marched up to the dance floor.

"Oh, there she is! Get your cute little ass up here, Tara Baby." Martina held her hand out to me, and I took hold and let her assist me on stage. She turned me toward the crowd, and I was about to lose my nerve and jump ship when Martina whispered, "A tigress is a queen in her own right. Draw them in and make a killing."

Her words strengthened my resolve as Martina introduced me to the audience. "This is my niece, Tara Raybrook, ya'll, and she's got a voice you would not believe."

She then passed me the microphone that felt foreign in my hand. Martina stepped back, the stage lights went out, and the familiar musical intro played. It was a song I knew well and heard my mother sing to my father many times when I was younger.

I saw them dance to this song, so in love with one another. They'd sway to the music holding each other in a passionate gaze. It made me want love so pure and true; my parent's love was an inspiration I aspired to know and have one day.

A single spotlight cast me in a haze of blue as I recalled the words to Etta James, At Last, and before my brain could protest, my mouth opened, and my voice broke the silent pause as I began to sing. I felt the words in my soul and let the harmony take me.

I sang to no one but the memories of the past.

But then, I looked out to the floor below and saw him. Dean walked toward the edge of the dancefloor before me and locked me in a stare. His eyes, face, and body held all the intentions for fulfilling the promise of the words I sang. And I felt it too. I pictured myself stepping down from the stage as the song continued on a loop, then Dean took me in his arms, and together we swayed to the music.

It was all too surreal like I was out of my body. Dean held me like a wingless angel, our hearts ready to take flight to hereafter, where we lived together in a paradise of our making. As I sang the final words, Dean's lips moved along.

You are mine. At last.

The beautiful melody drew to the last notes and faded into silence. A round of applause brought me back to reality. Dean was still before me with a smile as I clutched the microphone to my chest.

"Wasn't that beautiful? Take a bow, Tara." Martina applauded, and the crowd was on their feet, cheering and whistling loudly. I bowed and then handed to mic back to Martina.

"You killed it, girlfriend!" Martina hugged me. I stepped down from the stage and walked up to Dean.

"You are a nightingale, Tara. Your voice is mesmerizing," Dean complimented.

"Thank you." I blushed. I walked with him back to his seat. Along the way, people praised me, and I thanked them. I picked up the tray I had left on the table, ready to return to work, but Dean took my wrist, halting my steps.

"When is your shift over?"

"Four."

He smiled and nodded. I saw Danny sitting there, giving me a wicked, knowing grin with his thumbs up. I blushed with embarrassment, but at least I knew my uncle approved, which made the situation with Dean feel all the more dreamlike. Because in what reality would my family bring a total stranger into the fold with immediate trust?

My life has consisted of doubt and a lack of faith in people like Lyle, Asher, Gina, and Bren. Who else might come along and hurt my family or me? It was strange that Dean did feel like a person I could trust despite his prowling tendencies. There was a connection somewhere in the darkness.

Martina had the audience laughing as she told jokes. "My brothers and I are roosters. And though I'm always a rooster in my heart, at night, let me tell you, even a cock has to tuck his head in his tail feathers. All my queens know what I'm talking about, don't you ladies?"

The crowd was roaring with laughter.

"Cock a doodle doo!" Danny crowed loudly, adding to the hysteria.

Tonight was most undoubtedly special.

Chapter 10
DEAN

Desire To Devour

"It's now or never, or worst-case scenario, I lose control while you're wooing your girl." Zane had been waiting patiently all night for an opportunity to sate his thirst. These moments I detested most about sharing a body with my twin.

"Fine, Zane," I said irritably, "It has to be someone random and not from around here. You'll have to leave them standing and breathing and use your compulsion to send them off immediately. No playing with your food tonight."

We stood by the exit and waited for some unfortunate unsuspecting soul to go out for a breath of fresh air. I watched Tara run around the coop like a chicken with its head cut off. Occasionally, Zane made me turn my attention to Bren. And it was Bren who decided to step outside on her break.

"Oh, I do love a double endeavor." Zane pulled our body along, following Bren out the door.

"Not her, you idiot!"

"Don't worry. My compulsion will work on her like anybody else," Zane replied nonchalantly.

Despite my resistance, he continued his approach, and his lust was too intense for me to combat his monster. As he stood next to Bren, I lost all control. Zane was in charge now, and I could feel his incisors ache with the need to descend, to devour.

I thought you wanted her for more than another blood bag, Zane, I yelled in our head. But he ignored me as he turned on his charm, and Bren enamored under Zane's compulsion before I could say more. Zane took Bren's hand and led her into the forest as a trusting lamb led to slaughter.

He pushed Bren's back to a tree and kissed her. She moaned and latched her fingers into his shirt. The shirt Tara gave me, and it pissed me off. I was screaming in a fury, but it was all in vain, and Zane stooped lower and lower as he kissed a trail down Bren's body. She shivered and moaned as Zane lifted her skirt and leg over our shoulder. He kissed the inside of her thigh, moving closer to her panties.

Zane pulled Bren's panties aside and slid two fingers inside her, and she cried out. She panted and moaned as Zane worked her body into a frenzy, and he licked her inner thigh. His fangs descended, sinking into her tender flesh as she climaxed. Blood ran down her leg as Zane drank greedily.

Stop, Zane. You're going to kill her, I shouted desperately.

He got his fill just as Bren was on the verge of passing out, and he licked the wound closed and drug his tongue down her leg to clean up the trail of blood. Bren slumped against our body, and Zane lifted her over our shoulder.

Woody was exiting the building as we came out of the woods. Zane relinquished control back to me as I carried Bren toward Woody.

"What happened?" Woody asked in concern.

"I found her passed out," I said matter of factly.

"Shit," Woody cursed. "Quick, bring her inside to my office." I followed him with Bren draped over my shoulder and laid her on a plush leather sofa.

"I guess tonight was a bit more than she could handle," I surmised.

"Dammit, Dee! She was supposed to be here tonight to help. It's not the first time she's bailed on me, leaving me short on nights like this. I'm going to fire her ass," Woody said.

Anger ruled his tone, and he grabbed a water bottle from a minifridge and got to his knees. He tapped Bren's cheek. "Bren. Come on, open your eyes for me."

Bren moaned as her eyes cracked open. Woody opened the water and held it to her lips. "Drink!" He commanded. She did, and Woody and I both breathed a sigh of relief. Woody had Bren sitting as he held the bottle for her like feeding a helpless babe. I stewed in anger at Zane. I wanted to rip him out of my body. But then I could feel his remorse.

Shit. I'm sorry, Dean. I lost control. But she's alive.

Dammit, Zane! You nearly blew it for both of us. Don't talk to me anymore.

Zane slipped away into the dark recess of our mind.

I knew my way around a bar as I had experience from multiple gigs in the past. Stella took over on the floor to help Tara, and by the last call, Tara looked ready to drop. Only a small group was hanging around by three in the morning. After they left, Cannon went and locked the door.

"What happened to Bren?" Stella asked Woody.

"She passed out. Dean found her outside, and she's resting in my office." Woody replied.

"Poor girl. This night was the busiest we've ever had."

Tara was slumped over with her head in her arms. "Uncle Woody has got to hire more help if we have more nights like this."

"And I will. Dean offered to help behind the bar, so now he's on the payroll. I'm firing Dee and will look for a few more helpers on the floor," Woody offered. He counted out the tills while Stella and I cleaned up behind the bar. Cannon and Danny were bussing tables and cleaning.

Trey came out in a pair of black leggings and a long loose shirt with slippers on his feet. His face was void of make-up, and his natural black short-cropped hair had no covering. He yawned and stretched before sitting down on the barstool next to Tara. "Well, this was a glorious night. How did we do?"

"We did exceptionally well. Martina delivered on her promise and then some," Woody replied.

"Fabulous!" Trey beamed. "I told you, didn't I?"

Woody handed Trey a thick stack of bills, who fanned himself with it. "Oh, I do love the smell of greenery."

Woody passed hefty stacks of bills to everyone in the room. Tara lifted her head when Woody set money on the bar before her. Her eyes rounded in surprise. "Really?"

Stella fanned herself with her stack of cash. "You earned it. You busted your ass out there tonight. We all did. We should go shopping."

"Ooh, yes," Trey said, "I would love to take my best ladies out on an excursion. Perhaps we could go after we visit Rudy Bear at the hospital. Ooh, and before then too. I'd like to get him a get-well present. What do you say, Tara? You up for that?"

"I'd love that," Tara responded.

Trey and Stella squealed and clapped excitedly. Everyone in the room laughed. I watched Tara as her face lit up. She was so beautiful, even in her sleep-deprived state. All I wanted to do now was carry her to bed and hold her in my arms.

Bren stepped out of the hallway, still swaying on her feet. "Whoa there, girlie," Danny steadied her and then took her to a chair to sit.

"I feel horrible. I want to go home, but I can't drive," Bren said.

"Not before you get something in your stomach and drink more water," Woody said, "Danny, will you be able to drive her home?"

"Naw, man. I had a few too many tonight," Danny replied.

"Same," Cannon said.

"What about you, Dean?" Woody looked at me, and I nodded, unable to refuse. I intended to stay in his good graces and not let on that Zane was responsible for Bren's sickly state. Stella brought a plate with a sandwich, some fruit, and a glass of water. Bren ate ravenously. Then chugged the water.

"Do you have some orange juice and cookies? I feel like I donated half my blood to a vampire." Bren's statement made me freeze in place, but Stella chuckled.

"Sure thing, Sweetheart." She went back into the kitchen.

I turned and saw Tara looking at me with a questioning gaze. She knew something was up. My reaction to Bren's accurate statement threw up red flags, and I cursed Zane for his nature, which he couldn't control any better than I could my own.

I then realized my control over Zane's monster was weakening. I already knew this, though, as Zane has slowly developed resistance over the years. My powers over the dead and undead have been waning for some time.

Zane's blood was tainted by the venom of another vampire eighty years ago. The change happened to him, but not me. It was something I still didn't understand to this day. But at the time, I had full ability to control Zane's monster, so I didn't lose Zane to complete hysteria due to bloodlust.

As time progressed, I felt a trickling of my power seep away as my brother and I struggled within this body we shared. And, tonight proved that the scales have tipped in Zane's favor. I worried how much longer I had before Zane took over completely, and I would be lost forever to his control.

You know that is not my intention. I never asked for this curse. I feel like I'm losing control just as you are. I've depended on you to keep me in check, and I have the same fear. I'm sorry about Bren; I wanted more from her than her blood. I hate myself and this monster I am.

I forgive you. We need to figure this out together. In the meantime, you have to try harder. You've become too dependent on me to reel you back. You must step up and take responsibility.

I know. Believe me. I'm trying.

Woody had a set of keys in his hands. "You can take Cannon's Bronco. It's parked around back."

"Okay. I'll pull in around front." I accepted the keys and went outside.

I sensed something in the woods as I walked around the building. I knew it was something dark in nature, but it felt non-threatening and inquisitive. Its aura reached out to mine, and I felt a kindred likeness to my power. It wasn't dead or undead, but I could get a reading on it that told me it wanted something here, more like someone.

I stopped and turned my head, and Zane lent me his sharp vision as I stared deep into the trees. And there, I saw it peeking out from behind a one with its head tilted in curiosity as though it wanted to size me up and determine if I was a threat. I stood silently and observed it as it did the same. It came out from its hiding place, and I saw a tall human shadow figure.

I raised my hand in a peace sign, and it mimicked me. I heard Danny's voice calling for me, and the creature quickly morphed into a four-legged animal-like shadow and shot off at speed only Zane could match. I've never seen anything like it before, and I would've made chase if not for my prior obligation to take Bren home.

Zane zipped our body to the back of the clubhouse, got in Cannon's Bronco, and started the engine, giving it a few revs before driving it around the front. Danny was waiting with Bren leaning into him. He walked her to the passenger door, helped her inside, and buckled her seatbelt.

"Here's her address." He handed me a slip of paper and then moved to close the door. I put the address into the navigation system and then pulled away.

I looked in the rearview mirror and saw Tara halting her steps to her cabin as she watched me drive away with Bren. I couldn't help but feel guilty as I had asked her to join me for a drink after her shift, but I knew she was tired and needed to rest.

Bren closed her eyes and snored lightly with her head leaning against the window. Her apartment was only ten minutes away. I parked in the lot and shook her gently. "Bren, you're home. I need your apartment key, and I'll help you get there."

Bren groaned, and I felt like an ass as she fumbled around in her purse for her keys and then handed them to me. I helped her exit the vehicle, then carried her up the steps, inside, and laid her in bed. I took off her shoes and pulled the blankets over her body.

I left two bottles of water and some pain meds on her bedside table for the headache I knew she'd have when she woke. I plugged in her phone to charge, took her apartment key off the ring to lock her deadbolt, and slid it under the door. As I drove away, I repeatedly told myself she'd be okay.

Back at The Hillbilly Roost, I pulled Cannon's Bronco around and parked it where I found it. When I got out of the truck, I had a dire urge to knock on Tara's door. I approached her cabin, but I could hear her soft breaths of slumber as I got there.

"Looking for a place to crash?" Woody asked. I turned to see him observing me, which surprised me as I hadn't even realized he was there.

"You got a place for me?"

"Sure do, follow me." He led me over to a fifth-wheel camper and opened the door. I stepped inside the cozy accommodations. It was in good shape and a far cry from worse places I've stayed before. I didn't need much sleep, and there were plenty of woodlands to roam if I became restless. It would be an excellent opportunity to encourage Zane to hunt the wildlife instead of living it.

"Thanks a lot, Woody. I appreciate your generosity."

"I've had your kind through here before. I don't mind helping those who don't mind pitching in. I'm not anyone's benefactor, but I can afford to help out my fellow man as the need arises. How long do you plan on staying?" He folded his big arms across that broad chest, and I knew I couldn't bullshit him.

"I've never stayed anywhere longer than a few months," I admitted.

Woody accepted my answer with a nod. "Well, the camper is stocked with everything you'll need. I stay in the cabin down by the lake." He pointed out at a path past Tara's cabin. "If you need anything, don't bother me till at least half-past ten."

"Got it," I chuckled. "I can make do. Thanks."

"I figured as much." Woody closed the door and walked away.

I grabbed a beer from the fridge and sat on the sofa. I went to grab the television remote when I noticed a stack of books on the shelf above. I enjoyed reading better than the crap on the boob tube, so I picked up a book titled Generation Stone: Revelation Light Calling. A young girl in a world where she has to save everyone from a dark spirit falls in love with a deaf telepath. Not usually my jam, but I opened it and read the inscription.

Uncle Woody. I enjoyed this book and want to share it with you. Love, Tara.

That was enough to convince me. Women loved a man with a sensitive side; perhaps I could use a few pointers from the love interest. Not that I needed any, but I'd do anything for Tara. I've never been in love before. My longest relationship lasted five months; even then, Zane was too much of an interference.

As I read, Zane would interrupt, asking questions like an annoying person who wanted to jump ahead of the plot and didn't mind spoiler alerts. I shushed him several times as I got into the story before he finally gave up. I finished the book and looked at the clock, noting I had read non-stop for over five hours. I had to agree with Tara. It wasn't anything like I had expected, with a strong female protagonist battling darkness, falling for a pretty cool guy while tying two worlds together by soul-deep connections.

I could see Tara as a strong lead in her story, and I was more than happy to be her love interest.

Chapter 11
TARA

Grave Ambitions & Inhibitions

Three abrupt knocks came from the front door, and my mind immediately wondered if the dark shadow had returned. Nervously, I approached and looked through the small window. A man was standing there with his back turned, and I thought it was Danny because of his dark hair, height, and build. I opened the door while rubbing a dry itch in my eyes.

"Uncle Danny?"

My eyes came to focus, and he was no longer there. I stepped outside and the door shut behind me. I turned to open it, figuring a draft pushed it closed. But as I turned the handle, it wouldn't give. I struggled with it for a bit longer and cursed. I was locked out. I turned to walk down to Woody's to see if he had a spare key, only to find my bare feet standing on soft moss in unfamiliar surroundings.

A thick fog rolled in along the ground and engulfed my legs. Danny stood in the distance, and I called out. He didn't turn to acknowledge me as he lifted his arm and pointed. A large elaborate black metal gate appeared, and I felt pulled toward it on an unseen path with dense fog billowing around my lower body.

As I continued through the gate, my feet became damp and cold from the dewy moss. Danny led me in silence as the fog swirled and began to dissipate.

We were in a graveyard surrounded by headstones, and what was strange was I didn't even find it odd, nor did I feel frightened. That was until Danny pointed to a grave, and I suddenly stood by his side, having not recalled walking up to him.

Richard Ethan Raybrook
February 5, 1972-September 2011

I shook my head. "No, Dad's alive! They never found his body. Danny, why are you showing this to me?"

Danny was no longer there. I turned in a circle, searching, only to find myself alone and surrounded by graves.

"Hello?" I yelled; my voice echoed back to me. I walked toward the sound of a shovel scooping. Someone in a long dark hooded cape was digging a fresh grave. The cape swung with the movements of the shovel, breaking the earth, then sideways to deposit the clumps of soil into a pile.

"Hello?" I called. Again, ignored as the person continued to toil, the shallow pit grew with each break. I approached cautiously and stood mere feet behind the caped figure, who froze. They seemed to wait in anticipation of my next move, to which I reached up and snatched back the hood to reveal long dark hair. Their head turned, and I was shocked.

"Gina!"

"Hello, Tara. I'm digging my grave, but you're the one who's going to lie in it."

I opened my mouth to ask, "What are you talking about?" but then I knew the answer as Gina swung the shovel, hitting me in the back. I fell forward into the dark earth and found myself in a continuous descent. I screamed and flayed about for some time before landing on a pile of human remains. Bones clattered beneath my aching body. I moaned as I rolled, and the pile of bones shifted and slid like loose rocks on a treacherous climb. My hands and feet clamored for purchase, and I tried to stay calm.

"HELP! Gina?" I yelled. Why would she do this to me? I wasn't the one to betray her. Were my words to her so harsh? I'd never known her to be so vindictive. She wouldn't go so far as this. Would she?

I found it easier to army crawl atop the shifting bones, and as I made it to the dirt wall, a skeletal hand grasped my ankle. I screamed and shook my leg as bony fingers clutched tightly. Before I knew it, I was under full attack. A skull chomped its teeth, clamping onto my pants. More skeletal parts reached, surrounded, and grabbed me.

I screamed, scampered away from the assault, and began to climb a slope of bodies in various degrees of decomposition. The smell had my stomach roiling with a violent urgency to be sick. As I continued to ascend, the dead began to moan and made to grab hold of me. I continued to scream as I held onto anything to aid me, including a lower jaw that snapped and broke away. Eyelids opened, and shrouds of deathly grey rolled to look at me in accusation.

The corpse groaned, and I cried as it clutched me firmly. My feet were slipping, and in desperation, I reached up; my fingers sunk into eye sockets with a slimy residue. I threw up in my mouth at the sensation. Tears and sweat rolled down my face, and I cried in frightened desperation.

The higher I climbed, the more rotted flesh I encountered. I stood on a shoulder, and my foot slipped again as the flesh slid away like a filet from muscle and bone.

"Oh, no!" I groaned, feeling another wave of nausea. More hands gripped and pulled at me. My body began to backslide, and I would fall into the pits of Hell amongst the damned, desperate to have me join them in their eternal misery.

"HELP ME!" I reached up. I was so close to the top.

"PLEASE SAVE ME!" My body slipped, and just as I lost my grip, a hand caught me from above. A face cast in shadow appeared as two hands now held me by my arm. I let go of the wall of the dead and swung out freely, dangling in the air. Necrotic fingertips grazed my torso, legs, and feet.

"Don't let go!" the man yelled at me. I reached with my other hand and grabbed hold of his wrist. The man pulled me, and I landed on top of him with my cheek on his chest as he and I breathed heavily.

I heard his heartbeats. Wait? Heart Beats? As in two hearts as I could distinguish between the two. One beat slower than the other. I lifted my head to see my savior was none other than Dean. He put his hands on my back. "I've got you, Tara. You're safe now."

I rolled off his body and sat up. Looking back at the grave, it was once again shallow with no occupants. I shook my head in confusion. What's happening to me? Why?

Dean stood before me, offering his hand. I took hold, and he pulled me to my feet. "What is this?" I questioned.

He pointed, and I turned to see a tall shadow of a man. His presence felt welcoming, and I tilted my head. "Who is that?"

"Your destiny," Dean replied.

I walked toward the tall figure, and the darkness faded from its features, revealing a nose, mouth, and eyes, till I saw his entire face. My breath hitched. "Dad?"

He smiled at me. "Hi, Tara."

"Oh my god, Dad!" I threw my arms around him. "I knew it. I knew you were alive. I've never given up. I've been searching all these years."

"I know, baby girl." Dad held me tightly in his arms. He held my shoulders and gently pushed me away. I looked at him and knew there was something he wanted to say.

"Tara, I'm kind of in a state of limbo. There's something you need to do to bring me back. The shadow you saw won't hurt you."

"The shifter in the woods?"

"Yes," he replied. "I brought you a helper. Listen to what he tells you. But beware the second beating heart, as it grows strong every day. You must trust your instincts. He will need your help in return."

"Who will? None of this makes any sense. Why is this happening? Where are you?"

"You will find me, but you must start here." Dad pointed to a grave. The name gave me pause, and a dreadful feeling consumed me.

"No! Not that!" I shook my head. "There has to be another way. Please, Daddy!"

"It's time to face your past and your monsters, Tara. Some you will trust, and others you must battle. It's in your blood, and it's who you are. I'm sorry, this is all I can tell you. I love you, baby girl." Dad started to fade.

"No! Don't go!" I cried.

"Answer the door, Tara." Dad disappeared. Pounding on my door woke me, and I opened my eyes.

"Tara. It's me, Dean. Are you okay? Open the door." I looked around. Daylight peeked through the curtains, and the alarm clock flashed at 1:00 p.m. I opened the door to Dean, panting as though he ran here. "Are you okay? I was passing by and heard you yelling. You sounded frightened."

"Nightmare. Thank you for checking on me."

Dean gazed at me with his gorgeous baby blues. "You want to grab that drink? I mean not alcohol; perhaps have a coffee with me?"

He's here, and I'm a mess. The way Dean looked at me, he didn't seem bothered by my appearance. Dean looked at me hungrily, and I felt my body heat rise.

I want to grab you by your shirt, pull you inside, push you into my bed, and claim your sexy body.

"Tara?"

I blinked. "Huh?"

Dean chuckled. *Good gravy, that laugh!* His voice called to my inner primal tigress. *Trust your instincts, Tara, but don't lose control of yourself. You're not a she-beast in heat, high on catnip. Oh, but how I wish I could let myself go. I can tell he wants me, but in what capacity?*

"Would you like to come in?" I invited, hoping not to give myself away. "I can make some coffee."

"I would like that very much." Dean followed me inside and closed the door behind him, and I gestured to the kitchen table, but he went to put the coffee on instead. So, I excused myself to the bathroom. After finishing my business, I looked in the mirror.

"Awe hell!" I looked like I'd been to Hell and back.

"Everything okay in there? Do you need a rescue?" Dean asked.

"Ah, no, I'm fine."

I pulled my hair back, washed my face, and brushed my teeth, which didn't make much sense as I was about to drink coffee. But then you'd never know if the opportunity for some mouth-to-mouth action may arise, so better safe than sorry. I also put on some healthy swipes of deodorant. My legs needed a shave, but I had my pajama pants on, so at least that was covered.

Unless? Nevermind. Not happening, Tara! Not now. We just met for crying out loud.

Why did my mind keep going there?

I couldn't help but feel this incredible draw of attraction to Dean. What was it about him that made me want him so badly? Yes, he was gorgeous and charming and had a great smile and panty-melting voice. Fantastic kisser!

Oh my god, that kiss! Yes, I'm glad I brushed my teeth.

I stepped out to find him bringing our coffee to the table. He laid out sugar, creamer, spoons, and napkins. He also put some short-bread cookies on a plate.

Wow! Asher never did anything like this for me. I had always taken care of him, doted on him, and picked up after him. I cooked his dinners, made his lunches, and did his dishes and laundry. Asher? He took out the trash and mowed the lawn.

Dean pulled out my chair. "How do you like your coffee?"

"You don't have to…." I moved to take the mug, but he held it back with a mischievous grin.

"Tara, you waited on a large crowd of people last night with barely any help. Let me take care of you, would you?"

"Fine," I agreed. I sat back and took a cookie. "I take my coffee with one sugar and two spoons of creamer."

Dean smiled. "See now, that wasn't so hard, was it?"

I laughed and graciously accepted my coffee mug. I don't know what he did differently, but it smelled divine. I took a sip, and it tasted better than when I made it. And I could make a good cup of brew.

"This is very good. Thank you." I took another sip and hummed. I never knew coffee could soothe the soul like this. It felt like being in a cherished embrace in front of a warm, cozy fire.

"I'm glad you like it. I've worked in a few coffee shops and had the opportunity to perfect it over the years." Dean took a sip, and he groaned. "Mmm, the caffeinated beverage from the gods."

I laughed. "You think there's a coffee god?"

"There has to be! Only a deity of higher power could come up with such a perfect beverage," Dean declared.

"Indeed," I agreed, "Why else would the Bible talk about how God makes coffee? The answer is in Hebrews."

Dean chuckled. "Yes, I can see that. You're a funny gal."

"You're a funny guy," I returned. "So, Dean. What's your last name? Where did you come from? And how long will you be sticking around?"

"My last name is Perrish. I come from anywhere and everywhere. And I will be sticking around as long as you'll have me, Tara Raybrook."

"Am I the only reason you came?"

"You're the only reason I'd be willing to stay. But, that's entirely up to you." Dean grinned wickedly.

"Well, seeing how you just got here, and I don't know much about you, I suppose you could stay awhile while we get to know each other." I returned a smile that conveyed my hope to have him around for a long time.

"I have nowhere else I need or want to be!"

"Good."

"I concur." Dean winked.

We continued to drink our coffee and eat cookies in companionable silence. Dean kept giving me his eyes, and I never felt like sharing a coffee with a man could feel so seductive.

"I'll drink to that," Dean stated.

Did I say that out loud? I swear, I mean, I'm sure I didn't.

"Your eyes give you away, beautiful girl."

"Oh? And what did my eyes tell you?"

"That you feel the same way I do."

"And how do I feel?" Dean gave me a smoldering look, and my heart began to race.

"You feel like a woman who knows what she wants, and I know you feel a connection between us. I want to be whatever you need, fulfill your desires, and take you where you've never been. I want to show you your true self because we are the same, Tara. And I'll teach you. But I want something in return."

"What's that?" I quivered. Dean's words took me to the edge. My body, mind, and soul were reeling with a need so powerful I felt ready to detonate.

Dean's captivating blue eyes held mine. "To know you in every way a man in love could know a woman. I want to touch you, taste you, and consume you fully. I want you, mind, heart, body, and soul. You can tell me anything and everything because I want you as a friend, helper, and lover. I need your essence to course through my veins and mine through yours. I'm a drowning man, and I need you to save me."

I had to set my coffee down before I spilled it. My mouth opened and closed, but no words would come. What could I say to Dean's confession?

Well, that sounds good to me! Please, by all means, have me and do as you wish.

If only it were that simple. I just sent Asher out of my life for good, and on the same day, no, just moments after, Dean was there. I recalled the nightmare I had. My father told me he'd sent me a helper to trust. Was he talking about Dean? In my heart, it felt that way.

"Tell me, Tara. I'm teetering on edge here! Be my old lady. I'm an old man, and I'm not getting any younger." Dean looked at me imploringly as he waited for my answer, and I wanted to pounce on him like the tastiest prey.

Hell, if he could make coffee this good, what other good things could he do? Or perhaps I should say *bad things.* Would this bad boy break my heart? I felt like he'd do way more damage than Asher could if he did because Asher had never touched this place deep inside me, somewhere beyond the depth of my soul.

"You're not old, Dean. What are you, twenty-eight?" I asked in a coy tone. Why was I going on this rabbit trail? I wanted to say 'yes' and take him on the damn table and ride him like a stallion because hell, what woman wants to ride a pony?

And who needed a saddle when I could ride freestyle and hold on to that gorgeous mane? Dean smiled at me, and I felt he knew what I was thinking.

"Let's just say I'm much older than I look." Dean winked.

"Is that supposed to be a reference to your experience?"

"It is. And much more. As I said, I want to teach you everything I know. And before you ask, this is no joke about teaching a dog a new trick. There are things you should know about yourself, and the things I know go beyond the realm of mortal comprehension."

"Does it have anything to do with your tattoo?"

"In a way, it does."

"Great! Now you have me wanting to know more."

"And wanting?" Dean's wicked grin returned.

"Well." I shrugged nonchalantly.

Dean growled and stood abruptly, and his chair fell to its back on the floor with a loud clatter. He charged at me, and before I could scramble out of my chair, he grabbed my wrists and pulled me to him forcefully. And I wanted this from him, all his desires and promises, I wanted to fulfill. I wanted to be his anything and everything.

He crushed his lips to mine, and coffee breath be damned, I needed this! My heart already knew; my mind and body were catching up. And as he grazed my lips with his tongue, I wanted to taste him too. I had been so tired for so long, and I discovered that the coffee in my cup wasn't 'the best part of waking up.'

Dean's energy was like a shot of gourmet expresso that brought everything within me alive, and it was a flavor better than anything I had consumed before, plus the cream and sugar.

Mmm, yes, please!

Coffee references aside, I wanted more of what Dean wanted to dish and serve. Because now I was hungry, hungrier than I'd ever been before.

Dean lifted me, and my legs wrapped around his waist. He carried me to the bed. In his haste, he knocked the alarm clock off the bedside table. The song Knock On Wood was playing, and I had to laugh because the way Dean loved me was frightening and exciting. I reached up and knocked on the headboard, and Dean laughed.

Everything was happening so fast. And I felt this powerful urgency inside me to connect to Dean as though so much depended upon our union. There was something inside me I couldn't explain, but I knew it needed to be released, and Dean held the key.

Dean kissed me achingly slow as we took our time peeling our clothes off one another. His sensuality felt punishing in all the right ways. Dean trailed kisses down my body, each one a spark of electricity. I felt my core heating and charging, ready to be taken. Dean slipped off my panties and kissed me there. And, oh, this man knew how to kiss both pairs of my lips. I came undone in less than a minute, a new record. To the victor goes the spoils. But it was more like Dean was spoiling me, and he continued to lavish my body with his talented tongue and hands.

I need to install a fire extinguisher next to the bed for this inferno Dean created from my flesh. I was feverish, yet I needed more of him. "Dean, please!"

"Tell me what you want, Tara." His voice was husky, and he began to work his way back up my stomach. I grabbed Dean's golden locks and pulled him up to my face.

"I want to claim you!" I flipped him to his back and straddled his legs. I pulled him free of his briefs, took his generous length inside me, and gasped in pleasure. I rode him like a bareback wild stallion.

Dean grabbed my hips, and the fire in his eyes matched my passion for him as we crested the highest hill, jumped the ridge, and landed on the other side. I had never felt so free before. Our spirits collided and burst like a supernova. Then I felt the darkness as it enveloped me, and suddenly I knew. Dean and I were the same.

Our darkness made us what we were, and there was a life-awakening power within. It flowed through my veins. This life-giving essence also contained light and reminded me of Dean's tattoo. There still seemed to be more to Dean that I didn't know, another half.

There was a flash in his eyes that confirmed my intuitive thought. It looked as if he was battling something within as he closed his eyes, grunted, and strained.

"Dean? Are you okay?" My palms were on his chest, and there I felt it. Two heartbeats. One was running wild and the other slow and steady.

But beware the second beating heart, as it grows strong every day. It was the warning Dad had given. Two hearts in one body? Which was which? I felt the slower heartbeat pick up, and when Dean opened his eyes, I no longer recognized him. Blue flickered to silver, back and forth like a power struggle.

Dean's grip on my hips intensified as he lifted and slammed me to the mattress. I became frightened as his now silver eyes roamed my body, and he licked his lips.

"Mmm, I think I'll have a taste too." His voice sounded different, and I knew this wasn't him.

"Who are you?" My lips quivered, and I tried to pull my sheets to cover my nakedness. Dean, or whoever this was, grabbed my hands to stop me. He pinned my arms above my head and closed his eyes as he inhaled like a wild animal taking in my scent. I tried to struggle and break free, but my efforts were futile. I panted in fear as my heart hammered in my chest.

"I wonder if you taste as divine as you smell? Only one way to find out."

My eyes widened in horror as this monster opened his mouth wide, and his cuspid teeth grew in length. I screamed in terror as those fangs descended and bit me above my left breast. All he took was one gulp before pulling away and clutching his throat.

"Poison!" He choked before his grip on me released and fell back on the bed, gasping for air. He passed out, and I got to my knees and began to panic. I tapped his face and shook him.

"Dean?" Tears spilled down my face. *I killed him! Oh, dear God, no!*

His eyes opened, and he reared up and vomited.

"Holy shit!" I cried as a mixture of my blood, coffee and cookies spewed from his mouth. I grabbed the bedsheet and threw it over his lap as he continued to be sick. "Fuck!"

There was a frantic pounding on the door, and I heard Uncle Woody shouting. "Tara, open the fucking door. What the hell is going on in there?"

"Shit," I cursed. "Hold on; I'm coming!" I ran to the bathroom, threw on my robe, went to the front door, and opened it a crack.

"Who's in there?" Woody looked over my head, trying to see beyond me.

"No one. The television remote jammed, and the volume maxed."

"Don't lie to me." Woody pushed his way inside.

"Uncle Woody, please," I begged.

"What the hell is going on in here?" Woody looked around, and I was surprised to see the empty bed with the quilts pulled up to hide any evidence. The kitchen chair had been returned to its upright position and pushed in. In the bathroom, the shower was running.

"Who's in there?" Woody asked.

"Dean," I supplied.

"Why is he using your shower?" Woody folded his arms and stared me down.

"He was out for a run, and I invited him in for coffee. He asked if he could use my shower."

Well, at least the first part was true.

"Are you bleeding? Why is there blood on your robe?" Woody pointed to where the monster had bitten me, and I'd bled through the terry cloth material. How the hell would I explain this?

"Uh, a bad shaving incident?" I shrugged in uncertainty.

Just as Woody was about to call me out on my bullshit, the bathroom door opened and Dean stepped out fully dressed with wet hair and a piece of toilet paper pressed to his clean-shaven face. "I'm sorry about bleeding on your robe. I grabbed the first thing off the hook and thought it was a towel. Oh, hey, Woody, good morning!" Dean smiled innocently.

Woody didn't look convinced. "Morning. Now tell me what you're really doing here in my niece's cabin. The truth would make things go easier for you."

I swallowed as Woody wasn't looking at me. If he knew what happened, Dean might be a dead man walking. Not exactly, but he might receive a brandished fist to the face and get sent packing. I couldn't stand the thought of not seeing him again. But he certainly had some explaining to do.

"I was out running, and I heard Tara yelling inside, so I stopped to make sure she was okay. She'd had a nightmare evidently, and I asked if she wanted to talk, so she invited me in for coffee," Dean explained.

All completely true.

"So, you decided to shave and cut yourself and used Tara's robe to stop the bleeding?"

Dean lifted the tissue from his face to reveal a big nick still oozing with blood. "Yeah, again, I apologize for that. Honestly, though, Tara and I hit it off last night."

My face fell into my hands, mortified. Woody growled menacingly and stepped toward Dean, who backed up a step. I stepped in front of Dean and put a hand on Woody's chest.

"Woody, I'm a grown woman capable of deciding what I want."

Woody pointed at Dean threateningly. "He is a drifter, Tara. You just ended a bad relationship, and if he hurts you…."

"I'm okay. Honest!"

"Fine! Whatever is going on between the two of you better not affect business as usual. And, you!" He prodded Dean's chest. "If you hurt Tara in any way…."

"My intentions are honorable, Woody!" Dean replied.

Woody switched topics, clearly uncomfortable with the idea that his niece just had relations with a practical stranger. "Bren will be out the next few nights. She's still sick. I'll be interviewing new help today, so Tara, I may need you a little earlier to help."

"Okay. I'll be around."

Woody gave Dean one last threatening glare, and Dean returned it with a confident nod.

"You're on the clock tonight, too, Dean."

"I'll be there," Dean replied. Woody nodded, and walked out the door, closing it behind him.

Chapter 12
DEAN

The Monster In Me

Tara stood with her hands on her hips. "What the hell was that? And who am I talking to right now?"

"It's me, Dean. I promise. I'm sorry, Tara. I'll tell you everything." I moved to her, but she held up her hand to stop me. I desperately wanted to hold her in my arms and reassure her that I wasn't the monster who bit her.

"Please, Tara, let me check your wound." I approached slower this time, and she let down her guard. I gently pulled her robe back, and Tara hissed. I gave her an apologetic look as I exposed the bite mark clotted over. Her skin looked red and tender around the two puncture marks.

"Zane, you sonofabitch." I retrieved some ice, wrapped it in a kitchen towel, and gently applied it to the bite. I didn't have Zane's enzymes available to heal the wound over.

"Who's Zane? Dean, talk to me." Tara took my hand and guided me to the couch. "You should sit. You still look ill."

I allowed her to guide me and sat next to her. "This will sound strange, but I assure you it's not me who bit you. I know it doesn't make sense."

Tara nodded and prompted me to carry on. She took my words seriously, and I wondered why she hadn't run away screaming already.

"I'm freaked out, but I'm not going anywhere. I believe you; just explain this to me."

Why was she taking this so well? After everything she'd been through with that asshole, Asher, I couldn't understand her willingness to give me this opportunity.

"My twin brother, Zane, bit you. We share this body. Two hearts, two minds. He is a vampire, and I am something else. Until a few years ago, I could control his monster, but he's getting stronger, and it couldn't have happened at a worse time. It seems he had a reaction when he tried your blood."

"Vampire?" Tara looked shocked. But then she was quiet and looked like she was in a trance. "Monsters! Some I can trust." She blinked and looked at me. "I knew it wasn't you. I trust that. My father told me so."

"Your father?"

"The nightmare I woke from when you came to my door. My father has been missing for the last ten years, but he just came to me in my dream. He told me he sent a helper, and I believe it's you. He also told me to beware of the second heartbeat as it grows stronger. That's Zane's heart, isn't it?"

I was at a loss for the first time in my long existence. "Yes. But he didn't mean to hurts you. Tara, when I met Martina and decided to follow her here, I thought it was just a coincidence. But I felt drawn by something else I couldn't explain. And the moment I saw you, I knew. You are the reason I'm here. I believe somehow; that your father had a hand in this. The questions are how and what does it all mean?"

"I'm not sure, but he also told me it was time to face my past and monsters, some I can trust, others I must battle. There's something in me I can't explain, but it feels dark, and I'm not frightened, just confused."

"In what way?"

"Well, I'm sure it has something to do with my past. First, my father went missing, and my mom met and married Dr. Lyle Durst a couple of years later. He was very controlling over me. Lyle told me I had juvenile diabetes and controlled every aspect of my treatment, from testing my blood to administering my medications.

My mother ended up killing him to protect me. She said he was a demon, on the verge of draining me dry. She was ruled insane and sentenced to thirteen years in the psychiatric state prison."

"I don't believe your mother is crazy, and you never had diabetes, did you?" I asked, already knowing the answer.

"No, I don't believe she is. I didn't have diabetes, either. And yes, Lyle tested my blood, but I don't think it had anything to do with my glucose levels. The insulin he gave me wasn't at all. It was a saline solution. My mom was a nurse, and she found the saline and mislabeled bottles in his home office. Then there are my scars." Tara pointed out the faded lines up and down her forearms. "I was told I did it to myself. I'd have these blackout episodes and have fresh cuts on my arms when I came out of them. My therapist told me my blackouts were due to my anxiety, and 'supposedly' I cut myself because I was depressed due to missing my father."

"You believe your father is alive?"

"I know he is, Dean. I can feel it. I've never given up trying to find him."

"Is this the first dream you've had of him?"

"No. But it's the first one that felt entirely real, like all my senses connected somewhere between life and death. My dad told me he's in some kind of limbo. And you were there. You saved me from the grave. The dead were trying to take me away; it was terrifying."

"Tara, I sensed you were in peril. I ran here prepared to save you. When you answered, I was relieved, but you told me you had a nightmare, and I was certain you had been in danger. I was frightened for you. For our kind, our dreams are closer to reality than any mortals, and our nightmares take us closer to the veil between life and death. It can be a real danger."

"Our kind? What am I?"

"You are a necromancer."

Tara's eyes widened in shock. "A necromancer? How is that possible? How can you tell? Isn't that some kind of witch who can raise the dead?"

"We are not witches. We don't need to cast spells. Witches can bring back the dead, but it is not natural. What we are is in our blood; it's genetic, passed down through the generations. I know you are a necromancer because I recognize the power in your aura. It sounds to me like you inherited your necromancy through your father. I suspect more of your family members have capabilities but are nowhere near as strong as yours. Tara, your essence called to mine."

Tara placed her hand on my face and looked into my eyes. "I feel it too, Dean."

She took a deep breath and released it. "So, witches, vampires, and necromancers are real? But how is your twin a vampire and not you? How is it you share the same body? How does it work?" She looked at me, trying to find some physical trait that made my condition make sense.

"Zane and I were born this way. Zane's heart and circulatory system are separate from mine. When Zane was bitten, he changed, but I remained unaffected. I think it has something to do with my necromancer blood. It zeroed out the effects of the vampire venom. Zane's monster can take over this body, as you've seen. It's worse when the bloodlust is strong, and lately, it's getting out of control."

"So, you think when Zane bit me...?"

"Your blood knocked Zane out of commission, and your blood could be the answer to my dilemma," I answered hopefully.

"I didn't kill him, did I?" she asked worriedly. "I couldn't live with myself if I did that to you, Dean. I didn't invite him to make a feast of me, and he scared the shit out of me, but...."

"I'm so sorry this happened, and I'd never blame you. It wasn't your fault."

"Oh my god!" Tara's eyes widened. "Bren! I saw you carry her in the club over your shoulder last night. Then she made that comment about donating half her blood to a vampire. That was Zane's fault? Oh, shit!"

"Please, Tara. I hope you're not angry. I tried to stop him. It's like I said, my control over Zane is slipping." I waited as she processed this. I let out a breath of relief when she nodded.

"How can I be angry at you for something beyond your control? How do you think I can help?"

This woman was amazing! I didn't deserve Tara, but here she was, fully accepting everything I was sharing and taking it in stride. She's been through hell just as I have, and here I come with Zane in tow making things worse.

"Dean, I know you're thinking you're making things worse, but this explains so much in reality. Everything about my past. The blackouts, my scars, Lyle. Although, I'm not clear as to why my father disappeared. But I know he just visited me, and you showed up the day before. Do you think Lyle was taking my blood because he knew?"

"He may have run tests because he suspected something, but I can't say with certainty that he knew what you were. Maybe he found something in your blood, and he was doing some sort of research. I've never been to a hospital or donated my blood for fear something similar might happen."

"You said Zane is growing in strength. Do you think he's taken too much of your power because you've used it constantly, keeping his bloodlust in check? But Zane bit me and is now comatose?"

"You can't kill Zane that easily, and I don't think he'll be out for long. But I believe your blood is more potent than mine. You might help me with small doses of your blood, but only if you want to. I won't take from you unless you offer."

"I want to help you. My father said you'd need my help. I just didn't know how. So, how will it work?"

"You'll have to inject your blood straight into my heart. But we have to be careful. Zane's heart is slightly offset and to the right of mine. A small dose may knock him out of commission, but too much could be detrimental. Zane may be a parasitic bane on my existence, but he's still my brother, and I care for him. Hell, I even like him some days."

Tara maintained composure as she took this all in. I took her hand in mine and kissed it. "Whenever you're ready, Tara, we'll figure this out. Together."

Those beautiful brown eyes looked into mine, and Tara spoke with unwavering determination. "I couldn't be more ready."

<><><>

The fresh air made me feel better as Tara, and I walked through the woods. The sun's rays broke through the canopy of color, making Tara's hair shine with golden hues. The constant energy flow between us made me want to hold on to this precious gift forever.

There had to be some give and take with Zane, though. I knew he needed to feed to maintain his sanity, so I couldn't make his restrictions too stringent. I had to say it was nice to have a break from his constant interruptions. It was so peaceful. I could get used to this, but I would begin to miss him at some point.

"You sensed my family may have capabilities. Do you feel their power like you did mine?" Tara asked.

"It was more intuitive, but I felt an immense power flow through me when I shook Woody's hand, and he stared me down as if sizing me up."

Tara laughed. "That's Woody for ya. So, if he is like me, he's never said anything. Do you think he's aware? Or, perhaps he knows and has kept it a secret. But Woody has never hidden anything from me."

"I can't say for sure. But there may be a way to find out. If he knows and keeps it a secret, he must be willing to show his power. It isn't something I can make him do."

"Okay, but will you show me what I can do?"

"You most likely have used your power and haven't realized it. It could be something small. Like this." I picked up a dried brown dead leaf and held it before her. I closed my eyes, willing life back into it. I felt tingling when I touched the leaf between my finger and thumb and reopened my eyes. The leaf unfurled, and the vibrant green grew outward from the point of connection until the end.

Tara laughed with astonishment as I passed the leaf to her. "It's so soft. I've never seen a leaf so green. How beautiful! Show me!"

I picked up another dead leaf and took her hand in mine. With her palm up, I placed the shell of what once had been into her waiting hold. "First, see it as it is now. You must be aware of its current lifeless state. Next, picture the life it once contained."

Tara nodded.

"Now, close your eyes and tune into your heartbeat. See the life in your blood down to a cellular level. Follow how it moves, and concentrate on the power as it flows through your veins. Do you feel it?"

Tara held her eyes closed and concentrated. It took a minute before I could feel her take hold of her power. At first, it was just a tiny buzz, but then suddenly, she opened her eyes, and the leaf transformed instantly. It happened so fast; we were both amazed.

"Wow! I did that?"

"That was all you." I smiled. "You are amazing, Tara. How did it feel?"

"I felt just a tiny tingling coursing through me. Then suddenly, it pooled together in my chest and shot like a rocket to my hand. I felt the energy as it released through my fingertips. It's like an instant high. Not that I've ever been high, but it was like a shot of adrenaline or dopamine release."

Tara pressed both fresh leaves to her chest and sighed. "How can a power that feels so dark bring life so bright and vibrant?"

"Life and death are on opposite ends of the spectrum. One is dark and the other light. Thinking about it scientifically, it's like how you need both positive and negative ions to create a charge. Our energy acts like a natural defibrillator where the power in our blood creates a charge, and our touch releases it."

"That's what it felt like. The power inside me was surging and pinging. It gathered in my chest like a battery waiting to connect to a source."

"Exactly." I smiled at Tara. Her eyes filled with so much joy that tears ran down her cheeks. The sunlight made her tears glisten, and she looked like an angel.

"There may be darkness in us, Tara, but how we use it makes a difference." I leaned in to kiss her, and she met my lips willingly. I kissed her tenderly at first but needed more.

I still felt Zane sleeping heavily, so I knew he wouldn't ruin things this time. And I counted this as a blessing because I could be with Tara fully at this moment. She had claimed me, and now I wanted to claim her.

I toyed with the hem of her shirt, not sure if she was willing to give in to me so soon after what happened with Zane. But then she broke our kiss. "I want to be yours, Dean. Claim me."

I kissed her lips, and Tara met my tongue with hers, dueling, circling, tasting. Her taste was intoxicating. I would never get enough of the beautiful creature in my arms. Her actions reciprocated my feelings as she grasped my hair and pulled me in, letting me kiss her harder.

We pulled each other's clothes off with urgency. One of my hands moved to the soft flesh of her perfect round bottom, and I pulled her body flush to mine. Tara moaned in my mouth as my other hand massaged her breast, and I teased her nipple between my finger and thumb. I squeezed and gently tugged her hardened peak. She gasped with a breathy "ahh," to which my body reacted.

I lowered her to the forest floor on a bed of fallen leaves and continued to love her body, kissing, and needing more. She parted her legs, and I lay atop her, leaning on my elbows so I would not put my weight on her, but then she wrapped her arms around me, pulling me to her. "Give me everything. Make me yours. Please, I need you inside me."

I crushed Tara's lips with mine and entered her body with a demanding thrust. My tongue claimed her mouth with the same intensity. The buzz of energy started to build, and my heart was on the verge of bursting from our combined power building to a crescendo.

Tara's release came like a shockwave bursting forth like a rippling tide. The surrounding debris scattered with a violent gust of wind as the ground around our bodies cleared, and nothing but rich dark earth remained.

I followed her with my release, like nothing I'd experienced before. And I couldn't contain the words my heart already knew. "I love you, Tara."

Tara's eyes flashed a glowing amber and back to her dark rich brown. "I love you too. It doesn't even seem strange that we feel the way we do. Nothing in my life has ever felt so right before."

"I feel it too." I kissed Tara again, all fired up and ready for round two, and Tara was just as eager. So, we did as nature intended two bodies so compatible should do and merged as one, spirit, mind, body, and soul. And I knew my days as a sad wandering soul were through. If I went anywhere, Tara would be right there with me.

Tara laid her head on my chest, and I ran my fingers down her back. Something was sticking to her, and I peeled it away. It was another green leaf. I showed it to Tara, and she smiled. I pulled another leaf from her back, then another from her butt cheek. Tara sat up and turned to see an impression of her body made of living greenery. Leaves, grass, and small white flowers had sprung up from the earth.

Tara laughed. "Did I do that?"

"Yes, you did. You must be part fae," I teased.

"Are you telling me fairies are real too?"

"I suppose anything is possible. There are more curiosities to this world than most could imagine. You just have to look hard enough to find it. I've been roaming this world for over a century before I found you."

Tara's eyes widened in astonishment. "How old are you?"

"I'll tell you, but only because it isn't as bad as it may seem, considering." I gestured to my physical appearance. I passed as a young man between the ages of twenty-five and thirty, and I still felt like a teenager most days.

"I'm one hundred- and six years young. I've served my country in World War II, Korea, Vietnam, and Iraq, and I've seen many soldiers return home to their loved ones. On the other hand, Zane got his fill of violence and blood by taking down the enemy. No human enjoys war, but Zane thrives in it. It was the only time I could let Zane's monster be free. Zane thoroughly enjoyed the spoils of war."

Tara processed this information. "When did Zane turn?"

"In the early spring of 1942. It wasn't long after we enlisted in the Army. After training, we were partying at a club when a man in a lieutenant officers' uniform approached and bought us a few drinks. He set us up with a pretty brunette named Vivienne.

As the night went on, we danced and drank to the point of inebriation. Vivienne brought Zane and me back to a motel room, where she did a little seduction tease. She tied us down to the bed, and we were all for the kinky game she was playing. Vivienne performed a striptease getting down to her underwear before turning to answer a knock at the door. The man in uniform from the club stepped inside, and it turned out he was no lieutenant.

Zane and I struggled against our restraints. We thought he was some sick twisted fuck about to rape us, but then he hovered over our bodies and spoke. He went on about offering us a gift. Well, me. He didn't recognize or acknowledge Zane. Zane and I panicked as his fangs grew, and he struck, biting our neck. I didn't feel anything, but Zane cried in pain as the man drank from him and the venom hit his system.

Before the man left, he patted our head like a good dog and said, 'You'll make a fine addition to our ranks, soldier. I look forward to us working together.' Then he just left with no further explanation, no words of wisdom or guidance to help Zane through his transition. I felt Zane's loss, and it was unbearable. I stayed in that room the next few days and grieved. But then, on the third night, Zane awakened, and he was hungry.

I felt my power kick in, and somehow, I knew what I needed to do to help my brother. Zane went on a feeding frenzy, and I tried to reel him in the best I could. I figured out how to tap into my power over the undead on the next full moon and tethered a leash on Zane's appetite. But when we left for battle, I found Zane's strength and speed an asset, and we took down the enemy left and right together. We were awarded medals for our heroism, and it felt good to provide the service of protecting our fellow compatriots."

"That's quite the history you and Zane share. Now I understand why you've wondered all your life. Is it Zane's vampirism that kept you physically young?"

"It's that and my necromancer blood. We age slowly and live at least twice as long as the average human. You are very young and have many years ahead of you. We cannot be killed by any weapons formed against us, and only a necromancer can kill another by taking their power."

"How do they do that?"

"By draining their power from their blood."

"You mean like Lyle tried to do to me?"

"Which means…." I started.

"Lyle knew!" Tara's face grew pale and fearful. "My father. In my dream, he told me where to start."

"Where?"

"Lyle's grave."

Chapter 13
TARA

Bad Things

The atmosphere at The Hillbilly Roost was mainly back to the norm, except for Dean working with me behind the bar. We made a great team in a synchronized display, pouring, shaking, and serving. Dean was a magic mix master, like Tom Cruise in the movie Cocktail, and watching him mystified the crowd who oohed and ahhed.

Women occupied most of the seats around the bar, slipping big tips and phone numbers into Dean's shirt pocket. He'd tossed the money in my tips jar and trashed the phone numbers with a wink at me. I laughed and admitted to him how much he turned me on.

Dean whispered in my ear, "Just you wait. I've got something special planned for later."

I shivered, and the urgency Dean caused made me have to squeeze my thighs together. So unfair! *Payback!*

The new hire, Billie, bustled along, working the floor with a sugary smile. She was in her mid-thirties with dark hair, hazel eyes, and a killer body. I liked her already because she didn't take any shit from anyone. Her tips were meager until some jackass kept grabbing her ass and making lude comments.

Billie got fed up and introduced his head to the hardwood tabletop. The expertly timed face slam earned Billie applause and the douchewad a minor concussion. The patrons appreciated a woman with bravado, which earned Billie respect and better tips.

Fortunately, the guy was a new face, as our regulars knew how to behave, and Woody showed him the door. "Do you know how hard it is to find good help nowadays? Show some respect for the people who serve your sorry ass. Get the hell out of here, and don't show your ugly mug at my place again," he yelled.

"Tara, I've gotta say your Uncle Woody is my hero. My last boss was an asshole who took most of my tips and docked my hours whenever I complained. I'm feeling right at home here," Billie said.

"Yeah, stick around, Billie. Life tends to get a bit crazy here from time to time. The girl he hired the day before is already out sick for the rest of the week, and she couldn't hang for one busy night."

I didn't mention it was because a vampire half drained her. But Billie didn't need to know. I wasn't comfortable keeping secrets around my uncles, but what else could I do? I couldn't sell Zane out because that would affect Dean, and Woody would think I'd lost my mind.

Stella and Cannon were on the dancefloor while Danny flirted with a pretty redhead. "Your uncle Danny is hot. You think he'd be interested in going out with little ole me?" Billie asked.

"I can tell you that Danny is not interested in the redhead. Danny is just a big flirt at heart. You'd have a better chance than any of these women here."

"You're sweet, Tara. I'll wait till the night's end to stake my claim. It's only fair to allow Danny the opportunity to weed out the competition." Billie winked before sashaying away with a tray full of longnecks.

Dean pecked my cheek as he reached across to grab a glass, and I could see the menacing glares most of the women aimed in my direction. But I could care less. Those bitches were only looking for a one-night deal, which wouldn't be with my man. My man! I loved the sound of that. If Asher were here, I could hook these hussies up mighty quick.

As the night went on, Trey got up and called out for any takers on karaoke. A group of drunken girls sang Like A Virgin like a band of tone-deaf twats. I just rolled my eyes and looked at Dean, who laughed. "You should get up there and give them a singing lesson."

I laughed. "That's a big hell no."

"I loved what you sang to me last night."

"I wasn't singing it to you. Okay, well, I wasn't at first. Honestly, Martina picked it cause she knew it was my parent's song. They'd sing it to each other and slow dance. It's one of my favorite things to remember about them."

"That's romantic." Dean wrapped his arms around me from behind and swayed with me back and forth. It made me feel like doing all kinds of naughty things with him so close to me like this. I heard Woody clear his throat, and Dean gave a quick kiss on my neck before backing away.

Woody looked displeased. "Am I going to have to separate the two of you? You're behaving like a couple of randy teenagers when you're supposed to be working."

"Sorry Woody, Tara will behave, won't you, you greedy lass?" Dean smirked.

My mouth popped open in disbelief. "You ass! You've been back here harassing ME on the job. Don't make me file a complaint."

At this, both Woody and Dean laughed.

"Ahh, but I haven't heard you complain till now, my love. Woody shows up, and you're going to throw me under the bus?"

"A girl's gotta do what she must and all the jazz. I can't account for your actions."

"That is an absolute certainty, and I won't expect you to." Dean winked before whispering in Woody's ear. Woody laughed, nodded, and waved Dean away.

"What are you doing? Where are you going?" I watched as Dean hopped over the bar and headed toward the stage. I put my hands on my hips in a demanding stance. "Woody, what did he tell you?"

Woody's hands shot up in surrender. "It's like Dean said. You nor I can account for his actions."

Before I could ask, the intro for Bad Things began to play, and Dean stood on the stage with a mic in hand and eyes on me. He sang, and his moves were sexy as sin as his voice carried throughout the room like deep rich silk.

All the women in the room beheld the vision of my crooning Adonis as they leaned forward. They looked ready to pounce given the opportunity. But then again, so was I, because if anyone touched my man, they'd be getting their tits handed back in their handbags and booted out the door.

When Dean pointed straight at me and sang the naughty yet enticing lyrics, my cheeks flared, and I belted out a nervous laugh charged with sexual energy as Dean fueled my primal need. Woody saw my reaction and laughed, then nudged me.

"You better get up there before these women try to drag him off the stage and do bad things."

I jumped the bar 'politely' nudging a bitch aside who was drooling at Dean's ass as he dropped it like Magic Mike, jumping down to the dance floor and striding toward me like a man on a mission.

"Hey!" the woman screeched at me.

But I ignored her as Dean continued to sing, and I met him on the dance floor. Dean stood face to face with me, holding my eyes with his sexy baby blues as he traced his free hand down the side of my face and neck, then continued slowly down to my waist, and I shivered beneath his touch. He wrapped his arm around my back and started grinding into me, dirty dancing style, with his leg tucked between mine.

I grabbed Dean's broad shoulders and began swaying and grinding against his leg. Holy hot muffin! Dean was rocking me like a hunk of burning hot lava between my legs, and the center of my pants felt like they were about to catch fire for an entirely different reason. The way he made me feel was no lie!

The crowd was whistling and catcalling. Some women nearby yelled, "That is so hot. What a lucky bitch."

And it didn't bother me because, hell yeah, I was a lucky bitch, and if they only knew the hell I'd been through before meeting this sexy beast in front of me, they'd shut their yaps. Because I was overdue for something good in my life.

When Dean finished, I was flush from head to toe, and he crushed his lips to mine. The crowd went wild, shouting, "Hell yeah! Get you some!"

One asshole yelled, "I'll pay to watch!" I broke the kiss and laughed. I looked into Dean's eyes and was startled when his irises flashed to silver, and his voice changed.

"Was it good for you too, love?"

"Zane?"

His arm tightened around me before he said, "In the flesh, sweetheart."

I struggled to push away, and Zane laughed. "Oh, come on, Tara Baby. I'm just playing with you." He wouldn't let go, and he pressed another kiss to my mouth as I continued to struggle. When he backed his face from mine, I slapped him.

"I'm not a toy for you to play with, Asshole!" I shouted.

The crowd went quiet as I pushed free of Zane's grasp and turned to walk toward the exit. Looks of confusion shot at me, and a few women victoriously smiled as if they had won their chance.

As if! I thought as I charged toward the door.

"Tara!" Woody yelled.

"I'm going on break, Woody," I yelled back.

"What the fuck?" Billie asked in confusion as I passed her. I didn't owe anyone an explanation. I was pissed, and that's all anyone needed to know.

I took long fast strides toward the cabin and heard Zane yell behind me. "Tara, wait!" I unlocked the door, stepped inside, turned, and then screamed. Zane somehow bypassed me and stood before me in the kitchen. He held up his hands. "I'm not going to hurt you. I promise.

He pulled out a chair and sat down. "See, I'm going to sit here and not move a muscle."

"How do I know that? You can move pretty fast." I stood with my hands on my hips.

"You can come closer. I won't bite." He smiled wickedly. "Scouts honor!" Zane held up three fingers, then placed his hands flat on the tabletop to assure me he'd keep his word. I kept my eyes on Zane as I walked around him to the fridge to get a water bottle.

"May I please have one too? I'm parched."

"I'm sure you are," I retorted.

"I'm sorry I broke up the little love tryst you and Dean had going, but I just so happened to wake up during your sex-ka-pade song and dance, which I admit I quite enjoyed," Zane replied with a smirk.

"I'm not some reverse harem girl. I'm a one-man kind of woman, and I don't multi-task dicks like an over-sexed whore."

Zane burst out laughing. "I can see why Dean fancies you. You are a sexy woman and so very Caliente."

"You can save your cheesy compliments, Zane. What do you want? Realize, I'm only tolerating you because you and Dean are a one package deal."

I took a drink of water and set it down, then folded my arms across my chest. Zane's eyes zero in on my cleavage, and I quickly tugged the scoop of my tank top to cover up.

"You realize I already saw your lovely ladies." Zane smirked.

"And you'll never see them again," I replied

.

"Oh, contrare, Tara Dear. You forget Dean's eyes are my eyes, and I'm not always asleep when my brother is at play. So, in a way, you are in a threesome as I can just as effortlessly feel the pleasure and participate."

Zane smiled at my dismay. His words brought about an awareness that made my skin crawl, and I wanted to hear from Dean's mouth whether or not this was true. Had he and Zane shared women in the past?

Suddenly I felt so dirty. I don't know how other women handled two men or more at once. I'd read about it, but I just couldn't see myself capable of doing something so tawdry. Even if the female was madly in love with her men, it seemed far-fetched. One good man was all I needed.

I noticed Zane watching my facial expressions as my thoughts got away with me. His smile and mannerisms were entirely different from Dean's, making it easy for me to tell them apart. This whole situation was so peculiar.

"You going to tell me what's going on in the beautiful mind, Tara?" Zane leaned forward. "I can assure you, if I wanted to attack you, you'd be in my arms before you could flinch. Now, sit down, would you? I feel particularly predatory after that sexy dance, but I'm less likely to pounce if you're calm and seated."

I sat down with a huff and glared at Zane. "Tell me whatever it is you want to say."

"I just wanted to tell you I'm sorry for biting you. It was wrong of me to interfere. Dean and I have shared women in the past, but I know he is in love with you. So, I tried my best to back off. Lately, I've been having difficulty containing my bloodlust, as I'm sure Dean has already told you after what happened, and you're still here. I'm a creature of habit, Tara, and well, old habits die hard." Zane shrugged as if he were an innocent child incapable of claiming responsibility for his actions.

"That's a lame excuse. It's one men have used on me many times in the past, and it's not going to fly," I replied. "Look, I get the whole vampire bloodlust thing...."

Zane held up a hand to stop me. "Do you? I'm sure you can imagine, but you really have no idea what it's like."

Zane did have a point. I honestly didn't know what Zane felt when bloodlust consumed him, and I had to imagine it was beyond any emotion one could shut down by will alone.

"Okay. You've got me there. But Dean explained that he's always looked after you and constantly has to put the brakes on your actions. Because of that, his powers are drained as you continue to rely on him to cover your ass."

"You're right." Zane sighed and lowered his head. "I've been trying, but it's not as easy as you think."

"Then explain it to me. Because I'm willing to look past what you did to me for Dean's sake, but make no mistake, I know now how my blood affects you, so don't put it past me to make an example of your sorry ass. You don't get to play with me like that." I gave Zane a menacing gaze that brokered no argument. Zane looked taken aback by my declaration.

"Damn, Tara. You're badass to the core to talk to a vampire that way. Lucky for you, I like you so much."

I leaned forward and spoke in a low, deadly tone. "Don't tempt me, Zane. So, help me! You don't want to make me your enemy."

Zane swallowed nervously and nodded. "What can I say to that? You've got me between a rock and a hard place, and Dean might take a stake to my heart if I hurt you."

I arched my brow. "So, the old stake to the heart does work on vampires?"

"If I say yes, will you give me a pass?"

"Maybe. But my blood may be even more efficient at getting the job done." I smiled. At this, Zane smiled back at me, and I could feel an understanding pass between us.

"Did Dean mention that he once had an extra appendage removed that had belonged to me?"

"What was it? Where?"

Zane pointed down.

"What? Do you mean you and Dean had an extra?" I cleared my throat.

"Penis?" Zane supplied.

My eyes widened in astonishment. What the hell would that look like, let alone feel like? It would be like having two men at once. Yikes! I squeezed my knees together and clenched my ass cheeks tightly closed.

Zane started laughing hysterically. "Get your mind out of the gutter, woman! I was pointing to my foot. It was an extra pinky toe. And actually, we lost it in Vietnam. A stray bullet from friendly fire. No lie!"

I burst out laughing, and Zane joined me. After I caught my breath, Zane looked at me. "Truce?"

"Yeah." I chuckled. "Truce. But you still need to explain the whole bloodlust thing to me."

"I promise." Zane crossed his heart, mocked choking himself, and motioned as if he were sticking a needle in his eye. I laughed again.

Danny poked his head inside. "Trouble in paradise?"

"Just a little misunderstanding," Zane said.

I arched my brow and asked, "Just a little?"

Zane shrugged and rose slowly from his seat, still showing his hands like a magician would before pulling something from their sleeve. "No tricks," he said, gesturing for me to stand and lead the way. But I gave him a look that said, 'No way, Buck-O!'

Zane nodded and walked toward Danny and clapped him on the shoulder. "We're all good now." Zane walked out the door.

Danny assessed me. "Is everything okay? He didn't do anything to hurt you, did he?"

Technically, he did, but I'd never admit it to Danny. It felt wrong because I told myself long ago that I'd never be that girl who lets her boyfriend abuse her and make excuses for him. No, that shit would never fly.

It was Zane who'd done the damage, and it wasn't fair to Dean to constantly take the fall for his brother.

"No, Danny. Dean didn't hurt me," I said with absolute surety because it was the truth.

"You'd tell me if he ever hurt you, right?"

"Absolutely! I promise. No man will hurt me and get away with it."

Danny nodded his approval and hugged me. "You need to let Woody know you're okay. But first, I have a quick question."

"What is it?"

"The new girl, Billie, has been giving me the eye all night, and I was wondering whether or not it was my imagination?"

"Not your imagination. She's definitely into you."

Danny's eyes lit up, and he smiled. "Billie doesn't seem like the type to play around. I like that in a woman."

I smiled. "You need to ask her out. I know she's chomping at the bit to get to know you."

Danny deserved this; he's a good man. A bit crazy and rough around the edges, but genuine. I knew he and Billie would be good for each other.

I looked for Zane inside the bar but didn't see him anywhere. "Uncle Woody, did Dean come back?"

"I haven't seen him. Are you alright, Tara? I'm confused after seeing what happened between you and Dean. Care to explain?"

"It's complicated, but I assure you, I'm fine."

"Look, I don't want to get involved in your love life, but I'm here for you if you want to talk about anything else. And, know if Dean did anything to hurt you, he's gone."

"I know you're looking out for me. But I promise Dean hasn't hurt me. I've just had this conversation with Danny, and I'll tell you the same thing I told him. I'm not a person to be messed with or abused. You taught me to stand up for myself and make no excuses for the actions of others. And I'm letting you know if Dean ever hurts me, I'll throw him to the curb myself. I've already been hurt enough times in my life, and I'm making a stand."

"Good to hear. I've always been proud of you, but I must say, I'm prouder of the young woman you've become. You have a good heart, but don't let people walk all over you." Woody pulled me in for a hug, and it felt nice to have my uncles care so much.

Zane walked in from outside, wiping his mouth, and I silently groaned. He must have just fed, but on who? He went to the restroom and was in there for a few minutes before returning by my side.

"Really, Zane! Now?" I whispered.

"Sorry. You left me depleted, and I was starving. But, don't worry, it was some random dude, and he's still standing." Zane pointed to a big guy who was a new face as he swayed by the entrance door, trying to shake himself out of a stupor. "I didn't take more than two pints, so he'll be fine. See? I'm trying. I became weakened after what happened with you, yet I abstained from draining the guy dry, and I feel better."

"I suppose it's a start." How was I okay with this? A vampire walks into a bar and drinks Blood Light, and I am casually accepting this? At least it wasn't a woman, as Zane also seems to have an appetite for the opposite sex. I'd feel uncomfortable being with Dean after Zane used his body to be intimate with a woman and drink her blood. How was I supposed to deal with these feelings?

I suddenly felt queasy after realizing Zane had been with Bren the other night and Dean with me the following morning.

"Uhg!" My stomach clenched, and I had to ask. "Did you have sex with Bren when you know?"

"No, I didn't, but you must know I also have needs," Zane confessed. "I won't lie to you. I did kiss her and touched her intimately."

"I think I'm going to be sick." I ran to the ladies. Thankfully there wasn't a line, and I made it to the toilet just in time.

"Tara? You okay in there?" Billie asked. I spat a few times, flushed the toilet, and left the stall. Billie was leaning against the sink with a concerned look. "You're not pregnant, are you?"

"What? No! I've been working too hard and haven't eaten anything tonight." That was true, and as far as being pregnant, I hoped my birth control was doing its job. I hadn't had sex with Asher in over two weeks, and it was too soon with Dean to determine if I could be. No, I just had my period a little over a week ago. So, that's a hopeful, no. I'm not ready for motherhood yet.

"So, do you mind my asking what's up between Dean and you? You can tell me to mind my own business. But, you two have been all lovey-dovey all night, then you practically had sex with your clothes on during that dirty dancing display. Then you went kind of psycho and slapped the man."

"I don't want to come off bitchy, but things were going great, and Dean said something that pissed me off. I don't want to go into details, and it's complicated."

"Did he ask for a three-way?" I gave Billie an *are you kidding me* glare, and she shrugged. "Okay, I get it—none of my business. But, I just gotta say, you and Dean look so in love, and the way he only had eyes for you all night, it seems he just had a minor slip-up. It happens with men all the time."

"Yeah, I know you're right. Thanks, Billie." I left it at that. I didn't want to go deeper into this conversation. Billie was sweet and caring, but I needed to get her attention off me. So, I switched the topic to her and Danny.

"So, I talked to my uncle Danny. He's been checking you out all night, and I told him he should ask you out. I think the two of you would hit it off."

Billie smiled. "You think so? I have a feeling about Danny. He's a bit crazy and rough around the edges, but genuine."

"You've got him pegged. You should go chat him up," I urged. Billie still looked at me with concern. I put on my best smile. "I'm good, Billie. Promise."

"Okay. But promise me you'll get some food in your stomach."

"I'll get right on it," I swore.

Billie nodded, and I knew her mind was on Danny as she gleefully smiled while exiting the women's restroom. I blew out a relieved breath, no longer under scrutiny. I wanted to call it a night. It was late, and things were slowing down anyhow. Maybe I should tell Woody I'm tired and call it.

I went to the kitchen and made a grilled ham and cheese sandwich. Zane stepped into the kitchen. I looked over at him and recognized Dean's eyes looking back at me. "I'm sorry, Tara. I didn't know Zane was about to wake up. It was different this time, and I think it has to do with how your blood affected him."

"I'm not mad at you. Zane and I talked, and I believe we have an understanding."

Dean stood beside me and assembled two more sandwiches before placing them in the skillet and taking over. I heated a can of creamy tomato soup, then we sat and ate our dinner. I felt awkward now Dean had returned because I didn't know how to broach the topic of sex with him and his brother sharing at the moment.

Dean sensed my discomfort and placed his hand on mine. "You want to ask me something? There's no question I'd deny answering. I'm an open book; you can look at all my pages."

"Dean, you and Zane share a lot of history. He told me the two of you have shared many things. Even women."

"It's kind of hard to avoid. You understand why."

"Yeah, I get it's a physical thing, but with me?"

"It's different. Zane and I made a deal about you, and he promised to leave the room when we're intimate." Dean tapped a finger to the side of his head, indicating their combined consciousness.

"Then why did he show up our first time together?"

"Sex and blood go hand and hand for vampires. Zane wasn't present until the moment just after, and he has control issues and a bad habit of butting in at the most inopportune times. Our sexual energy triggered his blood lust, and I didn't anticipate it. I was so wrapped up in you. I wasn't paying attention to Zane."

"Zane and I talked about it and called a truce, but I can't help but feel all weirded out by this because I know Zane has needs. And, it's even more difficult because I ended things with Asher because he had his dick in another woman. It feels like a double standard; it confuses the hell out of me."

"I thought about this as well. I didn't feel worthy because I knew you were a woman who held her man to a higher standard. And you should. You deserve the best, and I want to be the kind of man who surpasses your needs and desires. I also know Zane's needs will complicate things. He seems to think Bren will be the woman who will turn his life around. I'm guessing you and Bren have a history that is not positive."

"Bren bullied me in high school. There's no love lost there. I was so relieved when she left for Texas. But it is four years later, and she returns out of the blue, begging for a job at The Hillbilly Roost of all places. She knew my family owned it, and I worked here. I don't get why she came back. I thought of the possibility she might have changed, but I didn't want to talk to her.

Knowing Zane is interested in her and sharing your body makes things worse. I hate to sound selfish, but isn't there someone else Zane could find an interest in, or perhaps just stick to snacking on guys?"

Dean chuckled, then became serious once more. "I wish it were that simple. Believe me, I don't like it any more than you, but I no longer have complete control when Zane takes over. When he was with Bren, I was aware, and I screamed and begged him to stop, but it was futile."

"Sorry about the pun, Dean, but this situation bites."

"I agree. Perhaps Zane needs an opportunity to get Bren out of his system. He's never committed to any woman, and his monster's bloodlust creates this illusion of love that never lasts. I understand if you need time to come to terms with this. It's the way it's always been with Zane and me, and I wish I could change it for you. If you want to abstain from intimacy, I'll understand. I'm so in love with you, Tara, and I'll do whatever you want."

"You make this so hard. I love you too, and I don't want to be apart from you. I need assurance Zane minds his business when we're together. And as hard a pill as it is to swallow, I'll allow Zane to fulfill his needs. I just don't want to be around when it happens, and I don't want to hear about it. I will shove my blood down his throat if he can't adhere to this compromise."

"This is a tremendous sacrifice on your part. I'm not happy about it, but I can't change it either. Zane has agreed to your terms and has also thrown in that he will compel Bren not to remember their encounters other than casual conversation and some flirting."

"So, he's been in on our conversation?"

"Yes, he has. I thought it was important for Zane to know how you feel, and he gets it. He wants things to work between you and me. He says he can be a noble person."

"I'm holding you to that, Zane. Otherwise, it's lights out.

Chapter 14
TARA

Confessions Of A High School Bully

The next few days went by without a hitch. Although he frequently interrupted Dean and my conversations, Zane remained faithful to his promises. In an attempt to further appease me, Zane took me out on a hunt in the forest. We sat perched together on a limb, and Zane jumped to the forest floor, taking down a young buck. I watched as Zane drained the blood from the poor animal's body in horrified fascination.

"Blahg! It tastes like gamey tofu." Zane wiped his tongue repeatedly on his long sleeve shirt. I climbed to the ground and looked at the buck's still body, its chest stained with blood, its eyes void of life. My heart broke for the deer.

Dean's voice returned, and his arm wrapped around my shoulder. "Think of it as a positive start in the right direction. Zane is making more effort than he has in the past because of you."

"Perhaps it's because he's afraid of me."

"Ha! Hardly," Zane huffed.

This constant switching back and forth was a tad disconcerting and would take some getting used to as Zane would always be third-wheeling.

"So, are you ready for your next lesson?" Dean asked.

"Yes. What are we doing today?"

"Do you see the stillness of death before you? It's different because, unlike the leaf, the deer had a heartbeat. You must focus on the heart this time, Tara. Reach out and lay your hands upon the deer's body." Dean instructed.

I did as Dean said. "But how will it return to a body without blood? It needs blood to survive."

"Don't think about that. With your power, it doesn't matter. Its blood will return because it is a part of the life source, and your power will recreate and reanimate."

With my hands upon the deer's chest, I felt the coldness seep in beneath the soft, warm brown coat. I pictured its once beating heart and a life of beauty in the wilderness as the deer peacefully foraged through the fallen leaves. A tear slid down my cheek.

"Why am I not feeling my power?"

"Remember what I told you. You have to see the lifelessness of its current state and work in reverse. Close your eyes and see its still heart, then tune into your heartbeat."

I closed my eyes, and it was like traveling into another universe as the darkness within the deer's chest cavity enveloped my senses. In the darkness, the shape and stillness of its heart took precedence, and I saw death. I held it in my sight for a moment before my vision turned inward toward my beating heart.

"Good. Now picture the deer's heart picking up where yours leaves off at the end of each beat, then will it into being," Dean instructed.

I watched my heart and heard the 'thump, thump,' then willing and guiding the upward rhythm to the dead heart inside the deer's chest. I began to feel the buzzing in my veins and saw the darkness of my power collide with my live red blood cells creating the collective sparks of light.

Thump, thump, thump, thump.

The energy level climbed, and I could see it travel backward through my extremities and gather like one large power cell in my chest. I drew in a huge breath as the power felt overwhelming, and I cried out as it shot down my arms and out through my hands.

It felt like an explosive had detonated, and the deer's body jerked as if shocked by a defibrillator. Suddenly its heart began beating, and I saw new blood magically seep back into its veins and begin to flow. As the heartbeat grew stronger, I felt my hands rise and fall as air pulled in and out of the animal's lungs.

The buck bellowed and moved its legs. It jerked its body upright, and its eyes observed me sitting beside it. I cried joyfully as the deer turned its head back to nuzzle its nose in my hair. It sniffed and then licked my cheek in a thankful gesture before standing and launching away at speed.

"That was exhilarating!" I cried breathlessly. I saw Dean's surprised reaction.

"Amazing! You're a natural. I've never seen a newly triggered necromancer's powers come so fast and effortless. There's something different about you, Tara."

Tears streamed down my face. I held my hand to my chest and took calming breaths. Dean squatted down beside me and ran his fingers through my hair. I looked at him, and he smiled at our shared joy. His hands cupped my face, pulling me in for a sweet, tender kiss.

"Can it always be like this?"

"Not always, I'm afraid."

"What do you mean?"

"What we are is both a gift and a curse. When death is traumatic, it's best to let the soul move on to the higher plane. I've experienced this when I brought back the mortally and psychologically wounded, and the memories return along with the life. It didn't fare well as some suffered from psychosis and lived out their days in misery. Others took their own lives because they'd seen the other side and no longer wanted to be here."

"Oh, no. That sounds awful. I'm so sorry you went through that." I placed my hand on Dean's chest and felt his and Zane's hearts. I could tell which was which now. I just knew.

"Sometimes, it was their time to go, and I couldn't accept it. I brought those people back, and it didn't bode well for them or me."

"How so?"

"Let's just say you can't compete with a higher power when other plans are made, and it's not in our best interest to interfere."

"Plans that entail making something good from something bad?"

"That's what I learned. We are instruments of two makers, and it is not our place to play God. But, what we're capable of doing has its time and purpose."

"Then why do we have this power?"

"I'm still trying to figure that out myself. Many necromancers were gifted by a goddess. Others from the demonic. My power feels too dark to explain as something heavenly."

"Wait? Are you saying I either have the blood of a goddess or a DEMON running through my veins? Shit! I don't like the sound of that. Not at all!" My chest tightened as panic took hold.

"Calm yourself, Tara. Remember what I told you. It's all in how we use our power. We can't help what flows through our veins. We didn't ask to be born this way. It's like Zane and me; it is beyond our control. Did you see what you just did? It was a beautiful thing. Everything, every life, exists for a reason. It's all part of a grand design, and we're small pieces on a universal chessboard. We can't predict the next move. We must embrace where we stand and wait for a grander hand to guide us."

Dean's words were a balm to my worries. I found myself calming in his strong arms. I wondered if my dad knew and why didn't he tell me. Was it a case where I had to become of age to understand? I was angry because my father had no control over what happened to him. Lost out there somewhere in the world and unable to find his way back again.

"I know. We will find him." Dean took my hand and guided me back to the cabin, where we spent the rest of the afternoon curled up and enjoying one another's company. We drank coffee and talked about the adventures of Dean and Zane.

He told me what went down after he met Martina, and I cracked up with laughter. Then Zane excused himself as Dean and I made love and fell asleep wrapped up in each other.

My phone woke me, and I groaned out of my blissful state. I hadn't slept so well in forever and didn't want to answer it. It stopped, and I sighed as Dean hugged me to his body like his treasured little spoon. Then Dean's phone began to ring, and he groaned. "Can't a man have his moment of bliss undisturbed?"

"Apparently not," I grumbled.

I felt the loss of Dean's heat at my back as he turned to grab his phone. He answered, and I heard Woody's voice. "Yeah. She was asleep. Okay, I'll put her on," Dean replied to Woody and then held his phone out to me. "Woody wants you."

I groaned again. Why? I wasn't due to work for another few hours. I held the phone to my ear. "Yeah? What's up, Woody?"

"I need you to pick up Bren for work tonight."

"Argh, why me? Isn't anyone else available? You know our history."

"No. Everyone else is busy. Bren called and asked if she could come in tonight. She needs the money. She had to pay to see a doctor, and she told me she wouldn't make her rent because of it."

I felt guilty because this was Zane's fault. "Dammit, Zane!"

"What did he do now?" Dean asked.

"Hold on," I told Dean.

"Who's Zane?" Woody asked.

Crap! I hadn't realized I cursed Zane's name aloud. Dean looked at me, encouraging me to answer Woody's question. "Zane is Dean's twin, brother."

"Why are you cursing Dean's brother?"

Think Tara. Okay, got it! "He's been texting Dean constantly the past few minutes and keeps interrupting our rest and this conversation."

Dean smirked at me, and I rolled my eyes. Yes, I was a low-down dirty liar. It was the best I could do on short notice.

"Okay. I need you to get to her place in an hour. She's going to be on light duty tonight. I'll text you the address," Woody said.

"Fine! I am going to get another thirty minutes of sleep now. Bye." I hung up and groaned.

"You want me to come with you?" Dean asked.

"No, I don't want Zane getting any ideas and popping in to start a flirty conversation with Bren while I'm driving. I might swerve off-road and plummet over a cliff. I'll just turn on the radio and pretend she's not there. Hopefully, she doesn't wear that same cloying perfume she did in high school."

Thankfully, Bren didn't live too far away. I could manage a ten-minute ride in awkward silence. I pulled up to the apartment complex, texted the number Woody provided, and waited.

Bren came out the door on the second landing a few minutes later. She saw me and looked nervous, which intrigued me because the Bren I knew from the past would have glared at me in hostility.

I unlocked the passenger side door, and Bren climbed inside with her purse and phone in hand. She closed the door, fastened her seatbelt, and remained quiet as she stared out the windshield. I didn't speak as I backed out of the parking space and began driving. Bren was texting someone as I glimpsed over to see Woody's name; I figured she let him know she was on her way.

Bren put her phone away and watched the road. I tried concentrating on the radio as an upbeat country song played and drummed my thumbs on the steering wheel. Bren cleared her throat a few times, and I tried my best to ignore her presence, but then she turned to me. "Thanks for picking me up, Tara."

I responded with a curt nod but kept my mouth shut. I could tell Bren wanted to talk, and my anxiety began to fill the space between us. I was white-knuckling the steering wheel while trying to keep my breathing steady. When Bren cleared her throat again, I'd reached my breaking point. I swerved off the road, into the gas station lot, and hit the brakes.

I turned to look at Bren. "Why did you come back? What's your agenda? It seems mighty suspicious that you return after four years and show up at The Roost of all places. You've always hated me and knew I worked there, so tell me?

Your life was looking good as you left for Texas, and I thought you'd have found yourself an oil tycoon by now and become a trophy wife, living it up in a Dallas high-rise."

Bren looked offended. "Is that what you think of me? That I'm some kind of floozy gold digger? I suppose how I behaved in high school would have brought you to such a conclusion. Look, I'm sorry I was such a bitch to you back then, but I have changed. It turns out Karma really is a bitch, and she dished her just deserts."

"Yeah, and you were a bitch, and I'm still sour about the four years you treated me like the dog shit on your shoes. You mocked my family's pain, and your actions and words were vile and heartless. But I figured you must have been hiding something, so now's your chance to spill and perhaps redeem yourself. I was weak back then, but I'm much stronger now, so don't put it past me to throw your ass to the curb."

Bren's jaw dropped in shock. She swallowed nervously and took a deep breath with her eyes closed. I could tell she was working up the nerve to speak her peace. It must be hard to swallow your pride when you finally admit what a lecherous snake you'd been. But something told me that perhaps Bren had changed. For the better? Well, that depended on what came out of her mouth next.

When Bren opened her eyes, tears fell down her cheeks. It's about time she felt remorse for her nefarious ways. I held my tongue and patiently waited for her to speak. Her lips quivered, and her hands twisted and fumbled. "Tara. You are right. I was in trouble back then, and I used you to hide my shame. This is difficult for me to talk about, but I'm confiding in you because I know I hurt you the most. You were going through something tragic, and my selfish, immature brain couldn't comprehend that your pain was worse than mine. But I was in pain, and I lashed out at you unjustly. For that, I'm truly sorry. I just wished I could make it up to you somehow."

"Then explain it to me. You pissed all over me, and I'm still pissed off. It's time to come clean. What happened to you, and why are you back here now?"

She had to know how I felt because I would no longer let my abusers off easy. And Bren saw as much with Asher and Gina. I knew that's why she averted her gaze when I looked at her. It was her admission of guilt and fear of my retribution. For four years, she sneered and jeered while holding me hostage to my pain and fears. She was getting off relatively easy for her crimes as far as I was concerned.

"You're right, and I deserve every word you're saying." Bren swallowed, then turned to look at me. "At first, it was petty shit. I was envious of you. Everyone talked about how smart and pretty you are, and all I had going for me was my body and clothes. I was never able to make friends as easily as you."

"What? Bren, you were always surrounded by people kissing your ass. I only had Gina and my brother. I felt squashed beneath your queen bee attitude, and you made it harder for me to make friends because of the nasty rumors you'd spread about me."

"None of those people were my friends. They were just a bunch of moochers because they thought I had money and could get them into places. And I was a total bitch for saying all those bad things about you, but again it was all petty, immature envy."

"Okay, I get that. So, you accomplished setting my reputation to a low standard because you were envious, though I'd never understood why it was me who'd never done anything to you to deserve such treatment. If things had gone differently, I would have been your friend, but you persisted in berating and belittling me. Why?"

Bren cleared her throat and released a breath. "By the time our Senior year had come, I felt I'd gone too far to make things right. I got myself into trouble, and it all began when I went to Principal Andrews to defend myself against another accusation. I confessed all my sins to a man who soothed me with his kind words. When his sympathy turned to endearments, then his endearments turned into intimate touches, I began to feel accepted for the first time in my life. We began an affair before I knew how to process Nick's affections and the feelings he incited. And I thought he loved me, and I was surely in love with him."

My jaw dropped. I'd known something was up by the rumors about Bren staying late after school and riding home in Principal Andrews' car. Students said she was having sex with some football players, was busted, and serving detention. Bren had put on a show around school and had everyone convinced she was the football team's trophy whore. It wasn't that after all. It was her cover story for what was happening between her and Andrews.

Bren took a moment to drink from a water bottle she pulled from her purse. It had to be a hard pill for her to swallow. She admitted guilt and bore her deepest, darkest secret to her adversary. If we were still in high school, I'd have let her fall into her pit of despair and sealed a heavy lid over the top because my rage for her wouldn't make me feel sympathy. But then again, I remembered feeling like I could relate to her at one point, having suspected she was hiding something.

Bren became emotional as she continued her story. "Nick told me he'd leave his wife and family once I graduated. I was so in love with him, so I foolishly bought into Nick's lies. I began stalking him at his home, needing proof that he would hold to his word.

I broke in one night when his wife took their kids out, and things got out of hand. He got angry with me, but then he made it up to me back at school. I thought he'd divorce his wife and marry me once he found out I was pregnant with his child. But when I told Nick, he told me to get rid of it and even gave me the money to take care of the abortion. I was devastated. I didn't go through with it; I couldn't. I convinced myself that he'd change his mind if he could only see what came of the love we shared." Bren was weeping, and the wall around my heart shattered for her.

"If you had confided in me sooner, I would have supported you. Yes, I was angry with you, but no one should go through what happened to you. He raped and used you. That fucking asshole! I never liked Principal Andrews."

Bren sniffed and nodded. "What's worse is when Nick found out I didn't have the abortion, he kicked me to the curb. I was so upset and stressed out I ended up having a miscarriage. I wanted our child so much, and my heart felt torn out twice."

"Shit, Bren!" I was crying, and I finally understood her motives against me. It was never about me. She was in so much pain, and though it wasn't right for her to take it out on me, I knew she had to release her pain somehow. She picked the unhealthiest way by putting a magnifying glass on someone else's. "So, you left for Texas. I understand needing to get away from the pain. But, no matter how far you run, it catches up to you."

"You're right about that. Nick took his wife and kids and left me behind in my misery. He hadn't known about the miscarriage, and I didn't want to give him the satisfaction. I went to college and started my new life and identity. I didn't tell anyone the truth about where I came from, and I partied, trying to drink my way through the pain.

In my Senior year, I met a guy I liked as a friend, but he felt more for me. He declared his undying love for me, and I told him I didn't feel the same way. His name is Bryan Connelly, and after I told Bryan I didn't want anything to do with him anymore, he began stalking me. I had a restraining order against him, but Bryan still attacked me. He raped me, and he whispered in my ear, 'Mr. A said to tell you, payback is a bitch, and if you dare come after him for child support, I have the green light to kill you.' I knew then that Nick sent Bryan to threaten me, but Bryan had taken his obsession with me too far, and I had to run."

"That's why you're back here? You need protection! Fuck, Bren! Are you sure this guy doesn't know you came back where you used to live? Have you told Woody about this?"

"No. I want to. I've been working up the nerve, but I need your help. I know it's a lot to ask after how I treated you, but your uncle is the only person I know who can. I've heard about The Rooster's reputation."

"Uncle Woody is not a hitman for hire."

"I know that. I just need to be surrounded by people where I can feel safe. I'm scared. It's hard enough knowing Bryan could find me and finish what he started. I hate living in that apartment by myself. But it was the best I could do when I got here. I don't want to lead this bastard to my family. My parents are getting older, and my little sister doesn't need to go through what I have."

"I just don't understand why Andrews would send someone to threaten and hurt you. You said you went on with your life. You didn't contact him after moving to Texas, did you?"

"That's the thing. I was stupid. I made one last attempt a year and a half later with a random baby picture and told him to see what he was missing, but I told Nick I expected nothing from him. I thought I was hitting him where it hurt, but it backfired."

"That was stupid."

Bren hung her head in shame, and I touched her shoulder. "Sorry. Look, we'll tell Woody together. He'll help you out. I know it, and he has a thing for damsels in distress."

Bren surprised me when she put her arms around me, hugged me tightly, and sobbed. "Thank you, Tara. I owe you big time. I want to make it up to you for every wrong I've done."

I hugged her back. "Let's just get this situation straightened out first. I've got your back. Bitches need to stick together."

Bren laughed. "I should have been your friend. I knew I saw something special in you; I was in a bad place and couldn't see past the shitstorm I put myself in."

I found myself saying something I never thought I'd say to my high school bully. "I forgive you. I think it's time we start fresh, don't you?"

"I do," she agreed. She wiped her face on her sleeves and smiled.

I pulled back onto the road with a change of perspective. I had a feeling that many more changes would come. From the moment I sat in my truck on that ravine, my life became a series of flips and turns.

I'd cut two people out of my life and invited two more. Well, three if I included Zane. In a way, Zane had done some damage even though Bren was unaware. I couldn't help feeling that this might come back to bite the vampire in his ass.

No one but Dean and I knew about him, but once he became revealed, shit would get real. He made a mistake by using Bren the way he did, so he had to know that she was off-limits because of the trauma she'd experienced. Hopefully, Dean could talk some sense into him.

As I pulled up to The Roost, I saw Zane's silver eyes as he ran up to my truck to greet us. Here we go!

Chapter 15
DEAN

Make No Mistake

"Get off your moral high horse, Dean. I made one mistake," Zane said.

"Two. You made two mistakes—First Bren and then Tara. Tara doesn't trust you to behave around Bren, so she went on her own," I said.

"It's only ten minutes away. Why aren't they back yet?" Zane had us pacing in Tara's cabin.

"Will you sit down? Your pacing is getting on my nerves."

"Yeah, and your complacency is getting on mine. I haven't seen Bren in over two days, and I want to know if she's alright."

"She would have been fine and working if you hadn't nearly killed her. You need to stop and consider these things before letting your bloodlust get the best of you."

Zane threw our hands up in frustration. "I get that I screwed up. You don't need to keep rubbing it in. I've been doing better these last few days. I only drank two pints human and feasted on venison juice, which is disgusting, by the way."

On that, I could agree. I had to brush and mouthwash twice to get the taste out of our mouth. Lights flashed past the window, and Zane zipped up to look outside. "Thank fuck; they're here!"

"Calm yourself before you step out that door." We went outside, and I struggled to keep Zane from running at Bren as she got out of the truck. I managed to slow Zane's pace and maintain a neutral expression on our face.

"Think before you speak."

"I'm not an idiot," Zane grumbled beneath our breath.

"That's debatable."

"Zip-it!" Zane whispered beneath our breath. I couldn't believe he had just said that to me! I held my tongue as Zane stopped a few feet before Bren and his eyes swung to Tara, who knew Zane was running the show at the moment. Zane nodded at Tara and winked, and Tara shook her head.

"How are you, Bren?" Zane asked.

"I'm feeling better," Bren replied. She averted her eyes, looking kind of weary in our presence.

"Glad to hear it. Hey, Tara." he acknowledged.

Tara put her hands on her hips and glared. "We're running a bit late, DEAN. I hope you don't mind, but we've got to talk to Woody. I'm sure you're needed behind the bar."

"Of course, ladies. Lead the way." Zane gestured. Tara walked by Bren's side, and it seemed as if she was protecting Bren. I thought she hated her. But then it occurred to me that something must have happened on the drive over.

We walked behind the two women at a distance. "I blew it," Zane said. "My compulsion didn't take full effect, and she's feeling awareness of what happened to her. She'll never trust me."

"Perhaps you need to back off, so you're not tempted to hurt her again. It seems to me she's already experienced enough pain in her life without you further complicating it. It looks as though Bren and Tara have come to an understanding."

I watched the exchange of body language as Tara held the door for Bren and nodded to her with encouragement. Bren looked nervous as she walked past Tara, but Tara put a hand on Bren's arm and guided her. We followed the girls inside and watched as they took the hallway to Woody's office. "I don't think we're wanted or needed in there."

Zane looked torn. "I really fucked things up this time. I hate this monster in me." Zane walked to the bar, poured a shot of whiskey, downed it, and then repeated twice more.

"Would you relax?"

"This is me relaxing. I need something to take the edge off." Zane took one more shot.

"And I need to work tonight. I don't need an inebriated vampire to make me look like an ass." I managed to knock the next shot out of Zane's hand. To any onlooker, this would be oddly comical. Zane and I have physically battled one another. He was left-body dominant, and I was right. How do you explain two black eyes? Thankfully we healed fast enough.

Zane paused and cocked our head. He was listening, more like eavesdropping on the conversation in Woody's office. Woody was speaking. "Bren, if you don't feel safe at your apartment, you can stay here. I've got a spare room or even the camper if you want. I'll put the word out about this guy who hurt you. He won't make it within fifty miles before someone spots him and grabs him off the street. He'll receive what he deserves."

Zane grimaced. "Shit! I thought he was speaking about me for a moment. Now, I want to hunt the asshole down who hurt Bren, but I missed the beginning of the conversation. I am an idiot!"

"You really do care about this girl, don't you?"

"Of course, I do! I have a heart. It's right next to yours. Remember?"

"Okay. So, I'm going out on a limb here and believing that what you're feeling is real for the first time in your existence. How are you planning to pursue a woman who's afraid of men due to the trauma she's suffered? Combine that with your predatory nature, and you've already attacked her."

"You make a valid point. I've never experienced this before, and I admit I'm stumped. You think Tara could give me some advice?"

I laughed. "You think Tara will give you advice on breaking down Bren's walls and attempting to woo her?"

"Another good point. Dammit! I have to try harder. I know being up in Bren's face isn't going to help. Maybe you're right. I need to back off and observe. Listen in on what she discusses with people she trusts. In the meantime, I'll try harder than I've ever tried before. I'll drink from rodents in I must."

"Wow! You've got it bad for Bren. Maybe I'm wrong, and you are capable of love!" We watched as Bren went into the kitchen to begin her shift. Tara came around the corner and saw Zane staring at the kitchen door. He visibly sighed, and our shoulders slumped in defeat. Tara came up to us and put a hand on our arm.

"I can't believe I'm saying this, but give her some time, Zane. Bren is scared and has been through some severe trauma. She's picking up on your monster vibes, and it's making her antsy," Tara said.

"She told you what happened to her? Did she say anything about remembering what I did?" Zane asked.

"Yes and no. Bren told me everything that happened prior to coming here but nothing about you. She doesn't remember, but I feel she's uncomfortable around you."

"Well, that's fucking fantastic!" Zane knocked back another shot. "Guess I'm going to call it a night then. Leave you love birds to your happiness." Zane sulked.

Zane slipped into the abyss as I came to, and Tara leaned into me. "I feel bad for Zane."

"Yeah, I do, too," I said. "Not sure what we can do about it, though. Zane kind of made his bed."

Tara wrapped her arms around me and breathed me in. I held her till Woody walked past us. "Get your asses to work. I'm docking those shots off of your pay, Dean."

"How did he know?"

"He's all about keeping an honest man honest." Tara pointed up at a camera hidden above the mirror.

"Dammit, Zane!"

"Luckily, there's no audio feed. Woody probably wondered why you were talking to yourself."

"Oh, hell. I didn't think about that. I know it isn't my business, but what happened between you and Bren? Are you friends now?"

"She confided in me and explained why she was such a bitch to me in high school. Bren went through a lot, and she admitted there wasn't any excuse for how she treated me. I just wished she'd have come to me then. But I think we can start over since she's come clean. Baby steps."

"I'm relieved to hear that. Just so you know, Zane was eavesdropping because, as you already know, that's what he does while taking advantage of his super hearing. Bren said something about a guy after her?"

"Yeah, Woody is putting the word out, and his connections with the network of clubs and gangs will help track this bastard down. Bren hasn't seen or heard anything since she's returned, but it's only been a couple of weeks."

"I'm willing to help. I know Zane will want to rip this guy's heart out if he catches him. Whoever he is, better pray someone else catches him first."

"All I have is a name, Bryan Connelly. Bren believes our high school principal, Mr. Andrews, sent this guy after her."

"Why the hell would your high school principal do that?"

Tara looked around to see if anyone was listening to our conversation, then whispered, "Principal Andrews took advantage of Bren, and she was pregnant with his child. She miscarried, but he didn't know. She thought she loved him, but he left her, and a year or so later, Bren sent him a picture of a random baby, which brought him to the conclusion she was threatening him. When Bryan attacked Bren, he told her Mr. Andrews said not to come after him for child support and threatened her life."

"He's on the hitlist too!" I snarled.

Zane began shouting in our head, *Let me loose on these assholes, Dean. They deserve no mercy!*

"Zane concurs," I told Tara.

"I figured as much. But we don't know where these jackholes are right now. If one has the guts to show, they will lead us to the other, and justice will be served. Right now, Bren is safe, and we'll help her in any way."

"You're a good person, Tara. You put aside your differences with Bren, and now you're helping her. Only someone with a pure heart could do that." I wrapped my arms around Tara and kissed her lips.

"Hello, lovebirds!" Martina approached. She sat at the bar. Tonight, she was Dolly with her big golden wig and large fake boobs in a sparkling white jumpsuit.

"Well, HELLO DOLLY!" I greeted. "What are you singing for us tonight?"

"Well, seeing how Miss Tara here stole you from me, loverboy, I'll call out Jolene on her thieving little ass." Martina teased Tara by giving her the stink eye while drumming her shimmery pink fingernails on the bar top. Tara stuck her tongue out at Martina, and they both laughed.

Not long after that, the bar started filling up with regulars and more new faces, part of the Qweenie Martini fan club, and the night was busy. This time, things went easier with Stella and Woody behind the bar with me while Tara stepped out to help Billie on the floor. Neither woman broke a sweat as the club reached capacity and the live act began.

Bren mainly stayed in the kitchen, prepping and cleaning. She did a few rounds on the floor, so she had the opportunity to earn some tip money, and things got wild when Martina took the stage.

"HELLO, COCKY ROOSTERS AND HOT HENS!" Martina shouted from behind the curtain. The crowd started crowing and cheering. "Your lady of country Dollyounce' is in The Roost tonight!" Martina stepped out on the stage, and a group of queens went into a conniption.

In the audience, several queens with big blond hair stood and screamed, "We love you, Dollyounce!"

"Ooh wee! I feel the love tonight! I love you, too, ladies! Tonight, I'm going to sing my heart out because, in a way, it's broken." Martina bowed her head and held a hand to her heart. The collective, 'Awe's,' was followed by a few chuckles.

"Yes, I know! My heartbreak is real. You see, I met a fine man less than a week ago, and he lit a flame in me when he stood up against a gang of blimpy butchers with bad breath to defend my honor as a queen. Dean, come up here, babydoll."

The crowd cheered and whistled. I laughed and obliged Martina. Without having met her, I wouldn't have met Tara. And for that, I'd always been in debt to her. I joined her on stage to the noise of whistles and catcalls, and I played bashfully and allowed Martina to do her thing.

"Hello, Dean Baby. How you doin' tonight?" Martina held the mic to me.

"I'm fine; now I'm standing next to you, Dolly." I flashed a seductive smile, and all the ladies in the house shouted and called out suggestive comments. I saw Tara standing next to Billie, both laughing.

Martina gave me an appreciative appraisal of my backside before delivering a stinging whack to my ass with her hand.

"Ow, Dolly! What the hell was that for?"

"As I said, Dean, my heart's broke, and it is your fault. You see that little she-devil out there looking at you. Martina pointed out Tara. Tara's face instantly changed from humor to 'Oh shit,' and Billie started cracking up. Tara tried to make a break for the kitchen, but Billie turned her around as the spotlight hit her.

"Not again, Martina!" Tara protested.

"Yes, you! Get up here! I want to have a word with you!" Martina demanded. I started laughing as Billie graciously 'assisted' Tara to the stage. Tara struggled as Billie pushed her from behind, and Tara's boots slid across the smooth wood dance floor. The whole place erupted with laughter.

"I'm gonna get you back for this, Billie!" Tara warned.

"Game on, sister!" Billie responded.

Martina pointed at me. "Why the hell are you laughing? You are in as much trouble as she is, Deany Baby. Look, folks. I bring my man home to meet my family, and sweet baby Tara here swooped in and got her claws in my boo."

"BOOOO!" the crowd yelled.

"Now, now!" Martina soothed the audience with a downward wave of her hands. "I've got something I want to say to these two. Have a seat." Martina pulled up two bar stools, sitting me in one and Tara across from me in the other. Tara sat with her face in her hands, looking embarrassed. She peeked through her fingers at me, and I just continued laughing because I was so into this.

"Payback," Tara mouthed at me, and I laughed harder.

"Now, what would Dolly do in this situation?" Martina asked. "She might sing Jolene." The audience began to chant, Jolene, Jolene, Jolene!" Martina interrupted, "But wait! There's something else you all should know."

Martina looked at Tara. "I'm sorry to put you on the spot, but truly, I want to say that you are my hero. What you've been through and how you handled it was dignified and awe-inspiring. The sad jackass who'd done you wrong got his just deserts. So, in truth," Martina turned to the audience, "I'd like to admit and my heart couldn't be happier for these two lovebirds you see before you."

Martina put her hand on Tara's shoulder. "This young woman here deserves happiness in her life. You know I love you, Tara, so I'd like to dedicate this song. Here's a little ditty Dolly sang called, Love Will Keep Us Together."

Everyone clapped and sang as Martina belted a convincing rendition of Dolly and her song version. She replaced the words, 'sweet talkin' girl' with 'sweet talkin' boy' and pointed in jest at Dean, which made Tara laugh.

By the second verse, Martina pulled Tara and me up to stand beside her as she encouraged us to sing along. I could tell Tara had forgiven Martina and Billie. Billie smiled and winked at Tara from the dance floor below.

Close to the end of the night, I let Tara know that Zane needed a snack, and Tara nodded in understanding. I felt the change as Tara watched our eyes flash from my blue to Zane's silver. Zane kissed Tara's cheek. "Dean couldn't have found anyone better."

Tara blushed. "Go! I'll see you both when you get back. Be careful."

Zane nodded, and we stepped outside. "I need a lighter fare tonight, Dean. The venison juice didn't settle right with me, and the guy had too much testosterone and alcohol flowing through his veins. I won't even dream about approaching Bren again till I get my shit together. There has to be a woman who fits my needs."

Zane walked out toward the parking lot and leaned against a sleek black vintage 1959 Fleetwood Cadillac while getting a whiff of the interior. Perfume permeated our nose. "This ought a do. Just got to wait it out."

It wasn't long before a gorgeous woman with dark hair and Asian features came out the door and started walking our way. Zane's fangs dropped, and his eyes flared. I could feel his predator ready to pounce as our muscles tightened. He did a quick scan of the parking lot to ensure no witnesses. After seeing it was clear aside from the woman coming our way, Zane dipped his head and pressed a hand to our temple as though he had a headache.

"Oh! Are you alright, Honey? I saw you up on the stage. I bet those lights got to you, didn't they?" the woman asked.

Zane nodded pathetically. "You wouldn't happen to have any painkillers, would you? I thought some fresh air might help, but...."

Real smooth, Zane. Don't forget your semi-sobriety pledge.
Zane nodded again in response.

The woman opened the front car door and climbed across the long bench seat to the glove box. "I've got just what you need, sweetie."

Zane looked at her ass. "Oh, I know you do."

As the woman turned with a baggie of random pills, Zane pounced on top of her. The woman yelped, but Zane clapped his hand over her mouth and looked into her startled, fearful gaze. Zane's eyes flashed, and the woman's eyes dilated, her body relaxing as she fell under his compulsion.

"I'm not going to hurt you. You just came out to get your pills and saw no one, and you decided to have a little party and passed out," Zane told her. Her eyes took on an intoxicated haze, and her head rolled back. Zane pulled the door shut and leaned into her neck, smelling her perfume. He sank his fangs into her flesh and began to drink.

The woman moaned and mumbled, "Oh, my fantasy come true." Her Asian accent was stronger, along with a deeper tone to her voice. Zane's gulps slowed as confusion set in, and he pulled away.

"She tastes strange!" He sucked on her neck and stopped again before licking her wounds closed. On closer inspection of her neck, the slight bump told Zane what he figured out by tasting the mixed male and female hormones in her blood.

"Ahh, hell!" Zane cursed.

I laughed and pointed out. *You did say lighter fare; you just didn't know it'd come in a unique blend.*

"I thought I could get a little more action than this. I can't do more now, knowing she's out for the count and still has carry-on luggage." Seeing the apparent bulge of aroused male genitalia made Zane stick his tongue out in disgust.

"I have nothing against chicks with dicks, but I still prefer vagina. No offense, love." Zane affectionately tapped her cheek. "Blah, too much going on in her blood for my taste. But I suppose it will have to do for tonight." Zane looked around to see if the coast was clear before getting out of the car.

"I'm proud of you, Zane."

"It's like the more I practice moderation, the better I get. Why didn't you have me do this before?"

"Really?" I asked in disbelief. "It's all I've been doing these past eighty years."

"Yeah, I know. But you know how it is with family? Nag, nag, nag. It just took an angel to come along and help me see the light."

The woman was snoring away carefree in the front seat of the car. "I think you fulfilled her fantasy tonight."

Zane smirked. "Yeah, but she'll think it was a wild wet dream. She should be happy when she wakes up."

"Sounds like a good thing," I agreed.

"Well, brother, enjoy the rest of your night with your angel." Zane retreated.

"Thanks. I will."

Chapter 16
TARA

Must Love Sundays

Another dark nightmare plagued my sleep, but waking in the safety of Dean's arms had all my fears drifting away like dissipating storm clouds. Usually, reality bites, but when my head gets stuck in those nightmarish confines, waking to reality makes me appreciate the land of the living more.

Sunbeams broke in through the cracks in the drawn curtains, which brought me another sigh of relief. Sunday afternoons meant church service, and I always found Uncle Woody's sermons enlightening. Maybe today's will provide an answer about my purpose.

Dear Lord, I know I'm a mess. That's how I always felt. But, some positive encouragement from the good book helped me realize I'm a person of worth in my maker's eyes.

Everyone here needed a tune-up and a spiritual top-off, so we visited our top mechanic weekly. Because let's face it, I've been putting on the miles lately. *Lord, help me!*

I nudged out of Dean's arms, and he mumbled. He looked so beautiful while he slept, like an angel. I made my way to the bathroom to get ready for the day. The hot shower felt divine. I hummed as I washed my hair with my eyes closed, and smiled when I heard the curtain pull back and Dean stepped inside.

A soapy washcloth gently caressed my chest, and I hummed in approval. "Good morning, beautiful," Dean's sultry voice greeted. "I heard a nightingale singing, and I had to come to investigate."

"Is that so?" I opened my eyes and took in Dean's sexy naked body. I traveled up to his face, and he smirked at me.

"Like what you see?" Dean wiggled, drawing my attention back down by making his special friend dance back and forth.

I laughed and replied, "Like what you see?" I bounced up and down, and my girls jiggled. Dean growled. He brought my body flush with his and kissed me while bringing the washcloth to my back and rubbing my skin with a lavish circular motion.

"Mmm, that feels good," I mumbled against his lips.

"I can make you feel good in many ways." Dean kissed me, and I delicately dragged my fingernails along his back. I felt goosebumps rise on his arms beneath mine. Our kiss deepened, and Dean grew hard against me. Dean pressed my back against the shower wall, lifted one of my legs, and entered my body. He squeezed the soap from the washcloth between us; the suds created a silky gliding sensation between my breasts and Dean's muscular chest. It slid down between our combined sex where Dean moved his hand and began working that magical place with skillful fingers making me lose all my senses.

Our eyes locked, and we panted heavily into each other's open mouths with fever-fueled breaths. Our tongues' touching, swirling, and tasting intensified. Dean's hips bucked faster, hitting the deepest sensual part of me, demanding more from my body.

"Sing for me, Nightingale!"

"Oh, Dean, yes! Don't stop!"

"Is this how you want me, Baby?" Dean's voice was deep and husky. He took me mercilessly. I panted and moaned. I cried and yearned for more. Every move Dean made was so hot! I didn't want this to end.

"Ohh, Dean, you feel so good inside of me!"

Dean's breaths came faster as his movements picked up a frantic pace. It hurt so damn good, and I begged him to keep going, rougher, faster, deeper. My body lit from head to toe with the most intense orgasm, and I screamed so loud my voice went hoarse. I shook and tightened around Dean's thick erection, and he continued relentlessly. Moments later, Dean growled and shuddered as he let go.

I slumped forward onto Dean's shoulder, and he tenderly kissed my neck. The movement of his hips changed to a slow rolling motion creating smooth gliding strokes both decadent and torturous. His mouth moved down and captured my nipple, and he began flicking it with his tongue—an aching spark shot to my core, and I came undone.

My head lolled against the wall. "Oh, Dean!"

He touched my sensitive spot again, and my body jumped. I giggled because he worked me so well, and I was ticklish. Dean knew this and continued torturing me. He chuckled and smiled against the overworked tender flesh of my breast.

"Stop it, Dean! You're only torturing me now." I tried desperately to wiggle free. He was still hard inside me, and I wondered how I would get him to cease. He began to move again till another wave rolled through me. My whole body lit up, and white-hot sparks went haywire through my veins. "Dean, you're going to kill me with sex!"

"But, what a way to go! Wouldn't you agree?" His husky voice was taunting, and he continued kissing me everywhere.

"You are wicked!"

Which only had him proving my point as he continued to touch me. He grabbed my ass, pulled out, then THRUST. I cried out, my back arched, and my breasts pressed forward. Dean captured my nipple, sucked it, and swirled his tongue around it.

He repeated this until I screamed into oblivion and officially lost my voice. I began to shudder and sob. Never have I ever felt like this! So spent and used in such a sublime way. Who knew being thoroughly devasted could feel so good?

Dean held me up in my depleted state. My legs were weak and shaky as I stood on the shower floor. He finished washing my body and paid extra attention to my womanhood. I continued to jerk as he worked between my oversensitive folds, and he placed a tender, loving kiss there. I nearly collapsed as I began throbbing with need and clutched Dean's hair.

"Greedy little songbird! You need more of this sweet nectar?" Dean cooed seductively.

"Oh, Dean! Please, no! YES!" I shouted hoarsely as his tongue thrust firmly between my folds and struck gold. His tongue worked magically around my sensitive flesh, then darted in and out repeatedly. He pushed two fingers inside, pumping fast and deep. I held on tight to his hair, my legs about to give out, but Dean held me steady with his other hand squeezing my ass in a firm hold, intensifying my pleasure.

I threw my head back and cried just as my legs collapsed, and Dean wrapped his strong arms around my waist. He shut off the shower, which ran out of hot water long ago, and I was shivering against his chest.

Dean grabbed a nearby towel, wrapped it around me, then lifted and carried me to our bed. He dried me, pulled the covers over my shivering body, and kissed my forehead. My eyes felt heavy, and I couldn't think, let alone speak.

Isn't there something I'm supposed to be doing today? Hell, I couldn't remember with all these endorphins pumping through my system. I felt warm and tingly and floated on a cloud of bliss. I wanted to fall back to sleep, almost forgetting I'd woke from another nightmare. I couldn't remember how long ago that was as I watched Dean's tight muscular ass move away. I felt myself drooling and had to wipe my mouth with my hand only to smear it on my pillow.

Dean returned with a towel around his waist and a glass of water. He helped me sit up and fluffed the pillows up behind my back.

"Thank you." I accepted with a smile and washed away the dry, parched feeling in my throat.

"You're welcome, my love!" Dean got dressed and went to the kitchen to start breakfast. I watched him curiously as he worked like a short-order cook whipping up eggs, bacon, and toast. Dean had lived a long time, done many things, and knew his way around a kitchen. In no time at all, Dean served me breakfast in bed. He sat next to me and started eating. I couldn't help but feel in awe of this beautiful man. How was it he hasn't landed a woman long before me?

Then I remembered Zane, and I sure hoped he'd been hiding deep in a tiny dark closet with earplugs and all the feels switched off. But then I wondered if the two of them shared women in the past; perhaps that's how Dean knew how to wind a woman's gears so tight her spring coils broke.

Dean was most definitely talented in everything he did. I have yet to experience what Zane could do other than move fast, compel, capture prey, and bite. Oh, he does talk a smooth game, and he's funny. And!

Oh, no, Tara, don't go there! Neither of us is into each other that way. Even though he shares the same hot body with Dean? Stop it, Tara! Zane is more of an annoyance than anything. And he's into Bren, which is another thing I'll never figure out, but I guess Bren may have some good qualities. Shit! Where am I going with this? It's wrong. So, so, very wrong!

"Did I wear you out so much that you don't have the energy to eat? Perhaps you should so you can build that energy back up for later." Dean smiled devilishly.

I piled my eggs on my toast and took a bite. My salivary glands had an orgasm, and I moaned. "Mmm, is everything you do so delicious?"

Dean smiled wide as he watched me eat. "I aim to please my beautiful lady!"

"About that! You know about Asher. Did you have another love you'd like to tell me about in your long life?"

"Hmm, let me see! What volume and page in the history of Dean Perrish might I find the answer to your question?"

Dean tapped his temple. "No. Not there. Nope, nope."

"What are you doing?"

"Turning through the pages. There's a lot to go through; give me a moment." Dean replied. "Oh, yeah, here it is. Yes!"

"Yes, you've been in love before, or yes, you found the right page?"

"The year was 1956. There was a woman named Shirley Owens. It was a case of unrequited affection, and she crushed me when she told me I needed psychiatric help for the voices in my head." Dean explained.

"Zane," I stated.

"Who else? But, alas, it was all for the best because Shirley found love with a police officer. They wed and live somewhere in Florida today. Six kids, twenty grandkids, and eight great-grandkids the last I checked. I wouldn't have been able to give her that life."

"Wow! That's quite the legacy!"

"Certainly is. Anything else you want to know?"

"I guess I'm good for the moment. So, we have Sunday service soon. Care to join me after our sin-filled morning?

"Tara, I love you. You know we're already joined in love. I vow to make an honest woman of you under the eyes of God with the traditional papers and ceremony if it's what you want, but with who and what we are, we're already together in every way we're supposed to be."

"I feel that way too, but you know I didn't grow up knowing what I am. So, it's not easy to look past the lessons I've learned and not hold to my beliefs. Though I know I'm not perfect." I admitted.

"That's where you're wrong. You are perfect to me. And, though I'm not a grand omnipotent deity to pass judgment over your life, I will always keep you the way you are, just as you have accepted me."

"Doesn't my being wrong make me flawed?"

"I never said you weren't without flaws. Hell knows I'm not always right. But that doesn't mean I don't think of you as anything other than perfect for me. You're brave, strong, mouthy, stubborn, intelligent, sexy, and beautiful. And Zane just added scary to the list." Dean chuckled.

"Well, those don't all sound like positive attributes, but I get what you're saying. As far as Zane goes, I wouldn't be so scary to him if it weren't for the fact my blood could do him some serious damage."

"Speaking of your blood, did you think about whether or not you wanted to help me? I don't expect it, Tara, but I will gladly accept anything you wish to offer."

"I already decided, and I want to help you. We just need the correct type of syringe to reach your heart. My mother is a nurse and told me how the doctors injected adrenalin. I suppose it would be like that. But why the heart and not your vein? The heart seems more intimidating."

"With necromancers, the heart is our epicenter of power, and since I know the exact location of my heart, it is also better because there's a slightly higher chance of hitting one of Zane's veins. I was a medic in the army once, so I did administer adrenalin shots. It wasn't exactly necessary due to my power, but I still had to keep up the pretense in front of my human counterparts."

"Makes sense," I concluded. "So, after church, I planned to visit my brother, Rudy, in the hospital. Perhaps we could find some supplies there."

"Tara, are you talking about pinching some syringes? You know that's stealing?" Dean teased.

"It's for the greater good. I can't feel guilty about that."

"No, Zane. Not happening," Dean said.

"What does Zane want?"

"To pick up some juice pouches from the blood bank. He said he doesn't mind hospital food."

I laughed. "Seriously, Zane? You know that it's there for emergency use only. Go. Find a snack in the woods."

"Zane said he'd rather drink the grape juice you call communion wine," Dean replied.

"Yeah, well, he's acting like a toddler, so if the shoe fits, drink the grape juice."

<><><>

The day was beautiful, so we sat in folding chairs by the lake. Uncle Woody opened the service with the Lord's prayer. Then Martina stood up wearing a purple choir robe with a glittering silver sash, and her hair was a Beyonce-style wig.

"Dearly beloved. We are gathered here today in the sight of the HIS grace and glory! Can I get an Amen!"

Everyone shouted, "AMEN!" Stella was clapping and bouncing in her seat, squealing with excitement, while Cannon leaned back with his arms crossed and a grin on his face. Bren sat next to Billie and Danny with a bible given to her by Woody.

I could only imagine what was going through Dean's head as he smiled at our congregation of bikers in black shirts and denim jeans with tattoos and chunky silver crosses worn around their necks.

Martina carried on like she was introducing the next stage act. "And there isn't any person, place, or thing in this world that can stand T'almightier than the maker of all man with a plan, the father above all fathers, brothers, sisters, and mothers.

He is above and beyond all space and full of grace, the Holy Ghost to which we raise a toast, and our Son Savior Sender, who pulled us out of sin's blender. Please give it up for the deity of every second, minute, and hour filled with Holy Power! Our Father who art in Heaven, Hallowed Be Thy Name! Our one and only! Goodness gracious and great God Almighty!"

After an introduction like that, we all shouted. "HALLELUJAH!"

"Anyone needing prayer?" Martina asked.

Danny jumped up and stood by Martina. Billie looked surprised, and Bren sat nervously rubbing her hands across her bible like she was making a wish on a crystal ball. Dean put his arm around me and gave my shoulder a gentle squeeze.

"I confess I'm a hot mess," Danny said. "I drink and swear and have recently fornicated." Billie dropped her head, and I could see her cheeks bloom and pinken with embarrassment. I couldn't help but snicker, and she turned to wag a finger at me.

"I wouldn't be laughing if I were you, sister. There's more than one ho in the house."

I bit my lips and tried not to burst.

Martina put her hand on Danny's shoulder. "Well, sweetheart, I can say to you, everyone here is in the same boat on the weekly. Nobody's perfect, but Jesus does want us to come to him as we are, repent and pray for forgiveness. Is there anything else you want to confess?"

"Yes. I wanted to commit murder, but I know I wasn't alone in these thoughts." Woody and Cannon stood up and clapped a hand on Danny's shoulders.

I knew they were talking about Asher, and suddenly Dean stood up and went to join them. I was shocked. I knew Dean had witnessed the fight between Asher and me. What I didn't realize was how it had affected him. He hadn't even met me yet and was ready to defend me.

All these beautiful men in my life stood willing to sacrifice the sanctity of their souls. It made me feel humbled, cherished, and at the same time, sad because of what they could lose by defending my honor. I didn't want that for them. I stood and went to them, and we all joined hands and bowed our heads to pray for forgiveness. I found myself wanting to forgive Gina and Asher. I realized if not for what happened, I'd be the one plagued with my feelings for Dean and feel trapped and resentful.

I knew I'd want Dean and sin in my heart with the desire to be with him while I was still with Asher, and I couldn't help but note the timing. After finding out about Asher and Gina, I met my true love. I found my heart grateful for the small mercy and knew meeting Dean was part of a grand design. I knew my dad had sent him, but he must have had help from our Lord to accomplish this feat.

Bren asked for prayer, and I realized it took incredible courage to come forward. Not everyone knew her story, but Woody, Cannon, and Danny pledged to protect her and asked for God's protection and peace.

Bren's face rolled with tears, and my heart went to her. I pulled Bren into a hug, and my heart felt lighter as I let go of the past and told her she was my sister. It was so good to have one heavy burden lifted off my chest from the past. I knew there was still more to face.

My dad's words came back to me. ***It's time to face your past and your monsters. Some you will trust, and others you must battle.*** Dean and Zane were self-proclaimed monsters I could count on to help me. Bren's monsters were her selfishness, pride, and the men who hurt her. She released her selfishness and pride. She and I could move on from our past. I thanked the Lord above for this mercy.

Martina led us in the song, Amazing Grace. Martina sounded like an angel, and Stella got up to join her. Stella lifted a hand in the air and swayed side to side. She always loved to hear Martina sing gospel songs. Amazing Grace was fitting, and for once, Danny didn't crack a joke about his inner wretch. There were two more women in his life now. I could tell he'd adopted Bren as his niece and Billie as his lady.

Woody stood and gave a short sermon on our battle with the enemy. He quoted. Ephesians 6:11. "Put on the whole armor of God, that you may be able to stand against the devil's wiles."

He closed in prayer and dismissed the service. We enjoyed a picnic lunch out in the sunshine. The combined feel of the warm rays and the cool, crisp air felt perfect. Woody approached Dean and me. Dean's head was in my lap, and I fed him cheese and grapes.

"Seems you two worked out your differences from the other night," Woody said.

"Yeah, I was being a jerk," Dean confessed on Zane's behalf.

"Are you coming with us today to see Rudy?" I asked Woody.

"It seems you have a group coming with you already. I'll see Rudy tomorrow with Cannon and Danny. I'm not getting stuck shopping with the ladies."

"You wouldn't have to do that if you took your bike."

"You know how Martina gets. She's insistent on having someone hold her purse in the dressing room, and I'm not falling into that trap."

Dean and I laughed. Woody pointed at Dean. "I don't know why you're laughing as that honor now falls to you."

Dean closed his mouth and looked at me with pleading eyes to save him. I laughed. "It's not that bad. Martina makes shopping fun, and I usually hate to shop. Besides, you can follow on your bike if you don't like it."

"I think I will. Just so long as you ride with me," Dean said.

"I'm good with that." I smiled.

"Be extra careful with my niece on the road," Woody said.

"I will. I promise," Dean said.

I stood up and hugged Woody. "We'll be safe. Love you."

"Love you too." Woody walked over to talk to his other congregants.

"Woody loves you fiercely. He's not a man of many words, but he gives a good short sermon, and I admire him," Dean confessed.

I smiled as I watched my uncle. "I admire him too."

Stella and Martina came up to us, and Dean stood up. "Are you ready to go?" Stella asked.

"Yes, Dean's coming with us, but we're taking his bike and following you in my truck." I tossed the key to Stella. "We'll need the extra space to bring back a haul with Martina's shopping habits."

Martina didn't take offense to my comment. "Girl, you know me well. We'll just have to go for a ride on my trike another time. Now let's get on the road. We're burning daylight."

Chapter 17
DEAN

Thick As Thieves With Good Intentions

Tara sat behind me with her arms wrapped around my waist. Her body pressed to my back made riding down the highway a most enjoyable experience. Tara was young, but her soul weighed heavy, knowing her past was catching up with her. I could see it in her aura as her spirit connected with mine. I wanted to take it away from her, but I knew she had to face her demons, and I'd be there by her side the whole way.

We followed Tara's truck with Stella driving and Martina gesturing wildly in the passenger seat. It looked like they were having a great time dancing and singing along with the music. Martina would often look back and wave as if she hadn't just seen us moments before. Tara laughed at Martina's crazy antics.

We pulled into the West Town Mall. Luckily, it was Sunday, and the mall would close in two hours. But I was to learn what Martina could do in two hours. Martina and Stella charged ahead as Tara and I followed.

We entered a large department store, and Martina went mad in the clearance clothing racks. She pushed through the clothing and slid hangers along the pole.

"No, no, nope. Oh, honey, no! This is sad." Martina found a shimmery pink top and handed it to Stella, who passed it to Tara. Tara held it up, scrutiny in her expression.

"Trust me, Tara Baby. You'll look fabulous in it." Martina continued her assault on the rack, repeating, "Hell no," with every metallic scrap of the hangers she pushed aside.

"We need to move on. I want to find something for Rudy Bear. Tara, I'm going to buy that top for you, and you'll wear it on a date with Dean."

"But, Martina," Tara protested.

Martina halted her with a finger to Tara's face with a hushing noise that sounded more like, "Psshutit. You will listen to your auntie Martina young lady. I know what I'm talking about. Now, the men's department."

Stella followed her, and Martina grabbed her hand. The women linked arms, thick as thieves on a mission to conquer. I laughed as Tara flung the garment over her shoulder and huffed in frustration.
"You want me to hold that for you?" I offered.

"No, Dean. Believe me when I say you'll regret that offer," Tara said. Stella snickered and looked back at us.

"Now, you have me worried," I said.

"Be afraid. Be very afraid!" Stella wooed.

At this, Tara laughed, and Martina made a chastising sound. "You all know me! That's why I bring my ladies along. They don't have shopping carts in the mall, and I can't carry everything. Plus, you know I treat you every time. So, no complaining. Comprender?"

"Damn, Martina doesn't play around, does she?" I asked.

"If shopping were an Olympic sport, she'd win gold. I love going with her because she finds the best things and gets the best deals. I'd be lost in here without her," Stella said.

"Awe, ain't that sweet, sugar. Martina kissed Stella's cheek. Martina didn't take long to find a nice men's button-up, a winter hat, and sleek black gloves. She went to the men's fragrance counter, selected a cologne, and went to pay.

"I need a gift bag, honey," Martina told the woman at the register, who appraised Martina's appearance with a rather rude judgy gaze.

"Who does your make-up?" the woman asked in an arrogant tone.

"Why, do you need a lesson?" Martina replied. Stella had an 'Oh shit' look and bit her lips closed.

The woman behind the counter looked offended. "No. I just thought I could show you...."

Martina cut her off, "Look, HONEY! You don't need to SHOW ME anything! If anything, you NEED to mind what you're about to say. I've been down this avenue before, and I know the shit you're selling, and I'm not buying. So, be a dear and just give me the gift bag I asked for, okay?"

"Ma'am, I wasn't trying to offend you; I was only going to show you how to tone down your look to something more natural," the lady rudely explained.

Martina smacked her hand on the glass counter and eyed the woman. Tara clutched my arm and struggled to contain her composure. It wasn't easy, as I wanted to bend over and take deep breaths to keep from bursting.

"Look, HONEY! I am a one-of-a-kind woman, unlike any other, but that doesn't entitle you to judge me so rudely. I'm also a loyal customer of this establishment, and the manager knows who I am."

Martina tapped her purple fingernail on the glass. "Get a pen and write this down." The woman looked confused, but Martina glared at her. "I'm waiting!" The woman quickly found a pen and paper.

"Mar-ti-na Doll-y-oun-ce," Martina enunciated slowly. The woman looked confused, and Martina tapped the paper and began to spell her name phonetically.

"M for Mariah. A for Astronomical, R for Right here in your face, T for Teaching you your place, I for I know I'm beautiful, R for Read this again when I'm through, and A for Ass because don't you feel like one right now?"

The woman looked angry, but Martina tapped the paper. "I'm not finished yet, honey. D for Damn I'm fine, O for Oh no you didn't, Double L' Looking Lovely, Y for You only live once, O for One day maybe you'll understand, U for Uranus. Get your head out of there, honey; it's not a good look on you! N for Need I remind you again, C for Child don't play with me, cause this is a game you won't win, and E for Everyone here will know who I am after this!"

The woman huffed, pulled a stylish blue gift bag from beneath the counter, and neatly put the items inside. "Will that be all, Miss Dollyounce?" she asked with her nostrils flaring.

Martina took the bag. "That's all," she read the woman's name tag, "Lin-da. Thank you for being so understanding and cooperative. You'll go a long way in customer service as long as you remember my name." Martina turned to walk away, and Stella burst out laughing. Tara and I were cracking up as we trailed behind.

"I don't think Linda will ever forget," I said.

"No, she won't." Tara laughed.

We went to a few more stores, where a few women squealed and embraced Martina. They punched in discount codes and exchanged endearments with kisses on Martina's cheeks. I carried several bags, and Tara, Stella, and Martina had a couple of bags each. People passed us and glimpsed at Martina, but no further rude encounters transpired.

We headed to the hospital as the daylight faded. As we entered Rudy's room, I looked around at the mass collection of balloons, flowers, cards, and party streamers. Martina walked into the room. "There's my sweet stud muffin. Rudy Bear, how are you?"

Rudy's face lit up. "Aunt Martina! I heard you were in town. Give me a hug, lady. Martina hugged Rudy and set the bag on his lap.

"I got a little something for you, sugar."

"Thanks, Martina." Rudy smiled. He pulled the shirt, hat, and gloves out. "Nice," Rudy commented. He pulled out the box of cologne. "Uh, thanks, Martina, but I don't use cologne."

"Oh, baby, you do now. You'll want to use this one. Believe me! It enhances your pheromones. You don't need any help in the looks department, but this cologne will bring out the wild in any she-beast. So, you got to use it sparingly. Just a dab behind each ear will do. It'll last you, and you'll be thanking me later." Martina winked.

Rudy laughed. "Alright, I'll give it a try." Rudy opened the bottle of cologne and tipped it on his finger before dabbing it behind each ear. "There's a pretty nurse here named Vera, and I've been giving it my all. I think she likes me, but she has to remain professional on the job. Maybe this is what I needed."

Stella leaned in to hug Rudy and sniffed. "Ooh, I like that. Maybe I should get some for Cannon. I'm always looking for things to keep it spicy in the bedroom."

"TMI, Stella," Tara said as she went to hug Rudy next and sniffed him curiously. "Ewe, and that'll be a pass for me."

Rudy laughed. "Thanks. I suppose that's a good thing. I don't need you getting all weird around me."

"You already weird me out, Rudy! But not in that way!"

Rudy laughed again and looked up at me. "Are you Dean? Stella told me about you."

"Yes," Tara answered for me and beamed. She took hold of my hand and pulled me closer. I observed Rudy's appearance; he and Tara had the same dark eyes. Not as lovely as Tara's, but the shape and tone were there. His hair was a dark brown to Tara's dark blond and sun-kissed highlights. Rudy had that protective brother vibe, although I could tell he was younger than Tara, but not by much. The cast on Rudy's leg had dozens of signatures and artwork, which told me he had no lack of visitors who loved him. He was lean muscle, and I could see all the football team references by looking around his room.

I reached out to shake Rudy's hand. "Nice to meet you, Rudy. Tara didn't mention you played football."

"Tara tends to get sidetracked. I suppose you might know something about that?" Rudy smiled knowingly, and Tara blushed.

"Shut up, Rudy." Tara slapped Rudy's arm.

"Ow! You hit harder than you used to. I'm calling Vera to tell her there's a crazy lady here abusing the patients."

"Whatever, Rudy. I see you've had a lot of visitors this week." Tara moved to grab a black sharpie off the bedside table and walked around to find a spot-on Rudy's cast, and she started scribbling with a mischievous grin. Stella and Martina watched and waited for their turns, laughing.

"Oh, hell! I can't possibly imagine what she's writing on there." Rudy complained. He ignored the women in the room as they continued to giggle.

"So, Dean, did you ever play?"

"Football?"

Rudy nodded and rolled his eyes as Stella started writing and Tara and Martina laughed.

"Yeah, I played a little in the Army."

"Who did you play for?"

"The Black Knights."

Rudy's eyes widened. "That's pretty impressive. You went to West Point?"

"For a stint, I got kicked out, though."

Tara gave me a knowing look. Yes, another Zane moment, but what could I do?

"That sucks. Did you serve over in Iraq?"

"Yeah, been there, done that."

"Well, thank you for your service, Dean." Rudy held out his hand, and I shook it.

"You're welcome, man." I didn't need to tell Rudy I was there during Desert Storm in the early nineties because it would be hard to explain why I looked the way I do.

A young brunette in a nurse's uniform popped in. I confirmed this was Vera as I zeroed in on her ID badge. She smiled at Rudy. "How is my favorite football player?"

"I'm feeling alright," Rudy responded with a wink, and Vera blushed.

She came up to him with an electronic device. "What's your pain level?

"Somewhere between a four and a six," Rudy replied. Vera nodded and made some notes.

"Do you need anything for the pain?"

Rudy shook his head. "No, but I do need your opinion on something. Could you take a whiff behind my ear and tell me if I smell weird?"

I looked over at Tara, Stella, and Martina, all grinning. Rudy tilted his head with an innocent look as Vera leaned in and sniffed.

"New cologne?"

Rudy smiled. "Yeah, my aunt Martina got it for me." Rudy gestured to Martina, and Vera smiled.

"Well, your aunt knows how to pick a good cologne." Vera winked at Martina, and Martina beamed.

"See, I told you, Rudy," Martina said. "Girl, this boy has been pining and over the moon for you. Don't leave my little Rudy Bear hanging!"

"Rudy Bear?" Vera giggled.

"Thanks a lot, Martina," Rudy said.

Tara smiled and looked at me, and as Vera passed, Tara's eyes widened in concern. Zane was salivating at the nurse's scent.

"Dean and I need to eat. I'm starving. Aren't you Dean?" Tara asked. My vision changed to HD as I felt placed in the back of our mind as Zane took control.

"I'm feeling ravenous." Zane took Tara's hand and kissed it. Tara scowled at him and pulled him along.

"See you in a little bit, guys." Tara pulled us out of the room and led us to the elevator. Once inside, Tara turned to look at Zane. "What the hell are you doing?"

"Isn't it obvious? Nurse Vera smells amazing! You're hungry, and I'm hungry. We should eat. My treat," Zane replied.

"You can't eat here at the hospital!" Tara spoke adamantly.

"Why not? If you're going to, so am I. If you don't let me do what comes naturally, I will have to raid the blood bank. Now, let's see." Zane mumbled the names of each department and the floor numbers.

"What are you doing?" Tara asked.

"Perusing the menu. However, it would be best if you let me get take-out. I hear the E.R. might be a good place to dine tonight, and they often have a new selection."

"Are you always so insensitive?"

"Not necessarily, and I care. Some of the time."

Tara looked shocked, then disgusted.

"Look, Tara, you know what I need to do to survive. Some poor bloke dies every second somewhere in the world, and I just so happen to have a talent for easing their transition to the hereafter. I bag, and Dean zaps when the situation calls. We make a great team, don't we, Dean?"

"I can't believe what you're implying," Tara said. The elevator doors opened, the E.R. sign came into view with an arrow pointing to the right, and Zane walked out with a casual stride down the hall. Tara quickened her steps to keep up.

"Zane, you can't do this, not here!"

Zane stopped. "Then where? Would you rather I go back up and stalk Vera, compel her, and take what I need?"

"No." Tara hung her head. "But, can't you wait till we leave and find someone, somewhere else?"

"I wish I could. I never got a chance to tell you about how bloodlust feels. It's not just a mind or emotional thing. The longer I go without feeding, the more intense the searing in my head and throat becomes. It's like burning hot acid injected with a thousand needles.

My monster loses control, and I feel like I'm being ripped to shreds from the inside out. I lose control of all my thoughts and emotions. I can't see straight, let alone think for myself, and I can't even fight him. Dean can't even stop him if I let my thirst go too far. Dean understands this, and now you must know. It's a necessary evil. Better to know this version of my demon than the other, Tara. Because for the love of God and the Devil, you never want to meet my monster."

Tara swallowed nervously. "Okay. What can I do to help?"

"Just keep a lookout. When I find the right person, do not interfere while I feed. Can you manage that?"

Tara nodded. "Okay."

"Follow me, love." Zane waited for a hospital staff member to open the door as we'd need an employee badge to enter. A custodial worker exited, pushing a cart ahead of him, and Zane stood in his line of sight.

"Good evening," Zane's eyes flashed. The man nodded as he held the door, and Zane and Tara slipped through. I was aware of everything that was happening. I couldn't speak aloud because Zane had complete control of our mouth at the moment. His thirst needed addressing asap.

There was a commotion down the hall as doctors and nurses scrambled to aid a young man with serious injuries. Blood was everywhere, and Tara walked cautiously behind Zane.

A woman approached as they drew closer to the victim. "You can't be back here."

Zane looked into her eyes, her mouth closed, and she walked in the other direction. Zane grabbed a white coat off a nearby hook, put it on, and walked directly to the man on the bed.

A doctor looked up and asked, "Who are you?" Zane gazed at the doctor, and the doctor froze.

"Doctor Lasling?" a nurse questioned. The injured man's vitals dropped as Doctor Lasling backed away and left the room.

"We need blood in here," Zane said with urgency. A woman rushed out and returned with two bags. Zane glanced up at Tara, who stood at the doorway mesmerized as Zane performed medical procedures and called out orders. But I knew it was all a farce. I knew this young man wouldn't make it, and so did Zane. I could already see his spirit separating from his body, and he was looking into the light.

"Mom. Grandpa. I'm coming!" he cried joyfully.

Zane glanced at Tara; her eyes widened, and I knew she could see the man's spirit. It's part of our abilities as necromancers to see the dead. A tear slipped from her eye, and Tara nodded in understanding.

The medical team did everything they could as the young man's heart flat-lined. They performed CPR and took the defib paddles to him four times, but it was all in vain as the young man's joyous spirit left his body and ascended into the light with reaching arms.

"Time of death, nineteen hundred hours, twelve minutes," Zane called. Everyone's heads hung, and a nurse began working on disconnecting everything from the young man's body.

"He is an organ donor. Call the transplant surgeon and arrange to have the body transported to the O.R."

Everyone else had left the room, and the last nurse was about to pull the line when Zane placed a gentle hand over hers. He looked into her eyes. "I've got this, Sara. Get cleaned up and check on 103, please."

"Thank you, doctor. As she headed out of the room, Zane stopped her once more.

"You did a good job, Sara." Sara looked at Zane and smiled with sadness in her eyes. She left the room, and Zane looked up at Tara. "Keep watch!" He pulled the curtain so Tara wouldn't see what he was about to do next.

I laid witness to scenes like this so many times in the past. It was the most humane way Zane fed. It was a mercy to everyone involved, including Tara. Zane wouldn't have waited till the last moment, choosing instead to compel the entire room and take what he needed. It didn't hurt Zane to drink the blood of the dead as long as it was a recent passing.

He pulled the I.V. and pinched it to reserve the blood he'd consumed from the bag after he drank from the vein, just enough to make it appear like most of the blood loss was due to the trauma.

He lifted and drank directly from the arm. He covered the body, pulled the blood bag off the hook, grabbed the extra, and tucked it inside our jacket. Zane quickly finished the first and tossed it in the red waste bag. He grabbed some syringes, pulled the curtain, and rolled the body out to the corridor. He stopped another staff member and told them to take the body to the OR for the transplant surgeon, and there wouldn't be a need to check for brain activity. The man was gone for good.

Tara gawked in amazement as Zane pulled off the white coat and went to the restroom to take care of any remaining evidence. He met Tara back out in the hallway.

"That was amazing, Zane. I didn't know. I mean, what you did in there and what I saw. It was merciful, beautiful even despite the terrible circumstances."

"Did you see why it's not always necessary for your power to intervene?" Zane asked.

"I did. I saw his spirit ascend, and it was glorious."

"And, had he been brought back, he'd have been brain dead, no life left in a shell kept alive on machines. His organs are going to save multiple lives. Dean knows these things, and it took him making a lot of mistakes in the past to learn his powers cannot save everyone," Zane explained.

"I understand now. But, how does he know who to save and who not to save?"

"That's something you'll have to ask, Dean."

"While we're still here, there's something else we need to get."

"You mean these?" Zane showed her the syringes inside our jacket.

"I've got to give you more credit. Tonight, I witnessed a side of you that's truly admirable."

"Shh. Don't tell anyone." Zane winked.

Chapter 18
TARA

An Invitation

I didn't have much of an appetite after what I had witnessed, so Zane and I went back up to visit Rudy. In the elevator, I remembered someone else I needed to see. I hit the button for the fourth floor.

"Why are we going there?" Zane asked.

"I have a friend here, Abigail. I met her last week and told her I'd come back to see her," I replied. The elevator doors opened, and Zane followed me to the nurses' station.

The man behind the desk asked, "May I help you?"

"I'm here to see Abigail in room 409."

The man looked confused. "We don't have an Abigail. Do you know the last name?"

"Uh, no. I met Abigail last week, and she told me she'd still be here and gave me that room number."

The man rechecked his computer. "No. I'm sorry. No Abigail, and without the last name, I'm afraid I can't give you any more information."

"Excuse me, but I believe you can," Zane said. The man looked up, and Zane's eyes flashed. The man nodded and tapped on the keyboard.

"Yes, here she is. Abigail Hensley. I'm sorry to tell you, but Ms. Hensley is gone."

"Gone? In what way?"

"Abigail was discharged and went home on Friday."

"Why was she here?" Zane asked. His eyes flashed again, and the man began tapping on the keyboard.

"Foot surgery. She had necrosis and was to have half of her foot removed. It was a misdiagnosis, and her foot was fine. So, the doctors had no choice but to release her," he replied. I was shocked. How do you misdiagnose necrosis?

"Do you have an address or phone number for Ms. Hensley?"

"I'm afraid there's a note here saying Ms. Hensley provided incorrect information, and her file needs updating."

"Just great! Thanks." I went back to the elevator and pushed the button to go down. Zane looked at me curiously.

"What?" I asked.

"Well, you're a necromancer. Did you touch Abigail at all when you met her?"

I thought about my interaction with Abigail and recalled touching her hand when I slipped the ring on her middle finger. "I did. I touched her hand. I didn't realize I could cure necrosis."

"Dead people, dead tissue, anything dead. Remember the leaf?"

"Oh, wow! This is great news! Does this mean I can heal anyone?" I asked excitedly.

"Not exactly. You can restore a dead body and repair the damage that led to death, but living tissue is another thing," Zane replied.

"So, I can't heal Rudy's broken leg?" I felt defeated.

"Afraid not. But there is something I can do to help."

"What's that?"

"Vampire blood has healing abilities. I can slip Rudy a few drops of my blood to help speed up his recovery. I'm afraid I can't heal him completely, it would raise many questions, and you don't want your brother to become a lab rat."

"Point taken. But you'd be willing to help my brother speed up his healing? I'd be so grateful. Rudy would be happy if he could be strong enough to get back on the field sooner." I leaned in and kissed Zane on his cheek.

"Yes, I'm happy to help out. The more you know I have a good side, the better chance I have at surviving your wrath the next time I piss you off." Zane chuckled.

"You have scored bonus points tonight. I'll remember what you did. I hope this isn't an attempt to butter me up because I will only make certain allowances. Do me wrong, and I'll revert to my previous promise," I threatened.

"Jeez, what else does a vampire need to do to earn your trust, woman?"

"Don't break it," I responded.

We returned to Rudy's room, where Martina, Stella, and Rudy played charades. Stella swung her hips, stepping back and forth in a dance.

"Dancing!" Martina called. "Ah, merengue, no, salsa!"

Stella nodded and tapped her nose as she kept dancing; she cupped a hand in a bowl shape and motioned as if dipping something with the other. She held the imaginary food to her mouth and took a bite of air.

"Chips! Salsa and chips!" Rudy cried.

Stella clapped and mimed, cheering for Rudy.

"Dammit! I was going to say that!" Martina exclaimed. "Okay! Let's see if you can get this one!" She stood up, put her hand over her right breast, and mimicked squeezing. Martina made a face that looked like she was in pain as she puckered her lips and held an imaginary glass beneath her breast. She lifted the invisible glass to her mouth to drink and shook her ass as she fanned herself with her other hand. Martina sighed audibly in relief.

"You feel like chicken tonight!" I shouted.

Martina looked at me in disbelief. "Really? I was drinking, not eating!"

"Well, you were squeezing at one of those chicken cutlets you wear in your bra. So, I thought you felt like chicken tonight." I shrugged.

Everyone laughed except Martina, who huffed. "Watch and pay attention, boys and girls. It's in the details you're not seeing." She did the routine again.

Stella shouted. "Ooh, I think I know! It's milkshake. Am I right?"

"Ah, NO!" Martina emphasized the boob squeeze and fanning herself while she drank, then sighed louder.

"Easy squeezy lemon breezy," Zane said.

Martina pointed at her nose.

"How in the hell did you get that?" Stella asked. "She looked like she was milking herself and shaking her ass to bring the boys to the floor."

I burst into laughter, and tears streamed down my face. Zane grinned at me, and he answered Stella. "Well, she puckered like she was eating something sour and squeezed her boob like a lemon juicer. Then she fanned herself, which represented a breeze."

Rudy chuckled. "I could see why Stella thought milkshake because boobs make milk, not lemon juice."

"These here titties are special, Rudy Bear. And haven't you ever shook when you ate something sour?" Martina asked.

"Okay, we get it now," Stella replied with an eye roll. "Your boob squeeze reference just threw me off a bit. What about you, Tara? We're naming foods."

"Okay, I've got one." I point to the floor. "Dean, stand here and turn your back to me, then bend forward and touch your toes." Zane smiled mischievously and did as I asked.

"Nobody wants to see you get your kink on," Rudy said.

"Oh, shut it, Rudy!" I stood to Zane's side, raised my hand in a curled grip like holding a whip, and pretended to crack strikes across Zane's ass. Stella and Martina were laughing.

"Ooh! Yeah! Set that fine ass on fire, girl!" Stella cheered. My roleplay cranked up a few notches as I moved like a tennis player in a tournament, and Zane's ass was the ball. Zane's body jerked with laughter as I continued my assault. I stopped abruptly, pretended to stir the contents in a giant bowl, then licked the spoon.

"Whipped Cream!" Martina shouted.

"I think I could get into this game. Okay, I've got one." Zane stood upright, wiggling his arms wildly in the air, then reached down and cupped his balls.

"Spaghetti and meatballs," Rudy shouted.

"I think we need to end this game. Your minds are in the gutter, and mine was the cleanest charade," Stella said.

"Girl, please! Your one of the trashiest sex talkin' hussies I know," Martina said. Stella gasped in mock offense. But we all knew better. Get a few drinks in Stella, and she'd talk about her and Cannon's bedroom activities in full detail. And that's why I've never entertained Stella with alcohol in my company.

Martina yawned. "Well, Rudy Bear, I think it's time we headed back to The Roost. It was good seeing you.

"You, too, Martina. Say hey to Trey for me," Rudy said.

Stella said goodbye to Rudy. "You and Dean coming back tonight?"

"We'll stay awhile longer, and we may even spend the night if it gets too late." I hugged her and Martina.

"Okay. Be safe!" Stella looked at Zane/Dean. "You take care of my niece."

Zane nodded. "Believe me. I will. I want to stay in your good graces, Stella."

Stella smiled and patted him on the back. "I knew you had a good head on your shoulders." Martina and Stella left the room, and I noticed Rudy smile as his eyes moved back and forth between Zane and me.

"I heard through the grapevine you gave Asher and Gina their dues. I would have loved to have seen that." Rudy grinned.

"Yeah, well, I held my ground just like Dad and Uncle Woody taught us. Asher was an asshole and couldn't take a hint, so our uncles gave him a civilized escort to his shitty car, and he didn't leave till Cannon threatened his life."

"The way Stella told it sounded more epic, but still, I'm proud of you, Sis!"

"Thanks, Rudy."

"And you, Dean. Martina told me about how you two met and then defended her. I've gotta say, you're a pretty righteous guy."

"Well, I do love to come to the aid of a lady. But Martina put that asswipe in his place. I wanted to kill Asher, but Tara already had an impressive backup crew. And if Stella got involved, I might have shit my pants if I got in her way," Zane answered.

I was impressed that none of my family had noticed the switch between Dean and Zane with the change of eye color. But I supposed they could think it was the lighting. Either that or Zane's compulsion was working on them.

Rudy laughed. "Yeah, man. I've seen Aunt Stella go to town on some guy one time. She sure knows how to wield that switchblade." Rudy looked at me. "So, you moved on fast."

"It wasn't like that, Rudy. Asher screwed up, and Dean just so happened to show up at the right time. Dean and I had an instant connection. I can't control fate."

"That's right, baby." Zane swaggered up beside me and put his arm around me possessively. "You're my old lady now."

Zane grinned at me before pulling me in for a kiss. I wanted to knee him in the sack, but he trapped me. I had no choice but to play along, even though it pissed me off that he was taking advantage. I pretended I was kissing Dean instead, but I could tell the difference. And I had to admit Zane was a good kisser, but still.

Shit, don't go there again, Tara.

"Break it up, you two, and get your own damn room. I don't want to watch your PDA," Rudy said.

My stomach growled so loud Rudy heard it. "I thought you went to get something to eat earlier?"

"Well, Dean did, but I got sidetracked. There was a person I met here last week. Her name is Abigail Hensley. I checked in on her, but she's no longer here, and they didn't have her correct phone number or address."

"Was she a little old lady?" Rudy asked.

"Yes. You saw her?"

"Yes. She came to visit me, and I forgot it until you mentioned her. She gave me this." Rudy held out an envelope, and I saw my name written on it as he passed it to me. I opened it and read the short letter aloud.

"Dear, Tara. I'm so glad we got the chance to meet the other day. I thought I'd still be at the hospital when you came for another visit, but I've returned home. I'd wanted to visit with you again, but we didn't exchange information. I guess we were both distracted, so it slipped our minds. You'll find my address on the back. I only have a house phone, so you might have to ring it a few times before I answer.

I look forward to seeing you again. Perhaps we can have lunch sometime. Your friend, Abigail."

"She seems nice," Rudy said.

I looked at the back of the page and saw an address and a phone number. "Yeah, Abigail is a very sweet lady. I want to visit her. Perhaps I'll call tomorrow. It's getting late, and I don't want to disturb her if she's resting. Did she tell you anything else? I wonder how she knew to bring this letter to you?"

"She didn't say much. She asked if I knew you. I guess she was asking around till she found the right person. She just gave me the letter to give to you, thanked me, and said she hoped I'd get well soon."

"Huh, sounds like a resourceful old gal," Zane said.

My stomach growled again, and Rudy laughed. "I think you need to take care of that."

"Yeah, I suppose I should. You want me to bring you anything?" I asked.

"Nah. My many visitors have been loading me up on snacks and drinks." Rudy pointed to a box by his bedside full of food. "You're welcome to it. There's no way I can eat all this. Plus, sitting in this bed all day, I gotta watch what I eat." Rudy patted his firm, flat abdomen.

"Looks like you've been maintaining," Zane said.

"Yeah, I've got to, man. I've been getting creative with my restrictive bed-ridden workouts." Rudy popped his biceps.

"Well, that will help you achieve a speedy recovery." Zane looked at me and winked. I knew he would be slipping some of his blood to Rudy, but I didn't know how.

"Tara, you're looking kind of tired, babe. Perhaps you should give your brother a hug goodnight, and we can go get a good meal and find a place to crash." Zane motioned to Rudy with an eager nudge. A saline bag hung above Rudy's bed with a line that ran down to Rudy's I.V.

I faked a yawn. "You're right. Perhaps we should go so Rudy can rest." I leaned in to hug my brother and watched Zane pull a syringe from his jacket pocket. A small amount of dark red liquid ran through the line as Zane injected his vampire blood into the port where a nurse would typically inject medications. Rudy's head turned away as I hugged him for a long moment in distraction. "Love ya, Rudy."

"I know what you're doing."

I froze. *Shit! Did he know what Zane was doing?*

I took a calming breath. "And what am I doing?"

"You two are naughty little children, and I should tell on you. Ma didn't raise you that way." Rudy grinned.

I laughed nervously. "Like you're any better. And I don't care if you tell Mom. She'll probably throw me a party and congratulate me."

Zane chuckled. "Ready to go?"

"Already?" I asked.

"Yes. Rudy's good to go. Aren't you, brother?" Zane clapped Rudy's shoulder.

"Sure, I feel great right now. Tonight's great company and laughter boosted my endorphins. Seriously, you both go and have a nice time. My leg isn't hurting, so I'll be able to sleep well tonight."

"Okay. See ya later, Rudy."

Zane and I left the room and got in an elevator. I turned to Zane and threw my arms around him in a grateful hug. "Thank you."

He returned the hug. "No problem. Sis!"

"If that's how you feel about me, you need to reconsider the whole kissing me thing."

"Oh, that was just for show. But I could tell you liked it." Zane smiled devilishly.

I punched him in the arm. "Did not!"

"Whatever you want to tell yourself, Tara. My work here is through, and now we return to our regularly scheduled programming. Up next is the Dean Perrish Show. This has been your gracious host, Zane Perrish, signing off. Goodnight, lovebirds." Zane winked, and his silver eyes flashed before Dean's beautiful blues returned.

"Well, that was an interesting evening," Dean said.

"It sure was," I agreed. "Did you catch the whole show?"

"I did, and I assure you, I'm not upset, Tara. You did what you had to, just like you've made exceptions for Zane. I want to tell you how amazing you are."

"Even if it means kissing your brother?"

"As Zane told you earlier, there are necessary evils. Sometimes we have to take risks for the greater good. And I don't want you to make a scene with my brother and have your family confused about how we feel for each other. Zane won't push things too far. He can be a pain in the ass, but he respects you."

"Okay. But, I'd rather Zane switch it over to you regarding the kissing parts."

"I agree, but tonight I have to admit I'm proud of my brother. He's seeing the light, and you're the beacon who's guiding him."

"That's beautiful. Enough about Zane. I've been dying to kiss YOU all night."

"I'll gladly accommodate you, sweet little songbird." Dean wrapped his arms around my waist and leaned down to kiss me. Dean's kisses were my true bliss. I missed this feeling. My stomach growled loudly, and Dean broke our kiss with a chuckle. The elevator door opened, and he motioned with his head.

"Come on, little nightingale. Let's feed you."

Chapter 19
TARA

Dark Interpretations

Dean treated me to a nice dinner at a late-night diner nearby. We found a nice hotel room where Dean spoiled me in every delectable way with his talented body. Satisfied in every way a woman could be, I fell asleep to the happy memories of the day's events, safe in Dean's arms. Unfortunately, it wouldn't last as I fell into the darkest nightmare.

I lay strapped down in a stark padded cell as my mother watched me from a chair in the far corner. Zane entered the room with a metal tray, sat in a chair beside my bed, and placed the tray down within view. I saw a selection of metal syringes and something else. It looked like a finger-length ring with an intricately carved design.

It was lovely at first glance, but Zane picked it up and slid it on his forefinger. A razor-sharp claw extended from the end, and suddenly an object of beauty became something deadly and frightening.

"Time to check your blood again, Tara." Zane began toying with me as he moved his clawed finger down my arm, and suddenly fear came rushing in as I knew what he intended to do to me. I've dreamt of this moment before. Wait! No, I've lived this moment before.

"No, You're not Zane! You're Lyle! Stop hiding, you fucking coward!

Zane laughed wickedly. "Ah, such a brave little girl you are. I see you're coming into your power and beginning to understand. Still, I need your cooperation. So just relax, love. This won't take long."

I spit at the monster's face. "You're not getting anything from me anymore. You're dead, dipshit. How do you like them apples?"

"Keep telling yourself that lie. I know you know what I am. We're the same, you and me. Your dear mother may have put me out of commission for a while, but I'll be coming to collect what's mine soon."

The metallic claw on Zane's finger grazed my flesh as he skimmed it lightly down my arm. It was enough to create a scratch where my blood welled to the surface. My mother came to stand behind Zane's form, this wretched wolf in vampire clothing. She gave me a worried look. "You see it now, don't you? The demon I killed to save you?"

"I do, and I'm so sorry that I didn't believe you. They told me all those things to make me see you as delusional." I began to cry.

Mom reached past Zane and stroked my hair. "I don't blame you, baby girl. I'm here to help." She grabbed Zane's hair roughly in her fist and yanked his head back.

Zane laughed as his eyes shifted to hers. "What? Do you think you can do anything to stop me this time, Lydia? You were weak then, and you're even weaker now."

My mother ignored his taunt as she pointed to my arm. "Those scars on your arms. You never put them there. That was all HIM!" She pulled on Zane's hair in an abusive grip. "I found him trying to bleed you out, and I did what I had to do to save you. I shot the bastard in the heart."

Zane smiled. "You just put me on a time-out. I already had what I needed to recuperate, but I'm afraid that source is nearly tapped out, so I'll be coming back for your daughter."

"Like hell, you will!" Mother shouted. A blade flashed in her other hand. She yanked Zane's head backward with brutal force and slid the sharp edge across his throat in a deadly slow motion. Zane's eyes widened in shock as the gaping slice in his neck gushed like a red waterfall. Blood poured from his mouth, and I screamed as Zane's silver eyes flashed to Dean's blue.

Dean's mouth moved to speak, but all that came was, "Ta, Ta!" I realized he was trying to say my name. He fell forward, and his head landed on my arm.

"DEAN!" I screamed. "No, no!" I sobbed.

"Sacrifices have to be made, Tara." Mom stood over Dean's slumped form.

"No! Why?" I cried.

"It's a necessary evil!" She smiled at me like a dark angel, satisfied in her vengeance. My mother dropped the sharp, bloody blade with a thump as it hit the padded cell floor. She turned and walked to the door, which swung open on its own and passed through the threshold.

"Mom! Come back!" I cried and struggled against my restraints. Dean's blood flooded and soaked down my arm, and I heard the steady dripping as it continued to drain from his dead body and hit the floor.

"AHHH!" I screamed, pulled, and tugged. I was left alone in my fear and pain. Dean's head shifted, and I heard the sickening gurgle and spill as more blood rushed from his open wound.

"Please! This is a nightmare! Wake up!" I yelled at myself. I shook my head back and forth rapidly. "WAKE THE FUCK UP!"

My eyes popped open in the dark, and Dean was above me. He shook my arms, yelling, "Tara, wake up! Oh, thank God! Jesus! You scared the life out of me!"

I sat up, and Dean pulled me into his lap and wrapped his arms around me. I hugged him to me tightly. "You were dead," I cried.

"Shh, I've got you. I'm not going anywhere. You hear me?" I nodded as my tears dripped on his shoulder.

"Shit, that was a bad one," Dean said. I continued to cry, and snot began to drip from my nose. I pushed at Dean, but he just held me tighter. "Just blow it on me, baby. I can take it." I began to laugh, and Dean let me back away enough to look at me.

"Here. Blow." He held the shirt he'd taken off earlier to my nose. I did, and he tended to me till I gathered myself. "Do you want to talk about it?"

"I'm sure this confirmed that Lyle's ghost is haunting my nightmares, or he is a necromancer who wants my blood and intends to steal my power. He appeared as Zane, but he didn't fool me. He threatened to return soon before my mother cut his throat, then his eyes changed to yours and, and."

"Remember what I told you. We can't die that way. Our bodies have a way of playing possum until our powers kick in, and we reboot. Your nightmares are getting worse, which tells me one thing."

"What?"

"Whether it's Lyle or someone else, they are accessing your mind through a necromancer's blood, and it has to be someone related to you."

"My father. All my nightmares began after my father went missing. When Lyle showed up in my life, the nightmares stopped till after Lyle died. Lately, they've returned with a vengeance. And my dad appears, telling me to face my past and the monsters. I knew who the monster was hiding behind Zane's image in this one. And I told him to fuck off because he would get nothing from me."

"Lyle sounds like a coward to me. I think it's time we investigate where your dad told you to go. I'm going to make a phone call."

"Who?"

"We need something heavy-duty to make the job easier, and I just so happen to know a guy."

"Are you telling me we'll dig up Lyle's grave?"

"That's exactly what I'm saying."

"I can't say I'm thrilled about that, but I know it's unavoidable."

"Zane and I can do this. You don't have to go."

"No, Dean, I have to be there too. It's like my father said, I have to face this. I need to know how and why this is all happening. I need to do this because I know it's linked to my father's disappearance, and it's best to have more eyes on the situation."

"You're right. I shouldn't treat you like you're incapable of facing your fears. I want to protect you, but at the same time, I can't hold you back from your potential to grow stronger in this."

"There's someone else I want to see first."

"Who?"

"Abigail Hensley. I didn't tell her, but she knew I was having nightmares. She told me she was sensitive. I don't know why I feel this way, but I think she could help us."

"There is always a reason to trust your feelings. I knew I had to follow Martina, and it was to find you." Dean ran his hands down my arms and lifted my chin to look into my eyes. He kissed my lips with sweet, tender affection.

"It's only going on six a.m. You should try to rest some more. Lay down with me." Dean gently guided me back, and I laid my head on his chest and heard the two heartbeats.

"Dean? When should we do the injection of my blood to your heart?" I lifted my head to look at him and pressed my palm to his chest. I felt his heart pick up as he looked into my eyes.

"Soon. But only if you're ready. I don't want to rush you. Even though Zane has shown great improvement, it could only be temporary."

"Why do you say that?"

"Because it could be a residual effect from your blood when he bit you, which created a hiatus from his monster. Decades of battling Zane's vices still wreaked havoc on my powers. And with everything happening with you, we don't need him losing control at an inopportune moment."

"Okay. I'm ready. We could do it now."

"Are you sure? I meant it when I said no rush. It's a big deal for a necromancer to share their blood with another."

"Why are you so hesitant, Dean? I'm confident about this. You need my help. What gives?"

"There's something you should know, Tara. I told you we linked in every way aside from this one thing."

"Okay. Tell me. Why would this make you hesitant?"

"Because once you share your blood with me, there's a possibility I may become extremely physical with you."

"What do you mean by extremely physical?"

"I mean sexually. Extremely more so than how we've already been together."

"You don't think I can handle it?"

"I'm sure you can handle it, but we might want to wait and go somewhere more. Secluded." Dean emphasized.

"OH! Are you saying your monster will come out to play?" I chimed.

Dean smiled. "Things might get wilder than usual. Someone might call the police on us if we were to try it here."

"Okay! I understand your concern. But for now, perhaps we could do a little practice run. Without the blood transfer. Maybe you could give me a little taste of what may come."

"So, what I told you doesn't scare you?"

"No. I think I'm beginning to understand that I don't have to accept my fears. It took you showing me what I'm capable of to see that. I can't wait to see what else we'll be able to accomplish together." I leaned in and pressed my lips to Dean's, and he pulled me on top of him.

"You are an amazing woman!" Dean held me and we ended up in the throes of passion once more. We continued to kiss and run our hands all over one another for some time before fatigue hit me. Dean laid back and pulled me down to his side, where I finally drifted back to sleep.

When Dean woke me again, it was ten in the morning. We went to breakfast, and while I ate pancakes, I listened to Dean's phone call to a guy who'd be willing to help excavate Lyle's grave.

Dean finished the call. "George works at the cemetery, and he's done a few exhumations and knows the best time to take care of our situation. He usually works at the graveyard digging fresh graves so it won't throw any red flags. He can mock up a work order for us if anyone comes to ask."

"He won't get in trouble for doing that?"

"Graves reopen when a spouse passes, and they share a plot. They don't tend to open the coffins as we plan, so George will have everything prepped beforehand. He'll get us in when the time comes and supply what we need to finish the job."

"Wow. Do you have many friends in very low places?"

"High, low, and everywhere in between." Dean winked.

"Fair enough. I'll call Abigail and see if she's up for company." I pulled the letter from my jacket and dialed her number. It rang several times with no answer, so I tried again. "Hmm. She's not answering. Maybe we should go check on her."

"Perhaps give it one more try."

I redialed Abigail's number. I let it ring six times, and just as I was about to hang up, I heard a frail feminine voice. "Hello."

"Abigail! It's Tara. How are you?"

"Tara? Oh, I'm so glad you got my letter. I'm fine, honey. Are you okay? I've been concerned about you."

"I'm okay. I was wondering if I could come to see you? Last night, I visited my brother at the hospital, and I'm still in town."

"So, the young man I gave the letter to was your brother?"

"Yes." I smiled. "His name is Rudy."

"Oh, dear! What happened to him? I saw the cast on his leg. Was it serious?"

"Rudy broke it while scoring a touchdown during a football game a little over a week ago, but he's making a speedy recovery. Abigail, I want to apologize for not exchanging information to get in touch. My head wasn't in a good place the day we met."

"It's okay. I wasn't in the best frame of mind either."

"Yeah, but I feel bad because you made such an effort to find me."

"Oh, Tara. It's fine. My foot was bad, you see, and I was scared about the surgery I was to have because my heart wasn't so good. But after meeting you, I don't know what happened because a few days after we met, my foot got better all on its own, and the doctors let me go home. It's a miracle if you think about it."

"That sounds miraculous!" I looked at Dean. "So, my boyfriend, Dean, and I just had breakfast, and I'd love to bring you something to eat if you don't mind. We can be over within the next thirty minutes."

"You have a boyfriend? But, of course, a beautiful young woman like yourself does. What am I thinking? Please, do come. I could use the company. I'll take some eggs over easy and some toast if you don't mind, dear. I don't eat much, so please make it a senior plate."

"Okay. We'll see you soon."

"Okay. Bye for now."

"Bye." I hung up and met Dean's smile.

"Abigail sound's charming. She reminds me of my granny Ruth Perrish."

"She's wonderful," I agreed. "I'm going to place a to-go order for her."

We pulled up in front of a quaint little blue house with a well-tended front garden. Dean parked his motorcycle before a white trellis and a walkway that led to a cheerful yellow door. As we made our way up the path, I saw hummingbirds and butterflies visiting the beautiful little wonderland of colorful flowers.

I pushed the doorbell with Dean standing behind me, and we waited till I heard Abigail's voice sing. "I'm coming!" She opened the door and beamed at me. "Oh, Tara, honey, I'm so happy to see you. Come inside." She stood back and waved me in, and Dean followed. "Oh, well, aren't you a handsome devil? Dean? Did I get that right?"

Dean smiled. "You did, Miss Abigail. Thank you for inviting us into your lovely home."

"I do love visitors. Please, come and sit with me in the parlor." Abigail guided us into her living room with furnishings that looked like what I'd seen in Victorian-era movies. There were vases with fresh flowers on her coffee and end tables with fancy lace doilies beneath. A sheer yellow curtain billowed with the breeze from the open window, and I could hear the clinking of a wind chime outside.

"I can tell you dedicate much time and care to your garden. Were those Charlie brown orchids I saw near the trellis? Dean asked.

"Yes, they are. I love the deep velvet brown color. Not many people appreciate brown flowers, yet it's the first thing you notice. That says something special about you."

"What's that?" Dean asked.

"You're an old soul who sees past a glamorous façade and looks for true exquisiteness." Abigail gestured to me, and I smiled graciously.

Abigail wore a vintage dress that ended just below the knee in a wildly colorful floral pattern reminiscent of the 1960s. The vivid tones of the blue, orange, yellow, and brown flowers popped out beneath a white button-up sweater. She had on stockings and yellow slippers. Abigail wore curls in her short silver-white hair like she'd put the curlers in the night before but hadn't tousled it out.

I held the take-out container to Abigail. "Here's your breakfast. Two eggs over easy, and a side of toast."

"Thank you, Tara. You two sit down while I warm this up. Do you want a drink? I have water, juice, and tea," Abigail offered.

"No, thank you," Dean and I said together. Abigail nodded and walked through the entryway to the kitchen. Dean and I sat down on a cream floral sofa with carved dark wood legs as she worked on plating her food and putting it in the microwave. Dean held my hand and smiled at me.

"I can sense something about her," Dean whispered to me.

"I do too." The microwave beeped, and I listened as Abigail opened and closed the door. She shuffled back into the living room with a plate and a glass of tea, and she sat down in a wooden rocking chair across from us and began to eat.

"Mm, you went to Popinmaya's Café. My husband, Jerold, and I used to go there on Sunday mornings. I always loved their breakfast." Abigail continued to eat, and Dean squeezed my hand and looked at me. I nodded in understanding. Abigail gave off a vibe that felt like a sonic wave reverberating off my power.

"I remember you told me about your husband and son. Do you have any other family members nearby?" I asked.

"It's just Ginger Rogers and me. She's hiding around here somewhere. Probably under the bed. She doesn't take well to strangers, but give her time; she might poke her head out from the hallway out of curiosity."

"Ginger Rogers? Why would she hide under a bed?" I asked, and Dean laughed.

"She's my cat, dear. I named her after one of my favorite early Hollywood actresses," Abigail said.

"Oh!" I laughed. "Sorry, I'm a millennial child, and I don't have many references before the 1980s from what my parents and uncles have told me."

"Well, I don't get what young people usually talk about these days, so I think we're alike. Maybe we could teach each other. Swap tales from the past for current events."

"That sounds good. There are a few things I'd like to know about you, Abigail."

"What's that, dear? I've lived long enough and don't have any secrets I plan to take to the grave. So, ask away!"

"Well, when we met, you knew about my nightmares. You said you were sensitive. In what way?"

"My great aunt Merna was a psychic. Merna claimed she could see and talk to the dead. People paid her to perform seances, and I was her assistant. I'd prepare beverages and snacks and set the table with candles. Merna told me I was sensitive but not as attuned to spirits as I was with premonitions and interpreting dreams," Abigail explained.

"And you can sense when someone has nightmares?"

"Tara, there's something different about you. I felt it when I first saw you. There's something or someone attached to you from your past. They are trying to find you, and I feel like they are a threat."

I looked at Dean. Abigail's words felt like a confirmation. How else would she know about my experiences? I didn't do social media unless it was helping to promote for The Hillbilly Roost, which wasn't often as Woody did most of it. I also posted updates about my dad, and there wasn't any positive feedback. Some asshole commented I should stop beating a dead horse, but I told him off and blocked him.

"Is there anything else?" I asked.

"It's a man with dark energy. I feel like he was hiding something, and I say 'he was' because he's dead, isn't he?"

"Yes," I confirmed. "My stepfather. My mother killed him before he killed me."

"Oh, dear!" Abigail clutched a hand to her chest. "I'm so sorry, Tara."

"I think I suppressed many bad memories, and they're returning to haunt my nightmares."

"But, it's more than that. Isn't it? You're under attack, and I believe your stepfather is a vengeful spirit. He wants something from you, and it's inside you."

I didn't confirm or deny Abigail's words because I could see it in her eyes, and she knew the truth. "Is there anything I can do to combat these attacks?"

"Hold on a moment." Abigail got up from her chair and walked down a hallway before turning into a room. A few minutes later, she returned, holding something in her hand. She motioned for me to stand and took my hand. I felt an object in my palm, and when Abigail's hand moved away, I saw an old brooch. It was sizable, transparent glass in an oval millegrain pearl setting.

"Blood knows blood. Take this brooch to the source of your pain and stick it to the heart of the matter. The looking glass will reveal what you need to know." Abigail tapped the glass, which made the brooch shift, and I felt the sharp jab of the needle in my palm.

"Ow!" I lifted the pin to see a dot of my blood well up from my hand.

"Oh, heavens! I'm so sorry. Here!" Abigail pulled a tissue from a nearby box and pressed it to my hand. "I'm not as graceful as I used to be."

"It's alright, accidents...." Just before I said 'happen,' Abigail's breath hitched, and I followed her eyes as she looked at the brooch in my other hand. Dean stood and came close to see what I now saw. The glass turned from clear to red, and I could see my power as it sparked like micro-lightning bolts through a sea of reds, golds, and pink.

"I've only seen this once before. My aunt Merna told me of a man she knew who could raise the dead. She called him a necromancer and said his blood had this power with something she called a life spark. Tell me, Tara. Is that what you are?" Abigail asked.

"I only found out a few days ago," I admitted.

"And you!" She pointed accusingly at Dean. "You're one as well, but something more. Tell the truth. I can feel it."

"I am a necromancer, and my brother is a vampire. He lives inside me," Dean said.

"Fascinating! I've seen a lot in my years, but this is a new one. Oh, my heart hasn't beat like this in some time." Abigail's body began to wobble, and Dean took her arm and helped her sit back in her chair.

"Are you okay, Abigail?" I asked.

"Honey, I haven't felt this alive in so long. This explains so much! You see my foot; they would take half of it off, and I had a bad case of necrosis." Abigail slipped her foot out of her slipper and rolled down her stocking before pulling it off her foot. "See! You did that, when you touched my hand, I felt something, and a few days later, my foot was good as new. I didn't think meeting you was a coincidence."

I kneeled and gently placed my hand on Abigail's knee. "I don't think so either."

Chapter 20
DEAN

Cold & Calculated

We sat on the sofa, and Abigail's eyes shifted back and forth between Tara and me like she was trying to figure out which of us was the chicken and who was the egg.

"So, what do we do next?" Tara asked Abigail.

"I have never heard of such a pairing as the two of you. Necromancers tend to hide their nature from their human family members unless they pass the gene and it is triggered," Abigail explained.

"Triggered how?" Tara asked.

"They come close to an unnatural death from which they rise by their awakened power. Or, they meet another necromancer who triggers it. I take it Dean has shown you what you are?" Abigail nodded at Dean.

"Yes. I feel my power was present in my blood without my knowledge years ago. My stepfather was testing my blood under pretense. He claimed I had diabetes. He was a doctor and had a god complex," Tara explained.

"A doctor? What was his name?" Abigail asked.

"Lyle Durst."

"I knew him, and I used to be a patient of his years ago. I never liked the S.O.B."

Tara froze, and her eyes turned glassy. "What is it?" I asked.

Tara blinked and looked at me. "I remember, Dean. I'd sit in the waiting room at Lyle's office for Mom to get off work. I remember that's where I saw you before, Abigail." Tara turned to the older woman.

"The pretty blond nurse, Lydia, was her name. She was your mother?"

"Yes." Tara nodded.

"I liked her a lot. Dr. Durst, though, there was something fishy about him. Oh, my, I read in the newspaper about his murder! It's all coming back now. It was your mother, sweet Lydia, who shot him. And you said he was testing your blood? Oh, this is bad!"

Tara leaned forward. "Tell me, Abigail. What do you know?"

"I felt evil within Dr. Durst. He always insisted on blood work for me, even though I was in good health. He'd tell me about these clinical trials that I might qualify for but never explained. He may have been looking for the same thing in me that he knew about you, Tara. He was a dangerous man, and he may still be."

"That's what I'm coming to realize. Dean and I have plans to see if he's really dead."

"That's the source I was talking about. That monster is the source of your pain and nightmares. You must exhume his body and use the brooch on his remains. Stick the pin where his heart once was, and it will show you if he is the true cause."

"It will change as it did with my blood?"

"If Durst were like you, it would pick up the residual energy. You'll see a slight change in the glass."

Tara turned to me. "But, Dean, you told me our kind is only killed another by draining their power. My mother shot Lyle. So, what does that mean if his body is there?"

"I'm not sure. It's possible he wasn't a necromancer after all," I admitted.

"There is another possibility," Abigail said.

"What?" I asked.

"Durst was a host."

"You mean he was like my brother and me?" I asked.

"No, he was possessed by a demon."

"That's what my mom called Lyle! A demon!" Tara exclaimed.

"Do you remember what happened?" Abigail asked Tara.

"No. I woke up in the hospital with bandages on my arms and thigh. The police interrogated me, but I didn't remember anything. But, my nightmares! I had one where a shadow person came into my room and cut my lip and arm with a sharp metal claw. And in my last one, Zane wore a metal finger-length ring with a sharp claw. It's the same thing, isn't it?" Tara asked.

"I think you're on to something," I said.

"Who is Zane?" Abigail asked.

"My twin brother," I supplied. "He would never do that to Tara."

"He is a vampire and does not desire Tara's blood?" Abigail asked.

For some reason, Abigail's question made me pause. I looked at Tara and shook my head, hoping she would understand not to answer. Tara held her lips closed and awaited my answer.

"Zane and I have an understanding. He doesn't touch what's mine. I have total control over my brother," I lied.

"I see," Abigail said. "Your necromancer trumps the undead being inside you. Very interesting. Well, I've got to say this is very enlightening."

"Why do you say that?" I had this growing unease with the direction this conversation was turning. Tara had just met this woman and opened up to her in complete trust based on Abigail's sweet nature and ability to detect the supernatural.

History has taught me to always be on guard when people begin asking too many questions. They always wanted something in return, and I had a feeling Abigail was no different. Perhaps she was just being helpful. But something kept prodding at my brain. Abigail happened to share a tiny piece from Tara's past, and the coincidence didn't pass my notice.

Abigail played up to Tara in her distaste for Dr. Durst, but what if that were a ruse? Tara was naïve in her hope that Abigail's offer to help was some fated reconvening.

"I feel I have a sense of closure knowing the truth about Dr. Durst. I'm so glad Tara came out of her ordeal alive. She has a gift that has helped me, and I'm very grateful. I feel better knowing you have the power and strength to pursue what's happening with Tara now. I want you to know I'm here anytime you need me."

"Thank you, Abigail. You've helped me more than you know," Tara said.

"You're welcome, honey. I'm so glad you stopped by, but I'm afraid I will need an early nap after the excitement." Abigail yawned and got up to show us out.

"Is there a trash bin where I can toss this?" Tara held out the tissue she'd used to stop the bleeding on her hand. I interrupted before Abigail could respond.

"I'll take care of it." I took the tissue from Tara's hand and stepped aside to let her pass. As Tara followed Abigail to the door, I put the tissue in my zipper pocket to ensure it stayed put. There was no way I was leaving evidence of Tara's blood and power behind with this woman. Abigail knew too much already, and we barely knew enough about her.

Tara hugged Abigail. "Thank you so much. I'd like to come by again soon. I've got to get home and catch up on some school work, and I'll be at my job the rest of my week."

"The bustling life of youth. I'm glad those days are in the past. My garden is work, but I love it," Abigail said. "Where do you work?"

"At my uncle's bar, The Hill…."

"Tara, I'm sorry to interrupt, but we need to get going. I just got a text from George," I lied as I held up my phone with my screen toward me.

"Oh, okay. Well, I'll see you soon, Abigail," Tara said.

"Okay, dear. Be safe on the road." Abigail stood at the door and waved as we got on the bike. I started the loud engine, which must have been too much for sweet Abigail because she quickly turned to go inside.

I smiled as I gave the engine a few more revs before putting up the kickstand. Tara had her helmet on and arms wrapped around me, and we took off down the road.

When we returned to The Hillbilly Roost in the middle of the afternoon, Bren was outside the camper hanging bedding on a line. She saw us and waved.

Tara waved back. "Hey, Bren! How are you acclimating?"

"This camper smells like an only men's club. I've been washing and cleaning all day. How was your visit with Rudy?" Bren asked.

"We had fun," Tara said. "Now I have to go catch up on some schoolwork."

Bren looked at Tara, then me, and smiled. "I see! You should let Dean help you since he's likely the reason you've fallen behind."

Tara laughed. "Not a bad idea. I'll see you later."

Bren beamed. "Much later, I'm sure. Don't have too much fun."

Tara smiled, pulled me inside the cabin, and then closed the door. "You care to explain what happened back there?"

"Nothing. I stood by while you and Bren had a pleasant conversation, and Zane clawed at our brain while I struggled to hold him back from sweeping Bren up in his arms and running away," I explained.

"Oh, good grief! That's not what I'm talking about. I meant the whole lying to Abigail thing. What was that about?"

"I know you think you can trust her, but think about the coincidence of the past you share with Lyle. I think she wanted you to believe she hated him to build up trust. Abigail wants something from you."

"Why would Abigail be so helpful and give me this?" Tara pulled the brooch out of her pocket. "I don't think she would give me something so valuable to help if she was trying to deceive us."

"Can you be sure that object's use is what she told you? For all we know, you could stick that thing in Lyle's dead body and bring back the demon who wanted to finish what he started. It already has your blood inside, and we have no clue how to clear it out. That's your power and what's needed to bring the dead back to life."

"I don't feel like Abigail is a threat. What would she have to gain?"

"You cured her necrosis. She went above and beyond all efforts, a woman her age would to find you. I feel she wants something more, and she used the brooch to confirm what you are. Then she insisted you use it on Lyle's corpse. I don't trust the situation."

Tara's expression conveyed thoughts turning in her mind as she tried to come up with an argument against my explanation. "Perhaps that's what I need to do to finish him for good. Lyle continues to haunt my nightmares, and I don't know how else to make him go away. They're getting worse, and you told me a necromancer's nightmares bring us close to the veil between life and death. How many nightmares do I have left before what's in my head becomes a reality?"

"I can't say. But I agree this situation is becoming more dangerous. Lyle might be close to figuring out how to make your dreams affect some aspect of your life in the living realm."

"How is that even possible?"

"Humans have died in their sleep. Who's to say it wasn't due to an attack in their nightmares? We wouldn't necessarily die, but it could affect something or someone else."

"Okay, so perhaps it's like Abigail said. We need to go to the source, and I use the pin. And whether not Lyle wakes, we'll still have the advantage and come closer to figuring this out."

"We must be prepared for all the ways this could go wrong, Tara. We need to do more research on that brooch before using it."

"Fine. In the meantime, we should do the injection." Tara unzipped my jacket and fished around inside before she pulled out the syringes Zane lifted from the hospital. She took off her jacket and sat at the kitchen table. Tara uncapped one syringe and aimed the needle at her arm.

"Stop!" I took hold of her hand.

"What? We've been over this."

"I know. It's not that. We should wait till nightfall and go out in the woods. Our powers work best under the moonlight, and we should distance ourselves just in case."

"Oh, okay. As long as we can make more of it, something romantic." Tara suggested with a seductive purr.

I gently took the syringe from her hand. "You can count on it. I'm going to pack a picnic and bring some sleeping bags. And we'll need to bring this." I reached into my jacket, pulled out the blood bag, and went to put it inside the refrigerator. "Zane will need to feed before you stick me in my heart."

"Okay. Since we have a few hours till dark, I need to finish some school work."

"Anything I can help with?"

"I have to watch the video from the live feed I missed and some reading."

"Okay, I guess I'll research the brooch."

"You can see if Woody will let you use his computer in his office."

"Okay." I leaned in to kiss Tara. I thought I was stealthy as I slid my hand beneath her shirt, but she halted my attempt by grabbing my hand and shaking her head.

"Later, big boy."

I hung my head like a pouty child, and she splayed her hand across my face and shoved me back.

"This BIG BOY is going to punish you for that." I smiled wickedly and smacked one hand across another to demonstrate my spanking her ass.

"Well, best bring your A-game because this girl will play dirty."

"Keep talking like that, and I'll unleash my demon on you, woman!" All this talk had me turned on, and Tara looked at the bulge in my pants and laughed.

"You better get that under control before you see Woody. He might think you have a crush on him."

"Ha Ha!" I laughed. "Just for that, I'm going to take a nice relaxing hot shower without you." I started stripping as I walked to the bathroom. I bent over to pick up my pants in front of Tara, sticking out my ass in an exaggerated motion, just beyond her reach. Tara whistled, and I flashed her a full moon before opening the bathroom door. Tara launched from her chair, and I quickly made it inside, shutting the door as she stopped short of getting smacked in the face.

"Dammit, Dean!" Tara cursed. I laughed and made sure she heard the lock click and started the shower. I took off my boxer briefs and shoved them under the door. Moments later, Tara reciprocated by pushing her bra under the door.

"Dammit!" How could I pass up this opportunity?

I unlocked the door and opened it wide, ready to claim my prize. Tara stood before me, still dressed with her hands behind her back, and an evil smile stretched across her lips. "My mom taught me how to deal with men who like to play with fire."

I smiled, leaned my arm against the doorframe, and reveled in Tara's appreciative gaze at all my naked glory. "Oh yeah, and how is that?" I asked.

"This!" Tara looked up, and my eyes followed.

"Huh?" My eyes dropped, and Tara threw ice water from a pitcher she'd hidden behind her back.

"Ahh, holy, fuck!" I screamed. I jumped around frantically to get the cold sensation to ease.

Tara cupped her hand over her mouth and talked into it like she was speaking into a walkie-talkie. "Danger, man shrinking! I mean sinking!" She started cracking up.

"You're in so much trouble, woman!" I slipped as I reached out to grab Tara. She squealed and ran from me toward the bed but didn't make it far as I wrapped her in a bear hug from behind and lifted her off her feet. Tara wiggled and fought to get free, but I held on tight. She kicked her feet in the air as I carried her to the bathroom.

"Dean, no! I'm sorry. Please! Put me down!"

"Payback, baby!" I said and nibbled her ear.

Tara kicked her feet apart and landed on either side of the doorframe, preventing me from pushing her inside the bathroom. I backed away and tried again with the same result. Since that didn't work, I set Tara down, flipped, and lifted her over my shoulder. Tara smacked my bare ass with her hands while she squealed and screamed. "Dean! Put me down!"

I passed through the doorway much easier. Tara grabbed the sides, halting me, but it was to no avail as her grip slowly slipped, and I smiled triumphantly. "You want me to put you down? Okay, no problem." I dumped Tara, clothing, shoes, and all into the tub beneath the cold running spray and started laughing.

"Ahhh! Asshole!" Tara screamed. She tried to heave herself upright, but I held her down till she was thoroughly soaked. I heard the front entry door burst open and quickly grabbed the shower curtain to cover up. The squeaking of shoes sounded across the wet floor as Cannon, Danny, and Stella slid to a stop and pushed their way through the bathroom entrance.

I held my hands up in surrender, and the shower curtain slid away. Stella looked at me and was the first to laugh, and I put my hands down to cover my cold shrunken, and embarrassed member. Danny and Cannon looked at Tara in the tub. She looked like a drowned pup—a sexy, pissed-off one.

"In my defense, she attacked me first!" I exclaimed. Cannon and Danny burst out laughing.

"Looks like she tried to pull a Lydia and failed." Danny pointed out the melting ice cubes scattered about the floor.

Stella had her phone out recording the scene while she continued to laugh. "Things have gotten more entertaining around here since Martina and Dean showed up."

Tara moved to turn on the hot water and, after a moment, sighed in relief. "Hey! No fair!" I called. Tara stuck her tongue out at me, but I could do nothing with her uncles and aunt watching.

"Uh, as you can see, she's not hurt. My pride is, but Tara's fine," I said. Cannon laughed as he handed me a towel, and I wrapped it around my waist.

"I think we need to start keeping score," Danny said.

"And taking bets," Stella said.

Cannon looked at Stella with a smirk. "Come on, let's leave these two to their villainy." Cannon pointed. "And clean this mess up! Woody will have both your asses if there's water damage."

"On it," I replied. Cannon and Danny left the room. Stella lingered for a moment longer with a big smile.

"Don't be embarrassed, big boy. I know how a man's anatomy shrinks from the elements, and I can tell you're packing." Stella winked. She walked away, and I heard the front door close and the trio's continued laughter as they continued away from the cabin.

I helped Tara up and aided her in stripping off her wet clothing. She was naked, shivering, and still looking at me with a promise of retaliation. I turned up the hot water, dropped my towel, and stepped into the tub with her. I put her beneath the hot shower and wrapped my arms around her. She started shaking, and I thought she was crying. I felt terrible.

"Baby, I'm sorry." I felt Tara's head shake back and forth, and she pushed away from my shoulder to look at me. She was smiling and shaking with laughter. Her laughter rose in volume, and I laughed with her.

Tara stopped abruptly, and her face turned serious. "Oh, you're going to be sorry, Dean. Just you wait. I'm going to get you when you least expect it." She smiled wickedly and burst into laughter again. I nervously swallowed as I began to think Tara was cracking, so I attempted to appease her.

"Truce?" I looked into her brown eyes and gulped when she shook her head. "Shit. I'm in serious trouble, aren't I?"

Tara nodded with a sly grin. "In the meantime, I'm going to be so good to you; you'll forget all about it." Tara shoved me back a few steps and dropped to her knees. She took me into her mouth, then slowly pulled back with the wet slide of her sweet lips. I hissed and sucked air in between my clenched teeth. I looked down, and Tara looked up with smiling eyes as she continued to caress me with her hands, lips, and tongue.

"Ooh, yeah, baby! You're full of surprises!" Tara drew me further, and my hands smacked at the wall and fisted the curtain. This beautiful doe-eyed seductress had me under her spell as I fought to hold back.

"Mmm-hmm," Tara hummed. She continued her oh-so-good merciless assault. She took me deeper and worked me into a frenzy. My hands took hold of her damp locks as I thrust my hips; I felt her moan in encouragement as she matched my pace.

"Ahh, Tara! I'm gonna…." I tried to pull back.

Tara's inhibitions were long gone. She grabbed my ass and dug her nails into my flesh in a ruthless grip. I lost control, and she hummed and moaned as she took every part of me. My legs quaked, and I groaned with the intensity of my release.

This woman would be my completion and undoing. Tara swallowed and then slid away with a pop of her lips. She smiled at me, batted her eyelashes, and stood. I became confused as fuck after Tara kissed my lips and turned away like she hadn't just given me the best blowjob of my life.

She washed her hair and then moved on to her body. She rubbed a soapy washcloth across her pert breasts with a seductive tease and worked her way down. I reached out, wanting to take over, but she turned away. "Nope."

"But, I…."

"I'm good, Dean."

"Tara, I…."

"We're all good here, baby." Tara patted my cheek, turned off the shower, and grabbed a towel. She wrapped her body and stepped out. I stood there, shrinking again, and began to shiver.

Suddenly, I heard Zane's laughter in my head.

"Fuck you!"

Tara whipped around. "What was that?"

"Not you."

"Oh. Hello, Zane. Enjoy the show, you perv?" Tara asked.

"Beat it, Zane," I yelled.

Zane was cracking up. *That was too good. I think I'm in love!*

"No, you're not, you sick bastard. You're not supposed to be spying, and you're breaking the rules," I yelled.

Chill out, Dean. I only caught the end.

"And that was more than enough, asshole!" I shouted.

"When do I get to have some fun? Huh, brother? It's not fair; you're getting all the action," Zane yelled.

"We haven't discounted your needs. I thought you wanted this for Tara and me. We've only just begun, and I know how you feel about Bren. We've got to figure out Tara's situation." I argued.

"I know, but the more time you spend with Tara alone, and I have to make scarce, the more I feel isolated and lonely."

"Awe, hell!" Tara stood in the doorway, fully clothed. "I'm so sorry, Zane. I didn't realize. Dean and I should be considering your feelings. I wish there were a better way to make this work. I can't believe I'm saying this, but I'll talk to Bren."

"You would do that for me?" Zane asked.

"Everyone deserves a chance at happiness and love. Even cocky, annoying bloodsuckers," Tara said.

Zane stepped out of the tub, our body still wet and naked, and walked to Tara with arms wide open. He wrapped Tara up in a hug. "You're an amazing woman, Tara. I couldn't have asked for a better sister."

Tara patted our back. "You should dry off. You're getting me all wet."

"Dean, your woman, is hitting on me again."

"Very funny, pervert. Now go cover your and Dean's fine ass."

Zane turned his head to look at our backside. "It is a fine ass, isn't it? You and Dean can thank me for that because I do most of the running."

"Okay, I'll be nice for once and let you have that one," I said.

Tara shook her head. "This is so confusing. I'm going back to my school work, and you two can take this conversation elsewhere."

"We're still on for our date tonight?" I asked.

"You bet your fine hiney we are," Tara replied.

Chapter 21
TARA

The Dead Move Swiftly

I pondered the drastic turn of events in my life since Dean and Zane showed up a week ago. Finding out I had this supernatural identity made me second guess what I wanted to do with my existence. I finished my schoolwork for the week in the hours Dean had gone to see Woody. What I thought I wanted seems so inconsequential now. Would my life ever fit in the normal category? I highly doubted it.

Dean returned and set the brooch down on the table. "How's your schoolwork going?"

"I'm ahead for the week, so one less worry. What did you find on the brooch?"

"There wasn't any information on the internet. But Woody had something to say when he saw it."

"Really?"

"Yes. It's a Raybrook family heirloom that went missing about eight years ago. Woody said the brooch dated back before the Revolutionary War and belonged to a great-great-grandmother named Camilla Raybrook. Your father was the first male heir to receive it."

"What? How did it end up in Abigail's possession?"

"After your parents married, your father gave it to your mother, and Woody believes Lyle stole it. Lyle might have given it to Abigail for safekeeping. If Lyle knew what the brooch does and told Abigail, that doesn't make Abigail trustworthy."

"Why would you say that?"

"Why would Abigail know about your nightmares, return the brooch, and insist you use it on Lyle's corpse? We can't be sure whether or not it's a means to bring him back. It could be Lyle's backup plan if something happened to him," Dean insisted.

Once again, I found myself asking that dreaded question. Why? Why would Abigail do this? What were her motives? Was she trying to catch me in a trap of Lyle's making? Maybe Dean was right. *Trust your instincts, Tara.* But then Abigail said the same thing to me.

"Did Woody know anything about Abigail?"

"No, he didn't. But Woody thinks it's a good omen that the brooch made its way back to you."

"A good omen? If my nightmares are any indication, good isn't the word I'd choose."

"Woody said it must mean something special about you because supposedly, the women in your family who possessed it lived long lives. Woody called them felines because of the whole nine-lives reference. There's a history of survival and close calls from what should have been fatal incidents. Does that sound familiar to you?"

"You mean they were necromancers?"

"You won the genetic lottery, Tara."

"Along with the maniac trying to drain me to death for my powers. Yay, me!"

"He won't get a chance to do that."

"Well, he came pretty damn close to it."

Dean huffed in frustration. He couldn't argue that truth, but together, we had a better chance of me surviving what may come next. I pray.

"Maybe we could check historical records at the library. Hopefully, we can find something helpful," I suggested.

"Yes. We can do that tomorrow. I have everything ready for tonight. I just need to grab Zane's snack pack." Dean went to the refrigeration and pulled out the blood. "I found a great spot on the other side of the lake where we won't be disturbed. Zane did a check of the area for any potential risks. I just need to give him a moment to take care of his needs before the injection."

"Okay. Should I wait here?"

"No. We can head out if you're ready."

I took Dean's hand, and we headed out the door. I was feeling a little nervous as we walked through the dark forest. I was ready before, but the more I thought about it, the anticipation of what I was about to do to Dean made me slightly anxious. What if I missed the mark and hurt Zane? What if I damaged Dean's heart? What if my blood had an adverse effect on Dean? What if it did nothing to help?

Dean picked up on my nervousness and gave my hand a reassuring squeeze. How could he know how or if this would work? He'd never done this before and only knew about others who shared blood.

The moonlight shone along the path before us, and we followed it around the lake and into a densely covered area, where we passed through some brush before coming to a small clearing. Two sleeping bags rolled out atop a blanket with a picnic basket. An electric lantern brightened the area with a few lit candles, and a romantic melody played from an old cd player. Dean had even stretched and draped a large bug net across and down the bushes surrounding our cozy little love nest so we could look up at the sky and not be disturbed.

"This is perfect, Dean. You thought of everything."

"Have a seat, little songbird." Dean held my hands, and I lowered myself atop the sleeping bag. He sat opposite me, popped a bottle of strawberry wine, poured two glasses, and handed one to me. "A toast to magic and romance."

We clinked glasses, and I took a sip. The wine accented the taste of the strawberries that Dean fed to me. "Mmm, this is good. But maybe I shouldn't indulge too much before, well, you know." Yeah, because stabbing someone you love with a large needle in the heart required a clear head. I was already shaking at the thought. Maybe I wasn't as ready as I thought, but I knew I had to do this for us.

"I promise it will be okay. I'll guide your hands, and it will be over before you have second thoughts. Just try to relax. Have some more to eat." Dean pulled out a thermos and poured a steaming au jus into the cup before unwrapping a French bread with melted cheese. He broke off a piece and dipped it before holding it to my mouth, and my taste buds savored the combined flavors.

"Mmm, were you a chef in France? This is amazing!" I broke off more of the cheesy goodness, dipped it in the au jus, and slurped at the dark brothy goodness that had run down my fingers. Dean looked disappointed, and I stopped mid-finger slurp, puzzled by his reaction. "What? Am I doing something wrong?" I know this isn't very ladylike, but I guess I never fully understood the concept of table manners."

"First of all, this is a picnic, and I could care less about table manners. Second, yes, there is one thing wrong with what you are doing!" He took my hand and guided it to his mouth, where he singled out my wet forefinger and sucked and licked it. I laughed as he continued to clean all my fingers this way. Dean nibbled on the pads of my fingertips which tickled, and I struggled to pull my hands free. He had a firm hold and didn't let go, and when he hit the pad on my ring finger with his lower teeth, I screamed with laughter. The nip of Dean's teeth sent a tingling sensation down to my core. Who knew fingertips were an erogenous zone?

"Mmm, I love the taste of ladyfingers dipped in au jus; Tara fingers are the best." Dean continued to torment me, and I was begging him to stop. A big smile graced his handsome face, and he kissed each of my fingers before letting go. Dean dipped a piece of bread and ate it. He offered me another, and I looked at him skeptically.

"I've had my fill for now." Dean waggled his eyebrows. I snatched the offering from him, popped it in my mouth, and then grabbed a napkin to wipe my hands. Dean laughed at me and stood up. He walked to the netting and lifted it.

"Where are you going?"

"Zane needs to feed." Dean held up the blood bag and shook it. "I prefer he doesn't do it in front of you."

"Dean, how am I ever supposed to get used to the fact that it's a part of our lives if I never witness it? I already saw him feed on the deer. Not to mention he also bit me."

"You're right." Dean sat across from me. His eyes flashed to Zane's silver, and Zane smiled at me.

"You always have to bring that up, don't you?" Zane asked.

"Just making a point. I'm feeling kind of nervous," I responded.

"About this?" Zane held up the blood.

"No. About the other thing. You know." I pointed at his chest.

Zane's brow arched. "Honestly, I'm a little nervous about it too."

"You are?"

"Yes, but I know it's necessary. Dean was right. I can feel the bloodlust growing again. Do you mind?" Zane shook the blood bag.

"Go ahead. I need to see and accept this as part of who you are."

"What I am," Zane corrected. He bit the tube, spit out the piece, then brought it between his lips and sucked. I watched as the bag drained in seconds, and Zane squeezed it to get the most he could.

"That was…." I started.

"Unremarkable," Zane finished.

"No. It was like watching a kid crush a juice pouch," I joked.

Zane chuckled. "I've heard such a comparison before. I think you called me a toddler in need of one."

I laughed. "Yeah, those things are too small to quench an adult. I suppose the same applies to the juice pouch you just finished."

"True. But it will hold me for the night."

"Zane, I want you to know I appreciate what you're doing for Dean and me. I don't want you to feel alone in all this. I know you've been helping more than you let on, and I want to thank you."

"You're welcome, Tara. Meeting you, this is the first time I've been considerate of my brother's needs, and you've helped me see that. Dean has always taken care of me. Of course, he has no choice since I live inside our body. It's time I do my part, and I want to thank you for helping him as well."

"I'm trying to conquer my fears and face my monsters. My father told me there would be those I could trust and help, but I think he was wrong about one thing."

"What's that?"

"I don't think you're a monster. If you'd never come across that vampire who did this to you, you would never have done what you needed to survive. And that's all we are trying to do here."

"I've done some bad things, and if you only knew, you wouldn't say that."

"Okay. But I have yet to find out what terrible things I may be capable of or have to do. So, tell me. Will it make me a horrible person, turn me into a monster?"

"Honestly, I don't know. Dean has faced these hardships and referred to himself as one, but I think it may be different for you." Zane's silver eyes stared at me intently, and I averted my gaze.

"Maybe. I do have your combined experiences to teach me how to deal. Have you and Dean faced adversaries such as Lyle before?"

"Dean and I have had a few enemies, but mostly we've fought men who were only doing what their countries expected. They were just regular people with families back home, praying for their safe return. For Dean, it was a matter of patriotism, but I murdered them for nothing other than their blood. I didn't think about it because my monster's bloodlust was satisfied, but I've had to deal with the nightmares in later years. Those nightmares still plague me and make me hate what I am."

I placed my hand on Zane's. "I'm so sorry."

Zane had a faraway look. "Sometimes I wish…." He stopped and pulled his hand from mine.

"What?"

Zane huffed out a breath. "Tara, sometimes I wish I could die and leave Dean's body so he can have a normal, well, as close to normal as possible life."

"Zane, no. Why would you say or even think that? Dean loves you, and he told me about how he grieved after that vampire bit you."

"I know. That's one thing I can say I've never done."

"What?"

"Yes, I've bitten thousands of people and killed hundreds in the wars, but I've never turned anyone."

"So, you mostly take what you need and compel them to forget?"

"Yeah, mostly. Do you mind if I do a quick run to lose some of these jitters? I promise I won't be gone for more than five minutes."

"I'll be here. I'm going to eat a little more and try some deep breathing to help." I placed my hand on my chest and took a shaky breath. Zane nodded, then he got up and lifted the net. He gave me one last look, then took off in a blink. I sat alone, listening to the music and the crickets chirping in the trees. I watched the moon hang in the night sky; it, too a witness to my intentions. I kept trying to convince myself this was right; I felt I needed a sign.

My father told me I'd have to help the one he sent, though he never said how. Dean filled in that piece of information, and I trusted him. Even though blood sharing occurred before among necromancers, it never happened to someone like Dean and Zane. Zane had a horrible reaction; who's to say my blood won't hurt Dean?

I heard a snap in the distance and turned my head in that direction. "Zane, is that you?" I stood up and looked into the trees. A shadow of a head peeked out several yards away, and I knew it was the shadow creature. I didn't leave the confines of the net, but I moved slowly in the creature's direction. It stepped out from hiding and moved toward me cautiously. I looked around to see if anyone else were nearby. I didn't want it frightened off like last time.

"My father told me not to be afraid of you. Who are you?"

The tall figure of a man rose, and it came closer, seeming as though it were curious. It stopped several feet before me and raised its hand in greeting. I felt like the cowgirl meeting the Indian in one of the stories Dad used to tell me about the old west.

"Hello, I'm Tara." I raised my hand in the same gesture. The shadow moved closer. I didn't feel afraid or threatened, and I wanted to reach out and make physical contact. Somehow, I knew this creature needed to tell me something. Its hand came closer as it took several more steps toward me. I moved closer and pressed my hand to the net.

"You won't hurt me, will you?" The shadow shook its head, and something in my heart told me to push forward. I pressed the net to stretch outward as the shadow's hand came closer and closer till its palm was mere inches before mine. I could feel energy like my own, and I saw the zapping charges and heard the crackling sound they produced.

I looked up at the face, dark and void of features. It was like looking at a blank television screen, a smoky haze like I could pass through it with my physical form. It felt cold, like a ghost despite the charges that passed back and forth.

"Do I know you?" I felt like I had the first night in the woods with Uncle Cannon. It was the same kinship I felt now in this shadow creature's presence. My heart slowed, and I felt serene. The shadow's head nodded at me, and I smiled.

"Are you able to speak?" Again, it shook its head. Its shoulders slumped as if disappointed, and I felt its sadness. I decide a game of twenty questions might help me figure out the creature's identity.

"Are you, or were you a person?" It nodded enthusiastically.

"Am I the person you've been looking for?" Head nod.

"Did my father send you?" Head nod.

"Do you know where he is?" It shrugged its shoulders.

"How could he have sent you, and you don't know where he is?" Shrug. Head shake.

"Do you jump back and forth between him and this place, and you can't remember?" Nod.

"Do you have a physical form other than this and the animal I've seen?" Nod.

"Are you able to go back to your physical form?" Nod.

"Are you able to animate your physical form? Head shake.

"No. So you're kind of stuck?" Nod.

"Where is your physical form?" It held its hands up and shrugged again.

"How can I help? I don't know what to do." It began miming. It pointed to its palm, then mine, like it wanted me to hold something. Then it poked at its chest and back at my hand. I thought about how I was to inject Dean in the heart with my blood. Did the shadow mean I needed to do the same to it?

"My blood?" It nodded and pointed back and forth between itself and me repeatedly. It motioned again to its cupped hand holding something, then back to its heart, trying to make me understand. My eyes widened as realization struck me. The brooch! I'd left it back at the cabin.

"The glass brooch!" It nodded enthusiastically. It motioned as if it held the brooch up to its chest and made a thumping motion.

"I need to use it on you, your heart?" It nodded again.

"Wait. How did you end up this way?"

It pointed to the sky and motioned as if playing the guitar. It put up its fists and punched out as if fighting against someone. Then, it pointed to me and held its arms like rocking a baby before patting its chest in ownership.

My breathing halted as my mind flashed back to that night when Dad and I sat out under the stars as he played guitar and sang to me. The image of his pocket knife covered with blood flashed before me, and I realized Dad must have put up a fight against someone before he went missing. The part of my nightmare replayed where my dad told me that he was in limbo.

"Dad?" A tear rolled down my cheek, and he reached out to capture it, but all I felt was a cold static sensation against my cheek.

"Who did this to you?" He shrugged again and shook his head.

"Are you like me? A necromancer?" He nodded. He motioned the word 'sorry' in sign language.

"It's okay, Dad. You sent Dean to help." He nodded again.

"Did you know about his twin, Zane?" He nodded.

Help him, Dad signed. The confirmation blew my mind because this was the sign I needed. There was a snapping of branches, and my father's shadow shifted to the four-legged creature. He took off so fast that I still could not make out distinguishable characteristics, which frustrated me.

"Come back," I yelled. I turned and screamed as Zane stood before me. I hadn't noticed his approach.

"Shit! Zane, could you not do that?" I yelled.

"I heard you talking to someone. Where did they go?" He looked around.

"It was…" Zane didn't wait for me to answer as he zipped away in the direction my father's shadow animal ran. Less than a minute later, Zane returned.

"What was that thing? In the distance, I made out a form that looked like a strange four-legged creature. It was so fast; even I couldn't catch up to it."

"That shadow creature was my father," I cried, "You scared him away!"

"Your father? You're certain?"

"Yes! It's my father's shadow form. His body must be in stasis, and his spirit is in limbo between life and death! I don't know how long he's been this way, and I'm scared, Zane." I dropped to my knees and sobbed. Zane joined me on the ground and wrapped me in his arms.

"Shh, Tara. Your father is alive, and we'll find him. What did he tell you?"

I sniffed and rubbed my nose on a napkin. "Dad couldn't speak in that form, but he showed me what I needed to do. I need to go back to the cabin and get the brooch."

"Okay, but what about Dean? Didn't you say your father wanted you to help him?"

"He did, and we need to take care of that now."

Zane nodded, and his eyes flashed. Dean stood before me and stroked my cheek with his hand, and my nervous jitters re-emerged as I looked into his blue eyes.

"Tara. I need you to focus, okay?" He took off his shirt and pulled a marker from the back pocket of his jeans. He made a circle on his chest over his heart, then took my hand and guided me to sit before him. He pulled out a syringe from a bag, then took out an alcohol wipe and swabbed the crook of my arm.

He looked me in my eyes and asked, "You're certain?"

I nodded, but my hands were shaking because I'd found my dad's spirit, and he'd been watching me for who knows how long now. He'd gone missing ten years ago.

Had he been alive for a while before this happened to him? How does a necromancer become the shadow creature my father is now?

"I'm ready." I held out my arm.

"Okay, Tara. You have to be willing to release your power as I draw your blood. Otherwise, this will hurt."

"You didn't tell me there would be pain involved."

"Just relax and breathe. I'll be gentle."

I sucked air into my lungs and breathed out. I willed my power to flow, giving it permission to be released. Dean positioned the syringe, and I felt the pinch of the needle go into my vein. He drew out the tiniest amount and held the syringe before me. I saw a pinpoint of light bobbing around within my blood.

"That's all?"

"Yes. We have to do this slow and easy. I'll be okay, but this is for Zane's sake." Dean laid down on his back and looked up at me. My hands still shook as I observed the syringe in my hold.

"You can do this. It might help if you straddle my hips. You'll have a direct and steadier aim in that position."

"Okay." I made my way to climb over Dean when he halted me.

"What?"

"Recap the syringe till you're in position," Dean instructed.

"Oh." I put the cap on and straddled Dean's hips. He put his hands on my thighs and looked up at me with his baby blues. When I didn't move, Dean took my hand with the syringe and guided it to the spot he'd marked without looking. He pulled the cap and held my shaking hand steady.

"I can do it myself if you need me to."

"No, Dean. We're in this together. I just need a moment."

"Okay. You have to give it a swift jab right here whenever you're ready." He pointed to the middle of the circle.

"Okay. I can do this!" I breathed. I held the needle a few inches above the mark and looked at Dean's eyes again with my hand still shaking.

"I have faith in you, Tara. As soon as you do it, you'll wonder why you were so nervous. Eyes here." Dean pointed to the middle of the circle again.

"Yeah. Okay. On the count of three. One, two, three!" I jabbed the needle into Dean's chest, and he grunted. I pushed the plunger, and Dean's lungs pulled in a fierce breath as his back arched drastically, and I leaned forward, taking grip of his shoulders to keep myself from landing atop the syringe still buried in his chest. When his body dropped back down, I pulled the needle out and pressed a napkin to the spot, and I could feel his heart pick up speed.

My eyes widened as I saw Dean's eyes illuminate with a brilliant glow, and his breaths turned frantic. His hands gripped my thighs, and his fingers bit into me. I bit my lips and grimaced at the tender pain, but his breathing began to calm, and his hands slackened. I felt his heart return to a normal rhythm as Dean snapped out of his trance.

"That was intense! Are you okay?"

Dean nodded but then looked at me like he wanted to devour me. He sat up, wrapped his arms around me, pulled me in tight, and kissed me like a man diving into a desert oasis. His tongue parted my lips and thrust into my mouth.

The way Dean's tongue swirled around mine was so combative it lit me up like a scorching white flame, and my core began to pulse with desperate need. His hard length rubbed against me, and I threw the syringe to the side and ran my fingers into his silky blonde hair.

He broke the kiss long enough to pull my shirt over my head, then crashed his lips back to mine as he pulled down my bra straps and cups to free my breasts. He quickly undid my jeans and pulled them off. Then he pulled his jeans down just enough to free himself before pushing me back, and parting my legs.

Dean's first thrust hit me like a surge, and he began to move his body with relentless urgency. I moaned, and Dean moved faster. Sweat dripped from his hair and down between our bodies as he continued to take me like he'd gone mad with passion. A cool breeze hit my flesh, but it couldn't touch the inferno Dean stirred up inside me. I cried out as my orgasm hit like lightning and sizzled throughout my body.

"DEAN! OH! OH!" I held him tight as he moved faster, panting heavily out of control. Dean looked possessed like a sex-starved demon had taken him over. His eyes glowed, and I thought he was about to suck the life out of me like a rabid and crazed incubus. He wouldn't stop, and I thought I would die from the intense pleasure rippling through me and the demand he was putting my body through.

I continued to cry, moan and sob. My body felt on fire, and I wanted to burn with Dean and melt away from the world around us. I orgasmed again, and my power burst out in a wave, causing an enormous wind gust that shook the trees and sent debris flying in a torrent. Thunder boomed, and lightning flashed above. Dark clouds rolled in from nowhere, and the moon disappeared.

Heavy rain poured, and I used every ounce of my will to hold on for dear life. I came again, knowing I had just died and gone to heaven. I screamed Dean's name and pleaded to him, but he'd become a mindless monster incapable of holding back. Thunder crashed, and lightning struck a tree in the distance. Our bodies became drenched.

"Dean, Dean. Oh, Dean, PLEEEEASE!" I cried and convulsed with my next orgasm.

Oh, God, help me! I prayed.

Finally, Dean cried out, and I could see his neck muscles strain as he came so hard that his hot semen gushed against my cervix and immediately ran back down my channel. He throbbed inside me, and the thundering pulse matched his heartbeat as his body slowed and quaked. My legs trembled, and Dean ran a hand down my side and hooked my leg, lifting it slightly and slowly rolling his hips. I was panting strenuously, and my heart galloped furiously against my ribs.

Dean kissed my bruised lips. "Mmm. I'm never going to get enough of you, Tara."

My voice was hoarse and shaky. "You're going to kill me."

Dean laughed and kissed me tenderly as he continued to move in and out slowly. "I doubt that, my love."

"Did my blood do that to you?"

"Mmm-hmm. I've never felt power so intense. Mine doesn't even compare to what you have running through your veins. It's a good thing we didn't put any more in me. I lost control and thought my heart would burst if I didn't take you."

"Your eyes glowed. Have they ever done that before?"

Dean stopped moving, and my body was still feverish. I was thankful for the cooling rain, but it slowed to a drizzle. I looked at our surroundings, and there was no way we could salvage what was left. And there wasn't much as my power had blown everything to smithereens.

"No, they've never glowed before. That is all you. You light me up hotter than a million Roman candles."

"I don't think I'll be able to walk for at least a week."

Dean laughed. "Was I too much for you? I can't say I'm sorry. Your power is an adrenalin junkie's wet dream."

I laughed. "I don't think there's another supernatural being out there who could have come close to annihilating me as you just did. I'm going to need an ice pack, strike that, an ice bath whenever we're able to move. I feel like you incinerated my body. Am I a pile of talking ash?"

My arms and legs were completely limp and useless. All I could feel were the slow ebbing waves of pleasure that continued to roll through my body. "I don't feel powerful right now. I don't think I can make it back to the cabin."

"I'll take care of you." Even though he was still rock solid, Dean reluctantly pulled out from my body. He helped me dress in my soaked clothing; the wet denim was challenging. Dean carried me piggyback. It was harder to see our surroundings as dark clouds loomed.

We approached the cabin, and I saw the lights inside the camper where Bren was staying. I needed to talk to her, but it was another thing on my growing to-do list, and I was too wiped out. Dean stripped me of my wet clothes, laid me in bed, and pulled the piled-up quilts to my chin. He undressed and climbed in beside me.

Bliss! Sweet and divine bliss was what I felt in Dean's arms. My body finally cooled, and I felt relaxed and ready to drift off.

Chapter 22
TARA

Deception and Revelation

My phone rang. Who would dare to interrupt my rare heavenly peace? "Ahh, nooo!" I groaned in irritation.

"Just let it go to voice mail." Dean hugged me tighter and breathed in the scent of earth and rain, which clung to my damp hair. The ringing stopped, and I sighed. My mind drifted into the deep recesses of my subconscious, and a weight lifted.

It was dark, so dark I couldn't see my hands as I reached out before me and searched for something to guide my steps. They glided along something smooth and pliable, and a gentle billowing breeze tickled my feet. I dragged my fingers down flowing satin, and I pushed forward. The fabric parted, and I stepped through.

My feet stood in something thick and wet. I continued to move till the surface became dry, but as I lifted my feet one by one, the substance felt tacky, and I heard the sticky peel. As I left prints behind from whatever covered my feet, my stomach clenched as I tried to convince myself I stepped in sugary syrup.

I heard a woman's scream and ran blindly in that direction. I had to help her. My arms moved through nothing but cold air. I held my breath and listened, but my heart was pounding in my ears. *Concentrate Tara!* I squeezed my eyes closed tight and slowed my breathing till my heart calmed, and I listened with earnest intent.

I heard a tapping that sounded like a metronome and let it guide me. I knew I was getting closer to it as the sound increased, and after a few more steps, it suddenly stopped. Someone whimpered.

"Help me," a female voice croaked. It sounded from my right, low to the ground, and I got down on my knees and crawled. My hands swept the floor from side to side, searching.

"I'm here to help you," I whispered. My palm smacked at the same thick wet substance I felt on my feet, and it splattered onto my face and mouth. I froze when I tasted and confirmed what my mind wanted to deny. Blood!

Why???

I spat and struggled to hold back the bile rising in my throat. My hands and knees submerged in a puddle, and the acrid metallic smell hit my nose.

"Oh, God!" I retched. *How in the hell did I get into this situation?*

"P-please, help me, Tara!"

I recognized that voice! "Gina! I'm almost there! Hang on!" I pushed myself faster with my hands slipping and searching. I slid, and my whole body splayed and landed in the pool of blood.

I struggled back to my hands and knees and continued to slip and slide. My hair stuck to my face, and my clothes pressed to my body. I vomited, and my hand slapped down on it.

"Fuck!" *Could this get any worse?*

"Tara," Gina called weakly.

I started crying. *Where was she?*

When I thought I'd never make it to her, a hand caught around my wrist, and I grabbed hold and slid onto my knees to pull myself to her. At least I hoped it was Gina, and I prayed I wasn't too late.

Wait! I am a necromancer! It is not too late! I can save her!

I felt her hair and moved along it till my hand pressed the top of Gina's head. "Gina! I'm so sorry. I wanted to tell you I've forgiven you. Don't die!"

Her body was so cold. Gina pulled my hand to her lips and kissed it. "It's alright, Tara. I know. I love you." Gina's breaths became shallow.

"Oh, God, no! Gina. I'm going to save you, okay? Do you hear me?"

"I 'h don ma-her an-mor," Gina slurred.

"It does matter! You matter to me! Don't give up!" I felt along her chest and went to press down, only my hands sunk through an open hole, and I screamed. "Holy! Oh, dear lord! Where's your heart?" There was an empty cavity where her heart should be. How was she still alive and talking to me?

"Gina!" I yelled.

She didn't respond.

"Gina?" I sobbed as I felt for her face, and my hand went to her mouth and nose. She was no longer breathing. What was I supposed to do? Gina's heart was gone. How do I fix this?

"DEAN!" I screamed.

I reached across Gina's body, searching for something, but I didn't know what till my hand landed on something that felt like a cold chunk of meat. That's when I realized I'd found Gina's heart. I picked it up carefully with both hands and leaned back on my knees. I grazed Gina's chest with the back of my cupped hands and found the hole. I couldn't tell how I was supposed to place her heart back inside her body, so I tried to feel for the aorta with my fingers. I remembered in grade school the 3D puzzled of the heart in science class, but this was nothing like it.

When my finger dipped into what felt like a spongy tube, I held it there and turned her heart until it felt correct before gently placing it into Gina's chest cavity. I didn't know if I was doing this right or not, but I wasn't going to give up on her.

"Come on, Gina!" I held my hands over her exposed heart, and my power came to life. Suddenly I could see everything as the electric charges lit beneath my skin and illuminated my surroundings. I cried out in shock, and horror seized my mind like a hot branding iron of torment. Blood was everywhere.

Gina's gapping chest splayed open with sharp jagged ribs cracked inward. It looked like some monster with incredibly massive hands had punched a hole in her. Her lifeless eyes stared up at me, and I couldn't see the color of her hair because the blood had soaked through it. I swallowed back the urge to hurl again and tried to concentrate.

I trembled as I closed my eyes and recognized the death I held in my hands. Then I turned inward to my heartbeat and listened.

Thump, thump. Thump, thump. Thump, thump.

I willed my power with it to Gina's heart by the third upward beat. The surge rolled from my extremities to my chest and shined like a beacon guiding life back home to Gina's body. It detonated, and my body seized as my power shot down my arms and through my fingertips.

Gina's heart jolted in my hands, then began to beat. I backed my hands away slowly, and her ribs mended back into place. The further I retreated, the more the damage to her body healed. Blood withdrew from around us and pulled back inside, and her skin closed over flawless.

Gina's chest moved up and down as her lungs pulled in oxygen, and I cried joyfully. Her eyelids had closed, and her eyes rolled back and forth before they reopened. Her lips parted, and she gasped a breath, looked at me, and smiled. "Tara, you saved me!"

I helped Gina sit up before wrapping my arms around her and sobbed with relief. "Gina. Oh, thank God! I'm so sorry. I love you so much!"

My cries became muffled as I buried my face into her shoulder. Gina embraced me and stroked my hair. "It's alright now, Tara. You brought me back, and I knew you would! Thank you!"

I pulled away. "How did you…? Do you know what I am? What I can do?"

"Dear, sweet little Tara. I always knew!" Gina's eyes turned dark, and a wicked smile spread across her lips.

"Gina?" My eyes widened in fear. I tried to back away, but she gripped my hair in a painful hold at the back of my head. I screamed as her hand transformed into something ghastly. Her skin turned a mottled gray and black, and her fingers grew into a knarled and boney length. Long sharp black talons grew from her fingertips.

She pulled my head closer, and a long bloody tongue struck my face like a viper. It dragged up my skin from my chin to my brow, and a putrid rotted smell hit my nose. Her voice doubled to that of her own and deep gravel. "Thanks for the charge, love! I'll be seeing you soon!"

Claws slammed into my chest, and I felt the fires of Hell wrap around my thundering heart. Her hand began to squeeze, and I screamed in agony. I shot up in bed, drenched in sweat. Hands grabbed my shoulders, and I started throwing my fists and kicking my legs.

"No! NO!" I screamed.

"Tara! Tara! Stop! It's me, Dean! You're awake! Breath, baby!"

"WHYYYY???" I broke down and sobbed uncontrollably. I began to hyperventilate, and Dean lifted me in his arms. The cool early morning air hit my bare legs as Dean ran to Woody's cabin with me, wrapped in a bedsheet.

"Dean, I, I!" I struggled for air, and my chest burned with pain.

"You're not going to die, Tara! Breath!" Dean kicked in the door, and Woody jumped up from bed and turned on the light.

"What the fuck?" Woody yelled.

"I need your help, Woody!" Dean cried.

Woody threw back his blankets. "Here! Lay her down."

Dean lowered my body into the warm impression of Uncle Woody's form. The bed dipped, and I looked up to see Woody's eyes filled with concern. "Tara. Look at me! Look in my eyes and listen to my voice."

"I, I," My head shook, and I was gasping. The air felt so thin. My heart slammed frantically, and my chest burned intensely.

Woody put his hands on either side of my head. "Look at me!" My eyes rolled, and my lids fluttered. I couldn't focus. I felt like I was going to die. Woody calmed and pleaded. "Look into my eyes, baby girl."

His voice was hoarse, and cold tears fell onto my cheek, cooling my skin. Woody's dark eyes flashed to a bright amber. For a moment, it felt like my heart had stopped. Then an icy cold gust filled my lungs, and my whole body tingled with cooling energy.

Woody was blowing a stream into me that looked like an arctic wind with frost particles in a continuous flow. The heat and pain in my chest began to subside, and my heartbeat returned to normal. I moaned, and Woody eased my head back onto his pillow.

"That's good. You're coming out of it. Keep breathing and looking at me," Woody soothed. He began to sing a lullaby in foreign words I could not understand, and it sounded like something old-world, ancient, but it eased my mind, and I pressed my hands onto Woody's. He moved his hands from my head and took mine into his as he continued to sing.

"What does it mean?" I rasped. Dean passed a glass of water to Woody, and Woody helped me raise enough to take a drink.

Woody chuckled. "And here I thought the first thing you'd ask was what the hell did I do to you?"

"Words first."

Dean laughed, and Woody gave me that 'smart-ass' smirk.

"It's an ancient Celtic lullaby asking for protection from the angels passed down through the generations. I don't remember all the word's meanings, but I know it mentions trust in the wings that wrap the slumbering babes and stretch wide to defend against the darkness."

"That's beautiful," I whispered.

"What happened to you, Tara?"

"I've been having nightmares, and they keep getting worse. A demon killed Gina, took her form, and tricked me into resurrecting it. It felt so real. Something wants me, and it's coming for me, and I don't know how to fight it." Tears rolled down my face, and Woody pulled me into his arms, cradling me like a small child.

"Hush now. You're not alone, baby girl."

I sunk into the warmth of my uncle's embrace, and it occurred to me that Woody had powers, but not like mine, and somehow Dean must have known. He rushed me to Woody with a steadfast determination, and it became clear that Woody had hidden this from me all these years. I should be angry, but it wasn't like I told Woody about my powers because I realized, in a way, I felt that keeping it a secret would protect my loved ones, and I didn't want them involved in my dilemma.

After all, my father knew, and he'd sent Dean to help. My mother was already damaged and paying the price for protecting me, and Rudy was innocent and did not know mine, Dean's, or Woody's abilities. I wanted to keep my brother as far from what was happening to me as possible.

But then I remembered that Zane had given Rudy his blood to help speed his healing, and I prayed that he didn't put a mark on Rudy somehow. Then there was Gina. Oh, God, I needed to call her and make sure she was alright, and I had to tell her I forgave her and work on mending our friendship.

Woody's phone began ringing, but he ignored it as he continued to soothe me. After several rings, it cut off, but it started ringing a moment later. An urgency grew in me, and I knew Woody needed to answer it.

"Here." Dean offered Woody his phone. Dean took Woody's place as Woody rose from the bed. I looked at Woody, his brow furrowed as he looked at the caller I.D.

"Asher," Woody answered. I lifted my head and listened to Asher's voice as he pleaded for Woody not to hang up. "What do you want?" Woody asked.

Asher sounded troubled, and I strained to listen to the muted conversation from his end. Woody huffed and ran his hand through his hair. I heard Gina's name mentioned, and I sat up.

"What is it, Woody?" Woody looked at me and shook his head.

"When?" he asked Asher. Asher was distraught, and I needed to know what was happening. Woody remained calm and composed as he looked at me, then turned away. Woody walked to the door; as he opened it and stepped outside, he said, "Tell me what happened."

"Let me up, Dean!" Dean tried to hold onto me as I struggled to push away.

"Tara, you have to remain calm. You've been through something traumatic, and Woody will be back." Dean tried to soothe me, but it felt more like he was trying to hide something. Something I already knew the answer to but wanted to deny more than anything in my heart.

Woody was pacing back and forth outside his window, and I heard him tell Asher, "She's not well enough to speak with you." Woody paused and responded, "Well, I don't need you to add any more stress to the situation with your pleading…."

He paused. "I will tell her and let her decide whether or not she wants to speak to you. No, Asher! She'll see you soon enough; just let her be. I'm sorry, Asher, but I have to go now. Bye."

Woody stepped back inside and closed the door. He looked conflicted, and I knew he was trying to find the right words to say, but I already knew.

"Gina?" Tears began rolling down my cheeks, and my lips quivered. Dean held me and Woody nodded.

"She's gone."

My throat felt tight as I struggled to swallow. "When? How?"

"A few hours ago. Tara, it's not…." Woody hesitated.

"How?" I demanded.

"Suicide. Gina shot herself." Woody approached the bed and kneeled.

I shook my head in denial. "No, no, no. Woody!"

"NOOO!" I shattered and fell into Dean's chest. I pounded my fists into Dean's body, and he took my pain till my hands fell limp. Dean nor Woody said a word as I let out my grief. It was consuming me from within, and I couldn't take it anymore.

WHY??? my soul screamed to the heavens. "I did, didn't get to tell her. I loved her, and I forgave her. Oh, God! I, I, I'm s, so sorry Gina." I was growing numb. I wanted to take that gun and shoot myself because the last words I exchanged with Gina were in anger. Guilt poured over my soul and burned holes through me.

"You killed our friendship, dug the grave, and now count yourself departed from my life." I had said those horrible words to her. Gina made a mistake, but I was the monster. My words had been the venom that slowly killed Gina. This was my fault.

"It's not your fault, Tara. He knows you're getting stronger, and he's playing to your fears. He's trying to break you down but doesn't realize how powerful you are."

"But this is real, Dean! I dreamt it, and it happened for real this time. It's like you told me. Our nightmares are dangerous, and you were right."

"You're a necromancer?" Woody asked.

"Yes," Dean answered.

"But, there's something else," Woody said.

Dean nodded. "My twin, Zane, is a vampire, and we share this body."

"Holy shit! Wait! Did your brother feed on Bren?" Woody asked.

"I'm sorry, Woody. I've been struggling to control Zane's bloodlust," Dean replied.

Woody's hands balled into fists, and he growled.

"Uncle Woody." I croaked. "That wasn't Dean's fault, and Zane feels terrible and hates what he is. Dad sent them here so I could help them, and they could help me."

"Dad? What does that mean?" Woody stood up and folded his arms across his chest. It was time to come clean as I realized Woody must get involved whether or not I wanted it, and he had some explaining to do as well.

My voice shook with grief as I answered. "In one of my nightmares, Dad came to me and told me he'd sent someone to help me. I've had these dreams for a while, and I am coming to understand they represent pieces from my past, memories I blocked out from the time before Mom killed Lyle. Only now, it is beginning to catch up with me, and Dad told me I must face the monsters that come with it. Lyle is coming back to finish what he started."

"Lyle is dead," Woody said. "He was not a necromancer. I knew he hurt you, but I found out too late; otherwise, I would have killed the fucker myself,"

"He was taking my blood, Woody. Why else would he do that if not to steal my power?" I asked.

Woody's brow arched, and he looked at Dean. "You've been teaching her?"

"Yes. Tara and I have combined our powers," Dean admitted.

Woody's jaw went back and forth, and it looked like he was contemplating attacking Dean, but he heaved a heavy sigh.

"It's what Dad told me I should do. If you're going to be angry, be angry at me too."

"I'm upset, Tara, but I'm reasonable. I'm just trying to understand."

"I am too. It's all getting too real. I can't believe Gina killed herself, and I feel like it's my fault because Lyle is trying to get to me. I'm scared for everyone I know and love. I was trying to keep everyone else out of this, but I realize now I can't. He's coming at me where it hurts the most."

"I'm telling you; it can't be Lyle. It had to be something else inside him, and it left his body when he died."

"This all started after Dad went missing, and a few years later, Lyle showed up. I believe Lyle is the one who took Dad, and Dad is alive somewhere. Uncle Woody, I saw him."

"You saw your father? When? Where?"

"Last night. No. Before that, I didn't know it was him the first time. Remember that night last week in the woods with Uncle Cannon? We told you we saw something. A shadow figure?"

"Yeah, I remember. Are you saying that strange shadow creature you and Cannon described was Richard?"

"Yes."

"What happened to him? How did he get that way?"

"Dad didn't know, and neither does Dean. All I know is he's stuck, and I have no idea how long he's been that way. I'm afraid we'll lose him for good if we don't find his body soon." I cried again as I felt the tremendous heartbreak of losing Gina and not knowing what would happen to Dad.

"Well, tell me what you do know, and we'll work from there," Woody encouraged.

I took a deep breath and blew it out. This conversation would be a long one as I struggled with my grief.

Chapter 23
DEAN

A Puzzled Past

Woody remained silent as Tara explained how her dad's body was somewhere in stasis, and his spirit was in limbo and unable to tell her where to find him. She told him about Abigail, the brooch, and everything she experienced with her power. When she told us about her latest nightmare, I became angry. Because whomever this monster was, he was messing with the wrong necromancer.

Zane and I would catch this coward and send him back to the bowels of Hell, where he belongs. Woody rubbed his face and tugged at the hairs on his chin. "So, tell me, Dean. In what way did you amalgamate Tara's powers with yours? And, did my brother specify that it was necessary?"

"Dad told me...." Tara started, but Woody held up a hand.

"I want to hear it from him," Woody said.

"Tara injected a trace of her blood into my heart," I admitted.

"Fuck! Do you have any clue what that does to a male necromancer? Especially coming from a mated female!" Woody stood up, and his footsteps pounded toward Dean. Tara jumped up and stood in Woody's path.

"He didn't hurt me! It was barely a few drops because we couldn't take a risk with Zane."

"What does that mean?" Woody's voice boomed.

"Zane's vampire is unable to drink my blood. It hurts him," Tara said.

"How would you know that, unless...." Woody halted. "Motherfucker!" Woody grabbed Tara's shoulders, stepped around her, and lunged at me. I jumped out of my seat and braced for impact. I wasn't going to fight Woody. I understood why he was pissed off, and I'd want to kick my ass if I were in his shoes.

Woody plowed into me, and Tara screamed. I struggled against Woody's assault, and the man was strong, but then Zane stepped in and took hold of Woody's fists before he could pummel our face in, and Woody's eyes widened in shock as he saw our eyes change from blue to silver. Zane was physically stronger than me, and Woody combined, and he held Woody's fist tight and squeezed till Woody grimaced in pain. Zane could have easily crushed Woody's bones.

"ZANE! Stop it! You're hurting him!" Tara screamed.

Zane glanced at Tara, but he still held on and looked back at Woody. Zane stared into his eyes till Woody conceded, and his arms slackened. Zane let go, and Woody dropped his arms but continued to glare at him.

"What did you do to my niece, vampire?" Woody growled.

"It was a mistake. I bit Tara, and I paid for it. Her blood poisoned me," Zane said.

"And you're not dead? Pity!"

"Woody!" Tara admonished.

"Don't interrupt, Tara! This asshole is lucky I haven't killed him." Woody warned.

Zane rolled his eyes. "I highly doubt you could."

"Want to try me, vampire?" Woody bumped his chest into Zane's.

"I'm not your enemy, Airmed's son," Zane replied. Woody's brows rose in surprise.

"That's right! I know what you are," Zane said.

"Airmed's son?" Tara asked.

Woody deflated and took a step back. "I am a descendant, and so is Richard, Tara's father, but I only inherited the healing gift, while my brother inherited the necromancer gift."

"So, you're not a necromancer?" Tara asked.

Woody shook his head. "Airmed is the Celtic Goddess of Healing, and she gifted our ancestors with abilities from her power. This gift of her power is passed down through the generations, and most are either one or the other. It's extremely rare for one born with both abilities."

"Tara! That must be why Lyle was stealing your blood. He must have known!" Zane said.

"What?"

"You are a daughter of Airmed!"

"How did you know about this? Dean never mentioned it before."

"Dean suspected. But he didn't mention it because he needed confirmation. The power your uncle used just did."

"So, my power is not from something evil?"

"No! Did you think that because it's what this jackwad told you?" Woody asked.

"Well, Zane and Dean were the only two who told me anything!" Tara retorted with her hands on her hips.

"That's not fair, Tara. We must swear to take our kind's secret to the grave, and we can only reveal it to another once their power has awakened or we use it on someone we trust," Woody said.

"If what we are isn't evil, why does it feel so dark?"

"Have you ever tried staring directly into the sun with your bare eyes? You can barely do it even with sunglasses on. It's the same concept; only the darkness isn't transparent or opaque. If that shield over our powers weren't there, the cataclysmic effect of your energy would scorch your human body. It's a protection."

"Holy shit! I didn't know that!" Zane exclaimed. "No wonder your blood affected me the way it did."

Tara looked surprised. "We are walking atomic bombs?"

"Only without our shield, only the goddess Airmed herself can live without one, but she can put in back if she chooses to reveal herself. But no one has seen her for centuries. Also, it's why no man can look upon God's face. The soul of man would obliterate," Woody said.

"So, if you can heal, why not help Rudy?"

"I have, but only as much as I can in his situation," Woody replied.

"Why? What about his situation makes him unable to be healed completely by your power?"

"For the same reason, you cannot intervene to revive Gina. Witnesses! Rudy's injury occurred in front of thousands of people, and he was already in surgery before we got there. It would cause a huge stir if I went in, and next thing you know, Rudy was up and running laps. I've done what I can to ease his pain and progress the natural healing process."

Tara hung her head, sniffed, and wiped her face.

"Ah, hell!" Zane said.

"What did you do, vampire?" Woody asked.

"Will you stop calling me vampire? I have a name!"

"Alright! What did you do? Zane!" Woody folded his arms.

"Well, I didn't know, or else I wouldn't have…." Zane swallowed nervously.

"Spit it out!" Woody demanded.

"Well, I may have slipped Rudy a little cocktail into his intravenous line," Zane admitted.

"You did WHAT?" Woody boomed.

"Calm down, Uncle Woody! He was only trying to help. And it was only a tiny amount so that it wouldn't be obvious," Tara said.

"And what if Rudy died? Do you know what vampire venom can do to a human?" Woody yelled.

Tara flinched and looked sorrowful.

"I didn't give Rudy my venom, and for the record, I have never injected venom into another living soul. I hate what I am and would never wish this curse upon my worst enemy," Zane said.

Woody huffed. "Well, you're the first of your kind to admit such a thing though I find it hard to believe. Vampires tend to flaunt their power and feel the need to collect trophies.

"Well, that's what I am. Only I was a discarded trophy, and I didn't even make it to the shelf."

"You were bitten and left on your own?" Woody asked.

"Not on my own. I had Dean to help me, and my death and transition triggered his necromancer powers. He was able to keep my bloodlust in check for several decades, but it has depleted Dean's powers, and that's why Tara gave him a boost."

"And you were okay with that?" Woody asked in surprise.

"I encouraged it. I want Dean and Tara to be happy without my interference," Zane admitted.

"A vampire with a conscience. If wonders never cease!" Woody shook his head.

"You see? Dean and Zane are here to help me. Dad already knew about Zane and told me to help them. With their help, I know we'll be able to find Dad and kill Lyle," Tara said.

"Lyle's dead," Woody repeated.

"Okay, I've considered his body may still be in the grave. But what if we dig up Lyle's coffin and see that he's not in it?"

"Tara, I was at the funeral. I saw his dead body in the coffin, and the same coffin went into the ground. I even watched the dirt get plowed over said coffin. There's no way his body isn't there."

Tara crossed her arms. "Well, Dean and I intend to check."

"What? Why?"

"Because I need to see it, Uncle Woody. I blocked out a lot of memories, and Lyles' funeral and burial were one of them. I blocked out too many things from back then. I thought I could move on from my past, but it's too deep inside me. All these missing pieces are returning to haunt me, and I need to put it all back together before it takes me apart."

"Fine. I get it. You need this closure, and I'll help you in any way you need," Woody said.

"That's all I'm asking."

"I understand how Dean can help, but what good is the vampire to us?"

"It's Zane, and I'm right here! I have my good uses."

"Oh, are you referring to biting the help? Because as I recall, Bren was out of it for days, and it would have been more if I hadn't intervened," Woody said.

"Bren was well enough; I knew she would be okay when Dean took her home," Zane argued.

"And that was because I helped her. No one could have survived what you took from her body," Woody said.

"Did you suspect a vampire attack?" Zane asked.

"I know the signs of a vampire attack, and I've scoured my property since. If I'd known that vampire was you, you'd be dead already. Be thankful Dean's life has value."

"I am thankful for my brother, and I realize his value. I know I'm a parasite in more ways than one, but I didn't ask to be born this way or bitten by a vampire, so could you back off? I'm sorry I bit and drank from Bren because, believe it or not, I care about her."

"And you'll stay away from her. Bren's been through enough. She came here for my protection, and I won't hesitate to take a stake to your heart if you come near her again," Woody threatened.

"My heart is right here!" Zane pointed at our chest, then shifted his finger left. "And this is Dean's. If you're going to kill me, remember that! Dean never did anything to deserve what I do."

"Hmm! Interesting. The vampire wants to be a martyr," Woody responded.

"Are you two finished ripping into each other?" Tara asked.

"I'm through!" Zane's eyes flashed, and Dean returned.

"Fascinating. You two trade-off like the flip of a switch. Where do you go when your brother takes charge?" Woody asked.

"I'm conscious of everything. It's how I can keep Zane from losing control, and Zane graciously bows out when necessary. He goes into something like a meditative trance and blocks everything out. It works both ways, but I'm dominant as it's mainly my body we share." I explained.

"I've heard about that. What's it called? It's not conjoined twins; it's a parasitic twin? You have no extra appendages or another head; it's all internal?" Woody asked.

"Well, I did have an extra appendage, but I lost it during the war." Dean pointed down.

Woody's eyes widened. "You're shitting me, aren't you?"

"Nope, it was an extra pinkie toe." Dean grinned.

Woody burst out laughing. "I thought you were pointing somewhere else."

Tara smiled at me. "Yeah, Zane got me with that one. Very funny."

"Works every time," I said. I watched Tara struggling to keep her spirits up, and I could tell she was tired. I pulled her into a hug, and she leaned into me. Woody noticed as well and went to make coffee. I had a feeling Tara didn't want to go back to sleep after the nightmare she had. And with the bad news about Gina, she needed some distraction.

We sat around Woody's kitchen table and played a few card games till daylight poured into the windows. Woody went to prepare for the day, and we followed him outside as he headed to his office.

Tara stood at the water's edge on the lakeshore and stared at the gentle ripples. I searched for some rocks I could skip, stood next to Tara, and started throwing them. The most skips I'd ever accomplished were seven. I got flustered when I sunk one, and Tara smiled.

"Impressive!" she teased.

"Let me see you skip one!" I handed a rock to her.

"This was one of Rudy's and my favorite pastimes when we were kids." She tossed her rock, and it skipped twice before plunking below the surface.

"Oh, yeah? Can you imagine Zane and me trying to play hide-and-seek when we were young?"

Tara laughed. "When did you know Zane was there inside you?"

"I remember my mother telling me I babbled a lot when I was two, and she said I sounded like I was arguing with myself all the time. But I didn't recognize Zane till we were three. Our mother always told everyone I had an imaginary friend who liked to pick fights."

"If your mom didn't realize what was happening, how did Zane get his name?"

"Kids picked on me a lot back then. They would call me coo-coo, crazy, or zany. I didn't like the first two words, but I didn't mind zany, so I replaced the y with an e and told my brother that his name was Zane. He told me he liked it, so it stuck."

"That's a good story. So, how did you make it through your teens and beyond?"

"When Zane and I had enough of being bullied, we discussed how we'd make it in a world where people would never understand us. At one point, we considered running away and joining a freak show, but our outside appearance wasn't convincing enough to make the cut.

So, we adapted, and when we argued in public places, people thought I was crazy and avoided us. But we got better at disguising our discussions as time went on, and in this modern era of technology, it became easier to talk aloud. People mostly ignore us now."

"So, you've only revealed this double life to people in the supernatural community or humans you could trust?"

"There's only a handful of people still living today who know everything about Zane and me, and that includes you and Woody."

"Wow! It sounds like a lonely life."

"It's not so bad. It's why we travel the world, and there are always new faces and new places. The world has changed so much over the years; it's amazing."

"I'd like to do that someday. I've been here all of my life. I want to manage a beautiful resort on a tropical island and bring my mother along."

"That sounds nice. I've been to a few. I did the Beach Boys tour."

"Where's that?"

"Have you heard the song, Kokomo?"

"I don't think so."

"I'll have to play it for you. The Beach Boys sang this song about all the islands throughout the Caribbean Sea, and it's one of my favorite songs."

"Oh, I think I remember hearing it played in the movie Cocktail. My mom loved that movie and let me watch it with her when I was thirteen. Remind me how the song goes?"

I took Tara's hand and pulled her into my arms. I started to sing and moved with the romantic melody in my head as we swayed back and forth together on the lakeshore.

Tara looked into my eyes and smiled as she listened to the words. By the second chorus, Tara sang along, and I delighted in my little nightingale's beautiful voice. When I finished singing, we continued to sway, and Tara repeated the chorus and few more times, and I felt her body relax.

"I think that's my new favorite song." Tara's eyes sparkled.

I leaned in to kiss her, and we swayed for several minutes to the gentle lapping at the water's edge. "One day, we'll dance to Kokomo on pristine white sand before the blue ocean. We'll walk the beach and sit and watch the sunset."

"Mmm, Dean! That's always been a dream of mine. I fantasize about making love on the beach at night with a small bonfire blazing. Just like the movie, except you don't knock me up," Tara joked.

I laughed. "We won't do that till you're ready, Love. Beach sex, then beach babies much, much later. I'm kind of a selfish man and want you all to myself for as long as possible."

"Awe, but, honey! We already have a toddler! His name is Zane." Tara smirked.

"Zane just said he resembles that remark."

Tara laughed. "Proves my point. Eavesdropper!"

"Zane's happy because you're laughing a smiling. He cares about you."

"I know. I care about him too. I might even let him party with us on the beach."

"He said he'll bring the booze." I smiled.

"Blood will have to go in a separate cooler."

I laughed. "We might have to find somewhere more secluded. A thief might try to steal a drink and find more than he bargained for."

"I guess the thief will have to stay for Zane's dinner party."

"Seclusion it is." I smiled.

Chapter 24
TARA

It's Hard To Say Goodbye

It felt good to have Dean take me away to an island paradise in my head. I felt so tired but didn't want to go back to sleep. We went back inside the cabin, and Dean helped me make breakfast. I didn't have to work tonight, which was good, and I didn't think Woody would have let me anyway. I was sure word had gotten around about Gina, and I prayed no one came knocking on the door to give condolences.

I tried desperately to keep my mind distracted. I didn't even want to look at my phone because I knew I'd see all those texts and voicemails, asking questions and sending prayers. I couldn't deal with it now.

After breakfast, Dean and I made love. It was tender and heartfelt, and I cried in his arms. Dean carried me to the bathroom, where he'd drawn a lavender and eucalyptus bubble bath.

I laughed as Dean made a production of squeezing into the tub with me, and the water overflowed with white foamy bubbles that cascaded onto the floor. We sat opposite one another with our legs bent and tangled in an awkward position, but it felt nice to have physical contact.

I scooped up bubbles and blew them as I used to when I was a kid. Dean and I constructed foamy hats and hairstyles on each other's heads and laughed at our goofball antics. I smiled on the outside, but my heart felt this constant ache. Sometimes I'd laugh, and the tears would come along as I recalled the good times Gina and I shared.

The worst part was knowing I could have saved her if I had only known. I could have brought her back if I had only found her before anyone else. Gina couldn't have killed herself, and I knew this. She and I talked about how there would be good and bad days. She promised me no matter how bad life got; she'd always hang on for the good days because those days always outnumbered the bad.

Dean saw me in my tear-induced reverie and smiled tenderly at me. He wiped at my tears and playfully patted at the bubbles atop my head. "I've got a surprise for you."

"You do?" my voice choked.

"Yeah! Watch the bubbles in front of you."

I looked down between us, and the suds bobbled up and down with the waves Dean created beneath. He started singing. "DUN, DUN. DUN, DUN."

I recognized the theme from Jaws and laughed. Something small and yellow emerged from the soapy suds, and Dean produced a rubber duckie with a loud squeaker. I cracked up as Dean squeezed it a few times, then snatched the duck from his hands.

"What should we name it?" Dean asked.

"I always liked the name, Charlie, like Charlie Chaplin."

"Okay! Charlie, it is! We'll take him on adventures as we travel the world, and he'll sit on top of my backpack as we ride through Europe. And everywhere we go, people will ask about him. He'll be famous, and everyone will say, Hello, Charlie!"

"You're ridiculous, Dean!" I laughed.

"But you like ridiculous, don't you?"

"I happen to love ridiculous," I agreed.

We sat in the tub till we turned into prunes, and the water became cold. Dean helped me out, dried me off, and wrapped me in my clean, soft robe. We sat out on the couch eating junk food and watching Cocktail until my eyes grew heavy. I struggled to stay awake but eventually drifted off.

By the time I woke, it was after 11 p.m. I yawned and stretched. Dean was sitting at the kitchen table browsing on my laptop. "What are you looking at?" I asked.

"Beachfront BNBs. I want to take you someplace special."

I got out of bed and walked to the kitchen. Dean pulled me onto his lap and began scrolling through pictures. It all looked inviting, I wished Dean and I could jump into those pictures and be the couple swinging in a hammock beneath the palm trees with coconut drinks in our hands.

The next few days and nights went by in a blur as my family and friends came and went. People prayed with me and spoke kind words. On the day of the funeral, Woody closed The Hillbilly Roost, and everyone went to the funeral home.

In the parking lot, an SUV pulled in, and I recognized the young men who got out. One man lifted the hatch and pulled out a wheelchair, and I was surprised when I saw Rudy slide out of the vehicle and hobbled on his good leg.

"Rudy!" I ran over to my brother as he sat in the wheelchair, and one of the men put the extension on to hold up Rudy's leg. I leaned in and hugged him. "I can't believe you're here!"

"I needed to be here for you and Gina. I loved her like a sister, and I couldn't leave you hanging. These are some of my teammates. Phillip, Ross, and Landon." Rudy motioned to the men behind him.

"I remember you all from the hospital. Thank you for coming and bringing Rudy. It means a lot to me."

The three men nodded. "We're sorry for your loss," Phillip said.

"Thank you." I walked alongside Rudy as Phillip pushed the wheelchair. We made our way up the ramp and went inside. Dean was talking to Cannon and Stella in the hallway, and he looked up and smiled at me. I smiled back and continued ahead.

There were so many people, and I recognized many faces from the past. I made small conversation, constantly aware of Gina's body lying in the open white casket. I hadn't worked up the courage yet to go there. From what I could glimpse, I recognized the dark plum dress she wore as one her mother had bought for her to wear to a formal dance in high school, and I remembered she hated that dress.

I approached her parents, Liz and Ryan, and hugged them. Liz cried on my shoulder and told me she loved me and was happy I'd been Gina's best friend. I supposed Gina didn't tell them what transpired between us, or Liz chose not to speak of it. Whether or not she knew, it didn't matter anymore. All that was left was my pain and guilt.

I spotted Asher walking in dressed in a dark gray suit. He looked at me and nodded as he walked past and went to stand before Gina's still form. I knew I should go up to and stand beside him, but I was a coward. A warm hand touched my back, and I turned around to see Trey standing there. It was the first time I'd seen him in a men's suit without any glamorous accessories, and it felt like I was looking at an alien who'd invaded his body.

"Wow, Uncle Trey! I didn't know you could pull off GQ!"

Trey smiled at me tenderly. "I can pull off anything when the occasion calls for it. I know I'm interfering, but you must do this, baby girl. If you don't, you won't have the closure you need, and you'll spend the rest of your life regretting it."

Trey put his arm around me and guided me forward. He stopped when he felt my hesitation, but he didn't leave my side. I looked at him, and his loving brown eyes reassured me. I took a deep breath and allowed him to ease me forward.

I focused on the movements of my feet with each step along the dark burgundy runner atop the cream carpet. I looked up and took in the back of Asher's jacket. I didn't want to expand my view beyond that focal point.

I clutched Trey's hand on my shoulder as my heart began to pound in my ears. Trey pulled me around to stand at Asher's side, and I squeezed my eyes closed because I didn't want to face the truth before me. Trey's hand tightened slightly on my shoulder. I heard a couple of sniffs and turned to look at Asher. His eyes were red, and tears spilled down his cheeks. He pulled a handkerchief from his pocket and dried his face.

"Shit! I told myself I wasn't going to do this." Asher sniffed. Before I knew what I was doing, my hand dropped, took hold of Asher's, and squeezed.

"Someone wise once told me it's okay to let go."

Asher sniffed again. "Yeah? Who was that?"

"Stella." I smiled.

Asher laughed. "Fuck! It had to be her, didn't it? She's the toughest woman I met besides you, Tara."

"Nah. Second place goes to Gina." I looked up, and for the first time, I saw the whole picture.

The beautiful girl I knew lay before me with her brunette hair in long loose curls with a purple Emperor Dahlia clipped to the side. Her eyes forever closed in eternal sleep; she looked like a princess awaiting her true love's first kiss. Her lips were full in shimmering soft pink, and her cheeks a natural blush. Her eyelids brushed with pale lavender.

She wore a heart-shaped amethyst crystal on a delicate gold chain around her neck, and a butterfly ring with multicolored sapphires on the first finger of her hand rested across the other just below her breasts. Her nails looked perfectly manicured in a clear natural coat with French tips. She lay there frozen in time atop a pristine white satin pillow.

"She looks like an angel."

"She does," Asher agreed.

"You loved her, didn't you? More than a friend." The way he looked at her now, I knew. Asher nodded, and his lips quivered.

"I can't believe she's gone. Fuck!" Asher let go of my hand, turned, and walked quickly down the aisle and out of the room. Trey still stood by my side, and he took my other hand.

"She is beautiful. I wouldn't have chosen that dress, but they did a great job on her hair and makeup." Trey commented in a way that was all too Martina.

A bark of laughter escaped my mouth, and I bit my lips closed. I took a deep breath through my nose and blew it out through my lips. Tears sprung from my eyes and rolled down my cheeks as I nodded in agreement. "Yeah! She hated that dress," I whispered.

"You should say what you need to," Trey encouraged.

"She can't hear me."

"Sure, she can. She may not be in that body anymore, but she's still lingering. She's probably watching and listening to what everyone is saying about her."

"You think so?" I sniffed. I looked around the room, hoping to see Gina's spirit, but saw nothing.

Trey pulled a handkerchief from his jacket pocket and handed it to me. "You can keep that! I don't want it back after you snot all over it."

"Thanks. Will you stay here with me? I don't think I can do this by myself."

"I'm not going anywhere." Trey stood by me as my rock as the floodgates opened and more tears spilled. I sniffed and made use of the handkerchief for which I was grateful. I wasn't sure if I should touch Gina's hands because I didn't know what my power might do with these intense emotions.

"Hey, Gina. I'm feeling a bit awkward standing here, but I always felt like the awkward one around you. You were always confident, beautiful, and headstrong—my rock and confidant. We had so much fun together, and I want you to know you always brought out the best in me. I want to tell you I'm—I'm so sorry for the last words I said to you. I was angry and in pain and didn't mean any of it. I forgive you and Asher because I now realize you were in love with each other. How could I not see it? I hope you forgive me for how I treated you, and I wish I had told you this before you left."

I broke down and began to sob. Trey pulled me into a hug and rubbed small circles on my back in a comforting motion.

"I've got you," Trey cooed tenderly. I nodded against his shoulder, and he let me go. I turned back to Gina's form and sniffed, and my breathing stuttered as I sucked in air and tried to calm myself.

"Gina, I love you. Always have and always will. I pray you find peace and live happily ever eternity in Heaven. While you're waiting for me, I'll always think about you." I let go of my fear and gently placed my hand on Gina's. It didn't feel real, and I couldn't feel HER anymore. It felt more like I was touching an object than a person. This body was nothing but a shell that once housed a soul. A beautiful soul full of love and everything good.

"Goodbye, my sweet sister."

I breathed and realized how often I took each breath for granted. I nodded to Trey and took his hand, and he led me away. More people stood and waited to pay their respects, and once everyone was seated, the ceremony began.

A pastor opened up in prayer and then talked about Gina and the more known things about her life. Gospel songs played on a piano, and people took turns speaking at the podium. I realize none of those people knew Gina the way I knew her. She showed the biggest and best parts of herself to me. She was brave, intelligent, funny, sassy, snarky, and could be a real bitch. But mostly, she was the best friend a girl could have as she stood up for me and had been my shoulder to cry on when my life fell to pieces.

It was my turn to speak, and I prayed I could get through this without breaking down. Dean kissed my hand, and I stood from my seat and walked to the podium. I looked out at the sea of tears in dark clothing and took a deep breath.

"Gina is and will always be my best friend. We grew up together. She and I were inseparable throughout high school, and we had the best and worst times together. We always understood each other whether we were getting along or fighting. Gina was easy to make amends with and was usually the first to apologize. Just like she did the last time we spoke.

Sometimes I make the wrong choices, and I was angry because Gina made a choice that I thought I'd never be able to forgive at the time. But, by the grace of God, I realized we all make mistakes, and good things can come from those choices. I planned on telling Gina I had forgiven her, but the opportunity passed in a blink of an eye, and now I live with the pain and regret. The choice to delay telling her how much I loved her came as the hardest lesson I've learned. From now on, I vow to forgive always and often because one never knows if they will get the chance tomorrow or even in the next minute."

I closed my eyes and pictured Gina's spirit before me, knowing in my heart that I would not see her there when I opened them. I didn't see or feel her anywhere, so she had to be on the other side. So, I prayed.

"Gina, I pray for your forgiveness. I love you, and I wish you were still here. I hope you find peace, my friend, my sister." I opened my eyes, and tears trickled down my cheeks.

Gina's mother nodded at me, her lips quivered, and her eyes glistened. She crossed her arms embracingly and patted her heart, and I placed my hand on my chest in acceptance.

I went back to my seat, and Dean held my hand. A few more people spoke, one last song played, and the pastor closed the service in prayer. A line formed to pay their final respects, and I glimpsed at the shell of the girl I once knew. I fought the need to place my hands on her body and send my power into her. I could imagine many more people dropping dead from a heart attack at the sight.

Dean's hand pressed the small of my back and ushered me forward. I hugged and kissed Gina's mom and dad on their cheeks and told them I was there for them if they needed me, which they reciprocated.

The funeral procession began with the pallbearers, including Asher and Uncle Woody, with four other men who carried Gina's casket to the hearse. Dean drove my truck, and Trey and Danny rode with us. The procession stretched with dozens of vehicles with headlights turned on and an escort to hold traffic as it passed. We pulled into the graveyard, the same one where Lyle was buried. Thankfully his plot was far on the other side away from Gina's.

It felt eerie returning here, and I tried to block out the small glimpses of the past that crept into my mind. I didn't want to remember it then, and I especially didn't want to recall it now. This time was about Gina's memory and everyone who loved her.

After the pastor read the 23Psalm, I took a rose and winced as a thorn punctured my thumb. Blood welled up, and I did my best to hide what happened with the handkerchief Trey gave me. I laid my rose on Gina's casket, told her I loved her, and said my final goodbye.

As everyone departed back to their vehicles, Asher approached Dean and me. He glimpsed at Dean and our joined hands, and I saw the acceptance in Asher's eyes. "Tara, can we talk?"

I looked at Dean, and he nodded as he let go of my hand and walked ahead to the truck. "Asher, I'm sorry I didn't realize what was going on and not considering your feelings for Gina. I felt like you and I were growing apart, and I was so busy all the time to give you a chance to talk. I want you to know I'm not angry with you anymore, and I forgive you."

"I know. I wanted to tell you, but I was afraid of the worst. But the worst happened, and I lost both of you. And now..." Asher's voice choked on a sob. "Now I'm alone and feel so lost and empty inside. I don't know what I'm going to do now." Asher looked so broken and sad, and my heart hurt for him. I put my arms around him, and we both cried. After a long moment, we let go.

"I'm still here for you, Asher."

"I know. And I'm sorry I was an asshole. What I did was wrong. I didn't have the courage to tell you how I felt. We had something good, but I don't know! This last year, you seemed to change somehow. I didn't understand what was happening or how to talk to you, but I could talk to Gina, and she was helping me get past so many hang-ups. And, well, you know the rest of the story."

I nodded. "It's okay. I think we've both learned a lot lately."

Asher glimpsed at Dean. "You've met someone. What's his name?"

"Dean."

"Is he treating you well?"

"Yes, he is."

"Good. You deserve to be happy, and I will no longer stand in your way. But, please remember the good times we shared. You'll always be in my heart."

"You have a good heart, Asher, and I will always remember the good times. I want you to know you're welcome to visit. Perhaps you and Dean could meet officially."

"I appreciated that. Maybe, I'll stop by at some point, but I don't know when."

"I understand. I know you need time. If you need to call me, I'll answer."

"Thank you, Tara." Asher hugged me once more, and then he walked away. Dean leaned against the truck and gave Asher a curt nod as he passed. He came to me and took my hand.

"You ready?"

I looked back once more as Gina's casket lowered into the ground, and the moment felt inconceivable.

"Yes, Dean. Let's go home."

Death is not the end, my dear
Oh no, it's not my friend
Your vaporous form
Bestills my fears
Your prompting
Soothes away my tears

End of Book One
Thank you for reading!
You have reached the end of Book One,
but not the end of the story.

Dark Trespass Book Two A Necromancer's Peril
is Available Now!

A dark threat will become real as the boundaries between
nightmares and reality are broken. Spirits and demons will
rise, and Tara will face her monsters.

The truth about Dr. Lyle Durst will come to light, and
new leads will show Tara the way to finding her father.

Tara will learn there is more to her uncles than meets the
eye when death pays a visit to The Hillbilly Roost.

Zane has a secret to reveal, and Bren will face her
nightmare in the flesh.

Misty Dawn Tackett is an avid reader and writer of paranormal romance and fantasy fiction. She lives in Texas with her husband, three children, two neurotic dogs, and a little fluffy potato parakeet. She is a self-described introvert with part-time extrovert tendencies. Her love for writing fiction stems from highly imaginative dreams.